INTO GOBLYN WOOD

INTO GOBLYN WOOD

ANNA KEMP
Illustrated by DAVID WYATT

SIMON & SCHUSTER

First published in Great Britain in 2022 by Simon & Schuster UK Ltd

1 3 5 7 9 10 8 6 4 2

Simon & Schuster UK Ltd
1st Floor, 222 Gray's Inn Road
London
WC1X 8HB

www.simonandschuster.co.uk
www.simonandschuster.com.au
www.simonandschuster.co.in

Simon & Schuster Australia, Sydney
Simon & Schuster India, New Delhi

A CIP catalogue record for this book is available from the British Library.

PB ISBN 978-1-3985-0383-0
eBook ISBN 978-1-3985-0384-7
eAudio ISBN 978-1-3985-0385-4

Printed and bound by CPI Group (UK) Ltd, Croydon, CR0 4YY

MIX
Paper from
responsible sources
FSC® C171272

For the Noisy Boys. Love you forever.

N

W   E

S

ARBOREANS

RUSHY BECK

THE WEALD

WESTERN EDGE

THE DEN

DITCHMOOR

School for the Wretched

GOBLYN WOOD

THE KNOLL
FAE DOMINION

WILDERMIST

WITHY HILL

NDERSTONE
Seely Village

MORROW RIVER

RIVERTON

DRUICS HERE
(sometimes)

TO BOGGART
HILL

TO LONDON

Fairytellings

SPOONS ARE REAL; WANDS ARE NOT. SPROUTS exist; magic beans do not. That flickering shape you saw out of the corner of your eye was a beetle, or a moth, or maybe falling leaves, but definitely not a fairy. Or so people say.

But people say a lot of things and often they are wrong. In fact, that shape you saw most likely *was* a fairy. Because, unlike wands and magic beans, fairies have always been amongst us. And we would do well to remember it.

Truth is, there was a time when people and fairies were tangled up together like the roots of a tree. They didn't always get on. Fairies are an irritable bunch and people even more so. But they jostled along side by side, the people in their villages, the fairies in their hills. Sometimes they even loved each other, and children were born with one foot in each world – magical children with the powers of both kinds leaping through their veins.

Then, after many years of jostling along together, suddenly there was war. The fairies whipped up the winds, made the rivers run backwards and rotted the apples on the trees. The people marched to the hills and caved them in. And those who were neither one thing nor the other were cast out and hunted down.

By the end of it, everything was broken and everyone was worn out. So a truce was made. The fairies crept back into the hills, the people sheltered in their villages and it was agreed that each would stay out of the other's way.

And so, over many long centuries, the two worlds untangled. People stopped believing in fairies, then forgot about them altogether. Then they started telling their children that what they saw out of the corner of their eye – what they *knew* they saw – was nothing but a common garden beetle. And the children, despite their better instincts for these sorts of things, believed them.

So that's where we find ourselves. In a truce, of sorts. But if we still trusted our instincts, if we looked and listened closely, we would read strange patterns on the surface of the rivers, and we would hear the warnings on the wind.

CHAPTER ONE

The Wretched

H AZEL QUINCE'S STORY BEGAN LONG BEFORE she was born. But this book begins at ten o'clock in the morning on her eleventh birthday. It was a good day for a birthday – bright and gusty, perfect for flying kites. But Hazel didn't know how to fly a kite. In fact, she didn't even know it was her birthday. Instead, she was sitting at a workbench in the Ditchmoor School for the Wretched, peeling vegetables.

If the Ditchmoor School for the Wretched doesn't sound like a nice place, that's because it wasn't. It was an awful place, and children were very unhappy there. And if you think peeling vegetables sounds dull, well you're right about that too. But it was better than having them thrown at you. And the matrons' aim was fearfully good.

That morning, Ditchmoor was silent save for the scraping of knives, the click of matrons' heels on flagstones and the occasional bout of coughing. Fingernails clogged with dirt,

Hazel worked quickly and mechanically, peeling the skin of a potato into curling ribbons. She had secured a good spot at the end of the bench, beneath a broken windowpane. There she could sit alone in a patch of yellow sunshine and breathe the autumn air that blew in from the countryside beyond. She was just about to set her knife to a particularly mucky turnip when a sudden squall sent a tiny bird tumbling through the window and onto the tabletop. As it shook out its flustered feathers, a smile of recognition broke across Hazel's face.

'Mr Robinson!' she whispered. The robin cocked his head and looked up at her with a soft, bright eye. Hazel put down her knife and stretched out a finger. With a glad chirrup, the bird hopped on, bounced up to her shoulder and pecked affectionately at her ear. 'Ow! Stop it!' said Hazel, starting to worry that the other children would notice. She caught him gently between her hands and brought him down into her lap. But it was too late.

'Those things are dirty, you know.' It was Elsie Pocket, leaning down the table, smiling the sort of smile that precedes a bite. 'They have diseases.'

'I don't think—' Hazel began. But Elsie wasn't done.

'If Miss Fitch catches you,' she whispered, 'she'll lock you in the coal shed and put *that thing* in the Warden's pie.' Hazel knew this was true. It had only been a week since she'd last been stuffed in the coal shed and she could still taste the soot in her mouth. She smoothed the indignant robin's ruffled feathers then popped him carefully out of the window. Silently, she returned to her peeling, hoping Elsie would lose interest. But she could sense the other children swapping glances.

'We know about those beetles in your drawer too,' Elsie said, wrinkling her nose.

'And the fleas in your bed!' sniggered Danny Huber.

Elsie tipped her head with a look of feigned concern. 'We're just trying to help you, Hazel.'

Hazel pressed her lips together and kept her eyes fixed on her turnip as if she couldn't hear, or didn't care. But she could feel her cheeks blazing. Elsie gave a snort of disgust and turned away, mouthing something to the others. There was a burst of laughter, followed by a yelp as Miss Fitch sent a cabbage whizzing overhead.

Hazel tried not to listen to what they were saying. What was the point? She'd heard it all before. They said she came from strange sorts; that she'd been born in a ditch; that she had insects, mice and birds in her drawer and pockets, even in her hair. *And, did you see her in the orchard yesterday, stock still, staring like an owl? Miss Fitch had to pull her ears to bring her round. Oh, and have you noticed her eyes? I swear, they change colour every time you look at them. So odd. So creepy. No wonder her mother dumped her here.*

No, it was nothing Hazel hadn't heard before. And on that day, her eleventh birthday, she did what she always did: curled up like a hedgehog, waited for danger to pass and felt raw with shame.

*

Hazel had no memories of her mother, not even a flicker. All she had been told was that her mother had left her at Ditchmoor when she was two years old. She had meant to come back for her, but never did. Almost everyone at the school had the same story. Nevertheless, Miss Fitch and her matrons remembered the day Hazel arrived. There had been the usual business – the knock at the door, the child on the step – but, when Mrs Mudge took her to the washroom for a scrub-down, she discovered something strange.

Around the child's throat hung a black stone pendant on which a curious symbol was engraved. Swirled like a snail shell with a strike through the middle, it looked like a letter from some ancient alphabet – though what it meant was anybody's guess. Mrs Mudge tried to remove the peculiar necklace, but quickly discovered that it had no clasp. Scissors, cutters, pliers – nothing could break its silvery chain. Some of the matrons feared witchcraft; others sensed riches, but from that day on they all regarded Hazel with a wary eye. And so, the necklace stayed with its tiny owner and, as she grew, it grew with her. And whenever she had a bad day, whenever the other children pulled her too-large ears or made fun of her small, sturdy frame, she would hold the pendant tightly in her hand and try to imagine the person who had given it to her.

Hazel's eleventh birthday had, without a doubt, been a bad day. So as soon as she was in bed, top-to-tail with snoring Sara Pandey, she tugged her necklace from her collar and closed her eyes. She always pictured the same scene: her and her mother by a roaring log fire, sharing a pot of rosehip tea. Hazel didn't know what a rosehip was, and Ditchmoor's fireplaces were invariably cold and black, but she had come across the scene in one of the school's rare storybooks, and it felt just right.

As she held the stone, smooth and warm in her hand, she embroidered a picture of her mother in her mind. She imagined thick, knotted hair, just like her own, the same subtly pointed features and, at the centre of each eye, a steady gleam of light, meant only for her. Usually, Hazel would follow these comforting thoughts down into the depths of sleep. Only that evening, sleep didn't come.

The night was strangely still. A chilly moon peered in through the dormitory window, illuminating the stiff ranks of bedsteads and the smooth faces of their occupants. Hazel squirmed onto her side, a vague unease weighing in her chest. She had felt it all afternoon – the faintest quivering in the air, a dim sense that the ground was less steady beneath her feet. She sighed heavily, blaming the greenish slop she'd been given for lunch. Clutching her pendant tighter, she tried to settle her tired limbs. Then, just as her muscles began to soften, she heard a sound in the courtyard outside.

Hazel's eyes flicked open. She sat up in bed, waiting, listening. The grey shapes of the sleeping children rose and fell with their breaths. Then she heard it again – a clear, three-note whistle. Anyone else would have thought it was the call of a nesting nightbird, but Hazel knew it was the sign.

CHAPTER TWO

The Belfry

HAZEL WRAPPED HER BLANKET ROUND HER shoulders and, taking care to avoid the creakiest floorboards, crept out of the dormitory. With a snick of the latch, she closed the door behind her and set off quickly down the moon-striped corridor. She had made this barefoot journey many times before, and flitted over the uncarpeted boards as quietly as a moth.

Once she reached the door to the corner tower, she glanced over her shoulder to check she had not been followed, then hurried up a musty staircase until she came to a small window with a rusted lock. One sharp shove and the window pushed open. Then, with a jump and a wriggle, she hauled herself up and out into the twinkling night.

As Hazel drew the cool air into her lungs, she felt a rush of happiness. Up on the roof, something inside her was able to uncurl and stretch its limbs. She leaned over the parapet, wondering what it would be like to sprout wings and soar high above Ditchmoor, looking down on the place as though it were nothing but a monstrous doll house. She was merrily imagining the shock on the matrons' faces, when she heard the whistle again, as bright and playful as a blackbird's call.

She looked over the courtyard towards the chapel roof. A boy with startling red hair was leaning out of the belfry, waving and beckoning to her.

'Pete!' Hazel bounced up on her tiptoes and waved eagerly back. Then she vaulted over a buttress and hurried along the parapet to join him.

Hazel and Pete were best friends. In fact, they were more like brother and sister. Pete's parents had died when he was a baby and, after being passed like a parcel from aunt, to uncle, to distant cousin, he'd ended up on Ditchmoor's icy doorstep on exactly the same day that Hazel arrived there. Within minutes of setting foot in the school's bare-walled nursery, the two infants had found each other and were sitting close together on a wooden pew, hand in tiny hand. Huffing with disapproval, Miss Fitch had tried to pull them apart, but they had both started up such a wild howling that she'd backed away in horror and never tried again. Since that time, Hazel and Pete had been inseparable.

'Get in quick! I've got something for you!' Pete reached out and pulled Hazel through a stone arch into the belfry.

'What is it?' she whispered.

He rubbed his hands together then rummaged in his battered old carpet bag. Hazel closed the makeshift curtains that draped the arches and lit the hurricane lantern that swung from a rafter beneath a huddled roost of bats. The flame flared, casting a warm orange light around the interior of the belfry, which, over the years, Hazel and Pete had turned into a snug little den.

Despite the cobwebs and the whiff of owl pellets, the place was comfort itself. The floorboards were covered by a worn, patterned rug and, scattered about, were squashed cushions and thick plaids, all stolen from the Warden's private quarters. Pete, a self-taught master-thief, had even managed to nab a briarwood chessboard and most of the pieces – though as neither of them knew how to play, they had to make up their own rules. It was a shabby little hideaway, but it was theirs alone, and their favourite place in the world.

'Ta-da!' said Pete, holding aloft a fat golden pear. 'Fresh from the Warden's garden!'

'You didn't!'

'Did!' He tossed it to Hazel who caught it with one hand. She flumped down on a dusty cushion and took a hungry bite.

'Thank you!' she said, through a juicy mouthful. 'Lovely.'

The children sat side by side, backs against the wall, and passed the stolen fruit between them. After the last drop of juice had been sucked from the core, Pete spilled more loot from the bag: a jar of pickled eggs, a tin of sardines, half a pot of marmalade and a dewy bottle of lemonade.

'Wow!' said Hazel, sitting up straight. 'That's a *lot*, Pete!' He puffed up with pride, but she shook her head. 'You'd better not get caught. You're on last chances, remember? If the Warden catches you with a haul like this, he'll send you to work for rat-catcher Pike, and I . . .'

Pete laughed. 'Can't catch me, Hazel,' he said. 'Too quick, too clever!' He unscrewed the jar of eggs and fished two out with his fingers. She gladly took one and gobbled it down. 'Anyway, I knew you'd need cheering up.'

'What do you mean?'

'Elsie, of course. I heard her lot were giving you trouble.'

Hazel shrugged and unscrewed the cap of the lemonade bottle.

'You should tell 'em where to get off,' he continued hotly, 'or *I* will!'

'It'd only make things worse,' she said. 'You know what they're like.'

'Oh, I dunno about that!' Pete replied. 'When Ed Truckle called me a gingernut, I dropped a frog down the back of his shirt. That was the last time he gave me any bother, and *that's* a fact!'

'Poor frog!' gasped Hazel, alarmed.

'Yes.' Pete nodded. 'Poor frog!' They looked at each other for a moment, then dissolved into snorting giggles.

As they caught their breath, Pete began to cough – a

deep, rattling cough that bent him double. Hazel frowned and passed him the lemonade. He took a swig, then briskly changed the subject.

'Anyway, listen . . .' he said. 'Did you hear about Mo and Kiran? They made it out!'

'What, really?!'

'They hid in one of the delivery carts, under some sacking. Rolled off the back once they were clear of the gates –' he smacked his hands together with glee – 'gone!'

'Where to?'

'The woods. They've gone to live with the Wild Children.'

Everyone at Ditchmoor had heard stories about the Wild Children. In fact, they were more than stories; they were legends. The Wild Children, so it was said, had escaped the clutches of wicked and negligent grown-ups and had gone to live in the ferny heart of Goblyn Wood. There, far beyond the reach of matrons or wardens, they hunted rabbits, scavenged for cherries and chestnuts and slept high in the trees. Everyone had heard the stories. Not everyone believed them.

'How do you know they made it?' asked Hazel.

'Well, I don't know *for sure*,' Pete continued, turning the bottle between fidgety fingers. 'The Warden told us they'd been got by wolves. But he *would* say that, wouldn't he?'

Hazel raised her eyebrows. Wolves were always a possibility.

'Just think,' said Pete, eyes shining. 'No Warden, no Fitch. We could make our own rules, live our *own* lives!'

Hazel sighed. They'd had this conversation before. 'But what if she came back?' she said. 'What if my mum came back for us, Pete, and we weren't here?'

He shook his head and puffed lightly through his nose. 'She wouldn't be coming for *me*, Hazel.'

'No, but . . .' She looked him in the eye. 'She'd take both of us, Pete. I *know* she would.'

His mouth twisted into a sad smile. 'They always *mean* to come back . . .'

Hazel's shoulders slumped. 'But they never do,' she finished.

Pete slipped his arm through hers and they sat for a while sharing the last sips of the lemonade between them. Moths flickered softly round the lantern; bats threaded in and out of the holes in the roof; below the floorboards a mouse hurried back and forth, storing up crumbs for winter.

'Let's go out on the ledge,' said Pete. 'It's almost midnight. You never know, we might see Miss Fitch whizzing about on her broomstick.'

Laughing, the children swung their legs out of the arch and dropped down onto a wide ledge where they sat side by side, feet dangling over the sharply sloping tiles below.

The moon hung full in the sky and they could see far into the night. Etched into the darkness were silver rivers and twinkling villages, glinting train tracks and chalk roads that led to who knew where. And, hovering black on the horizon, was the old forest with the ancient name: Goblyn Wood.

'You know I'd never leave without you,' Pete said, nudging her elbow. 'You'll think about it, though, won't you?'

But Hazel wasn't listening. She was gazing straight ahead, eyes fixed on the long, ragged smudge in the distance.

She had looked out at the forest many times before. She had felt drawn to it, warmed by it. She imagined leafy light, mossy roots and rock-strewn streams. But that night she felt a strange unease – the same unease she had felt all day. She strained her eyes towards the horizon. The woods were much darker than the rest of the night. An empty darkness. A darkness that bent everything towards it and swallowed it up.

Pete was talking about bonfires and dandelion soup. But she couldn't hear him. The shadows began to waver then spread, creeping quickly across the moorlands. She sucked in her breath as a shivery weakness gusted over her. And then, without knowing how or why, she knew:

There *was* something in Goblyn Wood. Not treetop villages or Wild Children, but something else. And it was dying.

CHAPTER THREE

The Ladies

THAT WAS THE FIRST TIME HAZEL HAD NEARLY fallen off the roof, but it was *not* the first time she had felt things – peculiar things that she couldn't explain. Since the spring, there had been several occasions when she had felt flickers and vibrations in the world around her. She never quite knew when it was going to happen, but when it did it was as if her nerves branched out of her body and joined up with the veins in the leaves and the roots of the trees. In those moments, she could hear each separate beat of a bee's wing, see berries ripening on the brambles, feel the sap rising through a thousand stems, until she no longer knew where she, Hazel Quince, ended and the world began.

Then, *snap!* It would pass, and she'd find herself being shaken by a matron, or surrounded by a crowd of whispering children. Which is why she didn't like to think about those feelings, and definitely didn't want to talk about them. So she shoved the whole chapel-roof episode into the corner of her mind and might have been able to forget about it altogether, had it not been for what happened a few weeks later.

It was Sunday after chapel. Ditchmoor's corridors, usually so blank and stern, echoed with excited chatter. *The Ladies were coming!* The Ladies – a mother and her two adult daughters – visited Ditchmoor once every few months and it was always an occasion. The night before a visit, the children were each given a lump of black soap to scrub themselves with. In the morning they had freshly laundered clothes, and hot porridge to put a flush in their cheeks. Then, at nine o'clock sharp, the Ladies would arrive in their purring white motorcar, take tea and ginger cake with a fluttery Miss Fitch, then glide into the stony courtyard where the children would be lined up in two smart rows, anxiously wondering if today would be *their* day.

For most of them, their day never came, but for a couple of lucky ones, Ladies Day would be the start of a whole new life. A smartly-gloved hand would pick them out and, after the right papers had been stamped, they would be whisked away to go and live with what Miss Fitch called 'a proper family'. But whereas most of the children counted down the days to the Ladies' visits with excitement, Hazel and Pete awaited them with a molten dread. Because what if one of them was chosen, but not the other? So, while the other children brushed and scrubbed, Hazel and Pete left their faces unwashed and made sure to clump their hair with extra tangles.

As the chapel bell tolled the quarter hour, Hazel cast her eye along the line of children opposite her – boys in brown jackets and long shorts; girls in tunics cut from the same coarse cloth – all holding their breath, imagining other possible lives, perhaps only minutes away. Elsie Pocket, who hadn't been at Ditchmoor long, had pulled her hair into two pretty braids and was picking anxiously at her fingernails. Hazel glanced at Pete, lined up next to her. His hair blazed brightly in the sunshine, but his face was pale and pinched. He winced as he stifled a cough.

Hazel frowned. 'Have you been to see Nurse yet?'

'What?' he scoffed. 'For more of her stinking cough syrup? No thanks. If anything's killing me it's that gunk.'

'But, Pete . . .'

'But nothing. Anyway –' he patted his cheeks and grinned – 'nothing like a deathly pallor to put the Ladies off!'

She didn't laugh.

'It's *all right*.' He thumped his chest. 'Fit as a flea, I am. Now don't forget the "stare"!'

Hazel blinked her strange, changeable eyes, now shifting like seawater from grey to blue to emerald green. 'I'm counting on it,' she said.

Before she could press Pete on his troubling cough, silvery chimes of laughter rang across the courtyard. The two friends swallowed hard, gave each other's hands a quick squeeze, then faced forward.

In their pastel skirts and laced-up boots the Ladies were the picture of elegance, yet there was something about them that made Hazel's flesh creep. Though their smiles were pearly bright, their teeth seemed too evenly set, and their finely sculpted faces were unnaturally smooth, as if poured and moulded from wax.

They approached the waiting alley of children and began their inspections, turning and gliding between the rows like dancers in a clockwork ballroom. The children stood silently to attention, heels together, puffing out their ribs. As usual, it wasn't long before one of the youngest began to cry – first a whimper, then a wail that shuddered round the courtyard walls. Miss Fitch swooped like a hawk on a baby rabbit and dragged the girl back indoors. Unflustered, the Ladies continued their inspections, cooing gently and ruffling hair.

Hazel drew a nervous breath as they drifted down the line towards her and Pete. She began her usual ritual, counting each step of the mother's kidskin boots, praying the rhythm wouldn't falter, willing them to walk on by as they had done every time before. But, on that day, the mother's footsteps slowed, then stopped.

Hazel looked up, ready to fix her with her off-putting stare. But, to her horror, the mother's china-doll eyes were fastened on Pete.

'So wan,' said the woman, brow creasing lightly as her daughters gathered round. She lifted his chin with a gloved finger. Hazel glanced across and met his eye, black with fear.

'Poor thing,' said one of the daughters, gazing at him as if he were an ailing puppy.

'Oh, Mama ...' cried the other, clasping her hands together. 'Couldn't we ... ?'

But she said no more, for at that moment, Pete launched into a bout of dramatic coughing and spluttering, made all the more convincing by the authentic rattle in his chest. The Ladies lurched away, lips curled in disgust. With a swish of silk, they turned their backs and crossed over to the opposite line.

Pete and Hazel exhaled simultaneously, hearts thudding. They reached their hands towards each other and discreetly locked fingers. They'd be safe now till winter, at least. Breath steadying, shoulders dropping, Hazel watched the Ladies finish their tour. Now it was Elsie's turn. She stood straight as a pin, blinking rapidly. As the Ladies approached, she took a small step forward and bobbed her head, but their soft gaze passed over her as if she wasn't even there.

In that moment, Hazel felt Elsie crumple. She didn't see it, she felt it – a painful tightness in the air. Then Elsie's eyes found hers and narrowed sharply.

Later that morning, after the Ladies had left with Zia Pinket and little Percy Thimble, Elsie hunted Hazel down.

The children were busy in the vegetable patch, digging up parsnips. It was raining hard – great glassy beads pitting the soil, drawing up the rich smell of the earth. Hazel rested on her spade as Mr Robinson bounced happily around her feet, tugging earthworms from the freshly turned clods. She was about to get back to work, when she felt a shove between her shoulder blades.

'Didn't I tell you to get rid of that thing?' It was Elsie, simmering with rage. 'I know you don't have any *actual* friends, but birds? Really?'

Offended, the robin shook out his feathers and bobbed away over the garden wall.

'We're outside,' said Hazel. 'I can't—'

Elsie pushed her harder, sending her tumbling backwards over her spade into the rain-soaked soil. 'Get yourself a real friend.'

Hazel sat up quickly, wiping mud away. 'Elsie!' she spluttered. 'If this is about the Ladies, then . . .'

The moment the words escaped her lips, she knew she'd made a mistake. Elsie's jaw tightened. Then, just as Hazel tensed up, ready for another assault, footsteps came splashing quickly towards them.

'*I'm* her friend!' Pete stepped between Elsie and Hazel, fists balled.

'It's all right.' Hazel scrambled to her feet. 'Really, I'm fine.'

'No, it's *not* all right!' Pete replied crossly. He turned to Elsie. '*I'm* her friend. Me! Now leave her alone, will you?'

The other children stopped digging and clustered around to watch.

Emboldened, Elsie took a step towards him. She was a head taller, and stronger. 'You?' she sniffed. 'You don't count.'

She tried to move past him, but Pete blocked her. She tried again, but Pete stood his ground. Elsie glared at him, outraged. With a violent shove, she thrust him sideways, face down into the mud.

And that's when something inside Hazel awoke. As she heard Pete coughing and spitting out clots of earth, everything grew clearer, brighter. She felt a bristling over her skin, a sharpening at her fingertips. Blood rushed hot in her veins, and her body, which moments before had been floating and uncertain, drew itself together into a solid mass of bunched-up energy.

Then a tremendous charge bolted through her limbs. And she sprang.

CHAPTER FOUR

Escape

'WITCHCRAFT!' MISS FITCH'S EYES POPPED with fear and fury. 'I'm telling you, Cecil, in all my years, I've never seen anything like it.'

Hazel stood in the Warden's office, dripping wet, shaking with fright and anger. Moments before she had been brawling in the mud and her body still brimmed with a terrifying ferocity – tiny lightning bolts sparking through every nerve.

The Warden looked up from his elevenses.

'Witchcraft?' he said, raising two caterpillar eyebrows.

'Yes indeed!' replied Miss Fitch, nodding vigorously. 'Unnatural, it was. Eyes flashing, snapping and snarling like a wild beast. It took four of us to pull her off. That Elsie girl's got bumps and bruises all over!'

The Warden chewed slowly on a crumpet and looked Hazel up and down. 'Explain yourself,' he muttered.

But Hazel couldn't explain a thing. She remembered the look of surprise, then terror, on Elsie's face. The rest was a blur of shrieks and blows before powerful arms had wrenched her away, feet kicking the air.

'I smelled it the very first day,' Miss Fitch continued, wagging a finger. 'Comes from odd folk, she does. Just look at those goblin eyes of hers! Green one day, brown the next. And how old is she now? Eleven? A wicked age. Know this, Cecil: this is just the beginning!' She folded her arms. 'Mr Pike will take her.'

'The rat-catcher?' the Warden confirmed.

Miss Fitch nodded. 'He prefers the small ones. Better for fishing rats out of rat-holes.'

'No!' gasped Hazel, turning to the Warden in desperation. 'Please!'

'Either *she* goes,' snapped the matron, 'or I leave this very day.'

The Warden dabbed a smear of butter from the corner of his mouth and gave Hazel a long, grim stare. He had no time for Miss Fitch's superstitions, but nor did he want to lose one of his most efficient matrons. He took in Hazel's oddly pointed features, her brambly hair and those strange, flickering eyes. Yes, the child probably was more trouble than she was worth. After forty years in the job, the Warden had a nose for that sort of thing and, in any case, he wanted to get back to his crumpet. He gave a grunt of assent, waved his visitors towards the door and stuck his spoon in the jam pot.

*

Papers needed to be shuffled and noises made about bad behaviour and last chances blown, but by lunchtime Hazel had been marched out of Ditchmoor's iron-studded doors with nothing but the boots on her feet and the clothes she stood up in.

Utterly bewildered, she blinked at the green landscape spreading out before her. Since the age of two, her entire life had been contained by Ditchmoor's granite walls. Eating, working, sleeping – a glum, grey life, but the only one she knew, spent with the only friend she had.

She turned and flung herself at the door, fists hammering, yelling to be let back in, but the oak was so thick that nobody could hear her cries. Frantic, she stumbled round the outside of the building. The clatter and murmur of lunch bubbled out of the refectory window, but it was too high up for her to see inside.

Not knowing what else to do, she returned to the doorstep and glanced down the roadway. Soon Pike would be along to collect her, then it would be off to the town's cellars to catch rodents with her bare hands and snap their wriggling spines. The thought of it made her legs go weak. Then, just as despair began to grip, she heard a bright, familiar whistle high above her.

She turned and looked up to the roofline. A small figure waved down.

'Pete!' she cried.

He put a finger to his lips then tossed down his old carpet

bag, swung his legs over the parapet and shimmied down a drainpipe.

As soon as his feet touched the ground, she wrapped him in a sudden hug.

'I said I'd never go without you,' he said in mock anger, 'I never thought *you'd* go without me!'

'They kicked me out!'

'I heard!' he said, impressed. 'Snuck out of lunch as soon as I could. Fitch is still raving about demons. I expect she'll hole up in the chapel till Christmas!' He hooted with laughter, but Hazel could only muster a giggle.

'You all right, Hazel?' he said, wiping his eyes. 'It's gonna be okay, you know. We're together, aren't we? And look! We're out! We're *out!*'

'It's not that, it's just . . .' She didn't know how to put it. 'I . . . I don't know what got into me.'

'I do!' Pete snorted. 'That Elsie had it coming and you gave it to her. About time!'

Hazel shook her head. All of a sudden, everything she had tried for so long to ignore pushed its way to the surface. 'I think there's something wrong with me,' she blurted. 'Really *wrong* with me.'

He looked at her, startled.

'Promise you won't think I'm weird?' she said.

Pete frowned. 'Course not. What is it?'

She glanced down the roadway. No sign of Pike, not yet. She sat on the doorstep and pulled Pete down beside her.

'It's hard to describe,' she said, fixing her eyes on the patch of stone between her feet, 'but I've been having these . . . *feelings.*'

'Feelings?'

'Not all the time, just sometimes, and then it's like . . .' She tapped her cheek, searching for the right words. 'Like . . . I can see the tiniest details – every grain in the floorboards, every speck of dust. And I can hear *everything*, all at once: spiders spinning webs, beetles burrowing in the rafters, mice sniffing crumbs on the floor . . . And do you remember the thunderstorm last week?'

Pete nodded.

'Well, I knew it was coming. Days earlier. I felt it in the weight of the air.'

'The weight of the air?' he said, scratching his head.

'Yes,' she said, everything pouring out now. 'Then today, in the vegetable patch, I was angry. So angry! Then all those feelings came rushing in at once, and I turned into somebody else, or *something* else. Something fierce, or . . . or wild. It wasn't me, Pete, but at the same time, it *was* me . . .'

She stopped speaking, breathless. For a moment she didn't dare look at him. When she did, he was grinning brightly.

'It's the thing, isn't it?'

'What thing?'

'You know, the same thing that makes sparrows sit on your shoulder, or squirrels eat out of your hand. You've always had it.' He folded his arms triumphantly. 'Ha! I knew you were special!'

'I don't know *what* it is, Pete.'

'Amazing, that's what!'

Hazel's eyes brimmed with relief. 'Really?'

'And magic,' Pete said, eyes rounding at the idea. 'Hey, maybe you *are* magic! Do you think it's magic? I bet it is!'

'*Pffft*, come off it!'

'Well, it wouldn't surprise *me*!'

Hazel shook her head and smiled.

The sky had cleared, and the late September sun was drawing up steam from the grassy meadows. She felt a weight lifting, the air around her brightening.

All of a sudden, they heard a rattle in the distance.

'Pike!' said Hazel. They sprang to their feet and stared down the roadway. A rickety pony-cart was cresting the hill.

'Right!' Pete swung his carpet bag over his shoulder. 'Let's go!'

'Where to?'

'The woods, of course!'

Hazel looked towards the bristling horizon. The strange sickness that had overcome her on the chapel roof had not returned and, once again, Goblyn Wood appeared as a soft, ferny haven. Pete was practically hovering with anticipation and, as she gazed towards the distant swathe of trees she felt it too – the promise of the forest, vast and green.

'The Wild Children?' asked Hazel.

Pete nodded.

Then they gripped each other's hands, darted across

the road and ran as fast as their legs would carry them towards what, until that day, had been the very edge of their world.

CHAPTER FIVE

Wolves

THE FOREST WAS DISTANT, AND THE WAY unmarked, but it was a golden afternoon and Hazel and Pete felt lighter and stronger with every step. They hopped over a wall into a gentle downhill meadow and breathed the unfamiliar air. A kestrel hovered high above them, pipits flittered in the jostling grasses, and all around was the fluting and humming of living things. As the granite block of Ditchmoor shrank down behind them, Hazel felt a shiver of energy rising through her, the world ripening with new beginnings.

'You can make cakes from acorn flour, you know,' said Pete as they rested on a stile. He pulled a hunk of bread from his bag and passed it to Hazel. 'Gather them up in the autumn, grind 'em between stones, add a drop of honey. Better than anything from the Warden's pantry, I'll bet!'

Hazel felt a pang as she remembered their cosy little belfry, with its soft cushions and half pot of marmalade suddenly abandoned. But Pete's excitement was infectious.

'We'll build a treehouse,' he said, 'up with the birds!'

'And the bats,' Hazel added.

'There'll be bonfires in the autumn . . .'

'And gooseberry jam!'

'In the winter, we'll make ice skates.'

'And, in the spring, we'll peel sticks for fishing rods.'

'You and me, Hazel,' said Pete.

Hazel smiled. 'Always!'

They breathed in the soft air and took in the space and light of the moorlands. The afternoon sun put fresh colour into Pete's cheeks. He dusted his hands and jumped down from the stile.

'Come on, then,' he said. 'Can't be late for the acorn-gathering!'

They walked quickly down the tussocky slope. Pete chattered breathlessly about edible mushrooms and the best way to build a treehouse and, as they drew closer to the forest edge, Hazel felt a new eagerness spreading through her limbs.

By the time they were deep in the valley the sun was low, lighting the edges of the clouds and stretching their shadows ahead of them. Soon, the ground softened beneath their feet and they heard the chatter of water over stone. A narrow stream rushed down into the valley's fold.

'How do we find them?' Hazel asked as they reached a boulder-strewn stretch of water.

'The Wild Children?' Pete replied. 'We don't. They find us.'

Leaping from stone to teetering stone, they crossed to the opposite bank. A shoulder of hillside rose up ahead, blue in the early twilight. Now that they were low in the valley, they had lost sight of the forest edge. Pete stopped and cast his eyes from left to right, uncertain. But, to Hazel's surprise, she knew which way to go. She didn't know how she knew it, she just did. She felt it there, waiting beyond the hill, drawing her irresistibly closer.

'This way!' she said.

'You sure?'

Hazel nodded and they pushed on, up the scrabbly slope.

The path was harder now – craggier, and tangled with low-lying shrubs. Pete began to slip behind, but the closer Hazel got to the forest, the stronger its magnetic pull became.

By the time they were halfway up the hillside, the shadows had meshed into night. Hazel was busily pushing ahead, feet pressing into the rising ground, when suddenly her senses prickled, alert. She caught the scent of rippling fur, steaming breath. A wet smell. Dogs.

She stopped in her tracks, all senses straining into the gloom. The wind rustled over the slope, swirling the fog-grass around her feet.

Pete scrambled up behind her. 'What is it? What's wrong?'

She didn't reply. Amongst the hissing grasses, there was a soft panting. Something – no, several things – were watching them, standing at a distance in the shadows.

31

Hazel took a step forward. The things moved too.

'Look!' Pete yelped, clutching her elbow. 'Wolves!' Keeping his eyes fixed on the ragged shapes, he rummaged in his bag and dragged out a clumsy-looking knife, stolen from Ditchmoor's kitchens.

Hazel had never seen a wolf before. She'd read the stories: jagged fur, lolling tongues – killers. But, as she met the amber gaze of the largest beast, something deep in her gut told her that those wolves weren't hunting.

For a moment she doubted her instincts, tried to rustle up some fear. But her heartbeat stayed steady.

'Don't startle them,' she whispered, cautiously motioning for Pete to put away the knife. 'Just keep moving. We're not far now.' Pete looked at her, astonished, but he stuffed the blade back in his bag and reached for her hand.

'Why are they following us?' he hissed nervously as they walked on.

'I don't know,' Hazel replied, 'but I don't think they'll hurt us.'

Pete squeezed her hand tighter as they trekked up the slope, their grey companions padding silently on either side.

As the ground levelled, trees rose up ahead. The air was cold now – a low wind rushing through the grass. They picked up the pace and made for the dense coverage of the forest.

*

The trees stood thick about them. Compared to the chill of the slope, the woods felt soft and warm. A green, mossy smell rose from the shaggy trunks and, in the gauzy darkness, Hazel could hear the rustle of small creatures breathing, feeding, growing.

They wandered further in, hand in hand, listening to the creak and rustle of the woods. Now that the moon was lost behind leaves, the wolves melted into the night – though a lingering scent of grizzled fur told Hazel they were not far off.

She pointed at a large hollow in the trunk of an oak. 'Let's set up camp,' she said.

Pete was still nervously scanning the trees. 'No,' he said. 'Let's find the Wild Children.'

'I thought they were supposed to find us,' she replied, confused.

'Yes, but maybe if we go further on they'll ... I don't know ... find us faster.'

She nodded and they wandered deeper in, waiting for a sign of some sort.

Pete cupped his hands and called out, 'Kiran? Mo? It's us! We made it!'

His voice vanished quickly into the leafy gloom. They trudged on, picking their way over twisted roots and mossy boulders. A barn owl floated silently across the path ahead. But there was no sign of treetop villages, or of any human life at all.

'Let's start again in the morning,' said Hazel, 'when it's light.'

But Pete didn't reply.

He was up on his toes, pointing excitedly. Hazel turned to see a small light bobbing in the middle distance. It looked like a lantern, but there was something strange about the shivering flame. Though it danced and flared, Hazel sensed that, rather than giving out warmth, the light was drawing it in.

She frowned and motioned for Pete to stay where he was, but his eyes were fixed on the flame and, before she could stop him, he rushed towards it, waving and shouting.

'Hey! Hi!' he called. 'We're friends! We've come to join you!' The light hovered for a moment, then skipped away through the trees. 'Quick, Hazel! They're showing us the way!'

'No, Pete, wait!' she urged. But he had already hared after the flame, determined not to let it out of his sight.

Hazel stumbled behind him, weaving between tree trunks and ducking low branches. As the light drew them into the heart of the woods, a shapeless fear stirred within her. Something was changing in the feel of the earth beneath her feet, in the ripple of the leaves around her. The warm pulse of life that she had felt on entering the forest was fading.

'Pete, stop!' she called after him, but he kept on running until, suddenly, they broke into a clearing. The light had vanished.

'Where did it go?' gasped Pete. 'Hazel?'

But she was not looking for the light. She was staring about her, eyes wide with horror.

The encircling trees were stripped of leaves and their barks were ghostly white. They looked as if they had been burned from the inside and would crumble to dust at the first breath of wind. Only there was no wind. The air was still. Everything was still. Even the soil beneath their feet was as dead and dusty as cinders. Hazel felt weaker and weaker, as if all the life was draining down through her body, into the parched earth. It was the same sickening feeling she'd had on the chapel roof.

Suddenly, there was a rushing in her ears and the world began to blacken and disintegrate. Then out of the woods came a clattering, unearthly laughter, and something was upon them.

A blinding force knocked Hazel to the ground and sent the forest whirling around her. She heard a shout and raised her head to see shadowy hands lift Pete high into the air. A cry of panic rose to her throat, but she could not make a sound. There were more than one of them, fast and agile, shrieking with dreadful laughter. Then one came reaching for her.

But something else now howled through the undergrowth towards the clearing. Out of the night came the molten forms of the wolves, leaping and springing fearlessly at the muscular shadows, hounding them back towards the trees. From far away, Hazel heard Pete calling her name. Then the night closed around her.

CHAPTER SIX

The Keeper's Lodge

THERE WAS A WALKER IN GOBLYN WOOD THAT morning. As usual, he'd packed his bag of equipment, made a flask of tea and set out with his cat in the hope of finding something rare or precious. And that is how he discovered her – cold and lifeless at the foot of a dead birch. After a panicked moment, he found her pulse. It was weak – no more than a trembling thread. He glanced up at the pale circle of trees and scratched his short white beard. *She's lucky*, he thought as he wrapped her in his jacket and hoisted her into his arms. Then, as he carried her out of the withered undergrowth, away from the dying woodland, he reflected that perhaps *he* had been lucky too. Very lucky indeed.

Hazel woke to an uncomfortable weight on her chest. Slowly, she opened her eyes to see two narrow pupils regarding her with cold disdain. She shrieked and sat bolt upright, sending an angry long-haired cat flying off the bed and out of the door. For a moment the world rocked and swayed like the deck of a ship. She had no idea how long she had been asleep, and her head was reeling. As shapes and objects drifted back to their places, she saw that she was in a bright and tidy bedroom.

Glancing around, she caught sight of her reflection in a tall mirror. She was dressed in a crisp white nightshirt and was sitting up in a brass bed, her legs tucked under a prettily embroidered quilt. The room was decorated with sweet-pea wallpaper and in the corner stood a mahogany washstand with pitcher and basin. Save for one dead wasp on the windowsill, everything was perfectly spick and span.

Now that the fright of waking had passed, her limbs felt drained and weak. She pushed back against the head of the bed to steady herself. A ghastly feeling was creeping up on her – the feeling of having woken from a hideous nightmare. Her mind groped around blindly. Something terrible had happened and now she was ... Where *was* she?

Footsteps clattered up a staircase.

'Blasted cat!' a voice muttered. There was a polite tap on the door and in stepped a portly gentleman with a neatly trimmed beard, followed by a rosy woman in a flour-dusted apron.

'Don't mind Purkiss.' The gentleman smiled. 'He's a little territorial, that's all.' Hazel stared at them, wide-eyed.

The woman bustled forward and touched Hazel's forehead with the back of her hand. 'Fever's down,' she said, nodding.

The gentleman pulled up a wicker chair by the side of the bed and looked at Hazel with soft blue eyes, greatly magnified by the thickness of his spectacles.

'I'm Professor Bartholomew Grinling,' he said gently, 'and this is my housekeeper, Mrs Plover.' The woman gave a small curtsey, then they both looked at her expectantly.

'Hazel,' she whispered, head in a whirl. The professor looked pleased.

'*Corylus avellana!*' He grinned. 'Pretty catkins, late summer nuts. One of my favourite trees.'

Hazel blinked at him, baffled.

'And where are you from, Hazel?' the professor continued. 'Your parents must be frantic.'

'I'm . . . I'm from Ditchmoor,' she stammered.

The professor nodded sadly and turned to Mrs Plover. 'A runaway,' he whispered. 'As I thought.'

Hazel looked around the bedroom again. 'Where am I?'

'I found you this morning,' said the professor, 'in the forest, half frozen to death.'

Her mind instantly sharpened. The forest. She remembered the dancing light, the ashen trees . . . her blood turned to ice.

'Pete!' she blurted. 'Where's Pete?'

'Who?' The professor looked startled.

'Pete! He was with me in the forest, he . . .' She trailed off as other fragments returned. She remembered the shadows, the wild laughter, the force of a blow.

'Oh!' she gasped. 'They took him! They . . . they came through the trees . . . and took him!'

'Who took him?'

'I don't know!' Hazel's voice was rising in fright. 'It was so fast.' She threw off her blankets and swung her legs out of the bed. 'I have to find him!'

But as soon as she was on her feet, the floorboards seemed to bend beneath her and her legs gave way. Her hosts quickly settled her back on the mattress. A thick nausea churned in her stomach.

'Steady now,' said Mrs Plover, rubbing her back. Hazel swallowed hard and tried to slow her choppy breathing.

Professor Grinling settled back down on his chair and looked at her with concern. 'Pete's your friend, is he?'

Hazel nodded rapidly.

'I see, I see.' He stroked his beard. 'And you say he was *taken*?'

Hazel tried to reply, but the only sound that escaped her lips was something between a gasp and a whimper.

'All right, my dear.' He put a gentle hand on her shoulder. 'This is a matter for the police. I'll report it to them straight away.'

Hazel stared at him. The police? But what if they sent Pete back to Ditchmoor? What if they packed her off to the rat-catcher?

'But I—' she protested.

Mrs Plover shook her head. 'You're in no fit state to go trudging about those woods.'

'But he—'

'The police have dogs; they have know-how,' said Grinling with a reassuring firmness. 'They're our best chance of finding him.'

Hazel hesitated, then nodded slowly. Better Pete was found by the police than not found at all.

'I'll call the station right away,' said the professor. 'In the meantime, Mrs Plover will make you a nice hot posset.' He stood up to leave. 'I dare say you're famished.'

Hazel could not remember the last time an adult had treated her with such kindness, and she didn't know what to say. She burbled something grateful as Mrs Plover tucked her back under the heavy quilt and hurried from the room.

As soon as the door closed, her thoughts swung back to the previous night. What had she seen in the forest? Pieces came together like shards of a broken mirror. She remembered the darting shadows, Pete snatched and lifted high in the air, shouting her name. Could it have been the Wild Children? Were they not the friendly tribe they had dreamed of? But that laughter – it wasn't human. It was more than human, or less . . .

As she lay there, trying to make sense of it all, Hazel became aware of a hubbub filtering in from outside. She sat up and tweaked the lace curtain by the window.

To her astonishment, she was not in some country cottage near the forest, but in the middle of what appeared to be a grand city. Finely dressed people hurried past swinging umbrellas, pigeons pecked at puddles and, all around, there was the chatter and hum of human life. Her gaze travelled across a cobbled forecourt towards what looked like a sprawling cathedral. Its arches and towers reminded her of Ditchmoor's chapel, only the gargoyles were not demons but lions, and the stone columns were carved with monkeys, frogs and snakes.

The door clicked open and Mrs Plover stepped back into the room with a steaming china mug.

'Where are we?' asked Hazel, baffled.

'We're in London, dear,' said Mrs Plover, setting the mug on the bedside table, 'and that –' she pointed towards the grand building – 'that's the Natural History Museum. The professor works there. He's the Head Keeper.' She saw that Hazel didn't understand. 'Oh, don't ask me,' she chuckled, fluffing Hazel's pillow. 'He collects beetles, beasties, that sort of thing. He was out in the forest this morning looking for some rare moth. Found you instead! Now drink your posset, please. You need to stay warm.'

Hazel took the mug and sipped the milky mixture, thickened up with soft white bread. It was like nothing she had tasted before: hot, sugary and frothy, all mixed with a warming spice. She drained the mug in a few hungry gulps.

'Good girl,' said Mrs Plover, straightening Hazel's quilt.

'Now, the professor says that the police are organising a search party. So we just need to sit tight and wait.'

'Thank you,' Hazel murmured as the comforting heat of the posset spread through her.

'Get some rest, my dear,' said Mrs Plover with a cheery smile. 'We'll let you know the minute we have news.'

Hazel wanted to ask more, but she was suddenly overcome by an irresistible drowsiness. As Mrs Plover took the empty mug from her hands, she felt her eyelids lowering, her head drooping, her limbs as heavy as clay. Then she fell back against the pillows and dropped like a stone into fathomless sleep.

It was many hours before something woke her: a sharp rattling, like a window being shaken. Hazel stirred and looked sleepily about the moon-washed room. For a moment, all was silent, but then she heard it again: rattling, then a high-pitched sound like a muffled cry. It seemed to be coming from the floor below.

'Professor? Mrs Plover?' she murmured. There was no reply. *Probably the cat*, she thought groggily, and slumped back into the eiderdown, where she slept solidly till morning.

CHAPTER SEVEN

The Door

'YOU LOOK SO MUCH BETTER TODAY,' SAID MRS Plover, ladling porridge into Hazel's bowl and topping it with apple compote. Hazel was sitting at the table in a comfortable green breakfast room, anxiously awaiting the professor and, with him, news of Pete.

As she devoured her porridge, she took in her surroundings – so different to Ditchmoor's echoing halls. There was soft carpet beneath her feet, a plump cushion behind her back. The reassuring light of morning streamed through the lattice windows illuminating a tidy crockery cabinet, on top of which stood a high-domed bell-jar. Hazel peered more closely at it, and startled at the contents. Staring down at her, with unblinking glass eyes, was a stuffed, long-eared owl.

The door opened and the professor trotted in. Hazel sprang to her feet.

'Nothing yet, I'm afraid,' he said.

Her heart contracted painfully.

'But the police have sent out the search party.' He gestured for her to sit down, then took his seat in front of a boiled egg.

'I should talk to them,' Hazel said. 'I could give them a description. Pete's the same age as me, he's got bright red hair and he's . . .' Her voice faltered.

Professor Grinling nodded kindly. 'You tell me what happened,' he said, tapping his egg with the back of a spoon, 'and I'll talk to the inspector.'

She hesitated. 'Don't you think I should speak to him myself?'

Grinling put down his spoon and took a notepad and pen from his jacket pocket. 'The inspector is a good friend of mine,' he said. 'It's best I speak with him directly. Now, tell me everything – every last detail. Try to remember.'

The professor was looking at her intently, pen poised. So Hazel took a deep breath and set her mind to the task. She told him about how they had come to leave Ditchmoor, their hopes of finding the Wild Children, the light in the woods and the terrible shrieking laughter.

As she told the story, she realised how absurd it all sounded. But the professor didn't show a flicker of surprise – he just listened closely, pen flying across the page.

'Very distressing for you,' he sighed, once she had finished. 'And now you have nowhere to go. No family, no friends?'

Hazel had barely had the chance to think about that. She shook her head.

Grinling screwed the lid slowly onto his pen and slipped it back into his pocket. He seemed to be weighing something in his mind. Then he cleared his throat.

'Mrs Plover could use a little more help about the place, couldn't you, Josephine?'

'Oh, yes,' laughed Mrs Plover, pouring the tea. 'Always glad for a helping hand.'

The professor slapped both palms down on the table. 'That's settled, then. You can stay here for as long as you need, Hazel, and in return you shall do a spot of dusting and scrubbing, that sort of thing. You know how to dust, don't you?'

Hazel could hardly believe her ears. She nodded slowly. 'Thank you,' she whispered.

'You're welcome.' Professor Grinling dunked a strip of toast into the crown of his egg. 'And don't you fret. We'll find your friend. I'm *certain* of it.'

If Ditchmoor had taught Hazel anything, it was how to dust, iron and scrub. After the breakfast table had been cleared, Mrs Plover cheerfully showed her around Grinling's neat and comfortable home. There would be vegetables to chop in the warm, herby kitchen; cobwebs to chase out of various nooks and crannies; and tasselled velvet cushions that needed to be arranged just so.

'He's a bit of a fusspot,' puffed Mrs Plover as she climbed the narrow stairs to the first floor, 'but he's got a heart of gold.' She showed Hazel how to smooth out ripples in the bedsheets and dust the gilt picture-frames, then she led her along the upstairs landing and past a firmly closed door.

As Hazel approached, she felt compelled to stop. It was panelled and varnished, just like every other door in the house. But as she stepped in front of it, she was seized by the powerful feeling that there was somebody on the other side, listening. There was no sound – no movement – just a charge in the air, an edgeless quivering that made her skin tingle and crisped the hairs on the back of her neck. She remembered the odd rattling sounds that had woken her in the night.

'What about that room?' she asked.

'Oh, you don't need to clean in there,' Mrs Plover replied briskly.

'Why not?'

'It's Professor Grinling's study. He doesn't like things muddled about.' The housekeeper gave a low chuckle. 'I haven't been in there for years. Lord knows it must be *thick* with dust! Now come with me. The bathroom taps want polishing.'

Resisting the urge to touch the handle, Hazel followed Mrs Plover down the hall to the professor's brass-and-marble bathroom. But, as she watched the housekeeper scrub the taps with vinegar water, her mind kept returning to the locked study door.

'Mrs Plover?' she asked. 'Is there anyone else living in this house?

Mrs Plover turned and looked at her, startled. 'No, my dear,' she said. 'Whatever makes you say that?'

Hazel instantly regretted asking. 'Oh, I heard some noises in the night, that's all. I thought there might be a lodger . . . or something.'

The housekeeper chuckled. 'It's an old house – grumbling pipes, squirrels in the attic. Now pour me some more salt, would you, dear?'

Hazel nodded and tried to force the study door from her mind. The last thing she wanted was to draw attention to her weird feelings. What if they kicked her out? Where would she go then? What would happen to Pete? *Be normal,* she urged herself, *Just be normal.* Then she mixed up the vinegar water and did her best to forget all about it.

CHAPTER EIGHT

Greenstone

A DAY PASSED. THEN ANOTHER, AND ANOTHER. Every morning Grinling would telephone the police but, so far, all they had found was Pete's old carpet bag. The professor had brought it home for Hazel to inspect the contents. She recognised the plaid blankets from their belfry, the half-empty jar of eggs and tin of sardines and finally, to her dismay, a golden pear from the Warden's orchard, its skin now bruised and torn.

As she waited for news, Hazel was grateful for the tasks that kept her legs moving and her mind busy. She polished the silverware, tended the herb garden and checked the larder for stocks of eggs, biscuits and butter beans. But the best distraction of all were the books that the professor brought back from the museum's library.

'I thought you might enjoy these,' he said, hauling a pile of enormous tomes onto the breakfast table. Each was bound in richly coloured leather and embossed with glinting gold-leaf. Curious, she peeked inside the burgundy volume on the top of the pile. It was a gloriously illustrated encyclopaedia of birds.

'Go on! Take a proper look,' he said with a grin. She kneeled up on her chair so that she could better see the pages and began to leaf through. The glossy spreads displayed dozens of species in the finest detail, each line of each feather drawn with a sharp, living precision. She ran her fingers over pictures of hummingbirds gleaming like jewels, macaws as bright as splashes of paint.

'This one's on insects,' said the professor, tapping the spine of the next book in the pile. 'And this is about life in the deep oceans.'

'Thank you,' she breathed, unable to peel her eyes away.

'And this one,' said the professor, drawing out a dark blue volume and opening it up, 'is about the extinct wildlife of the British Isles.'

'Extinct?' asked Hazel, turning her attention to the detailed illustrations of leopards, jaguars, bison and bears.

'Indeed,' sighed the professor, 'all of these beasts used to roam our fields and forests, would you believe it? Then they were hunted to extinction, every last one.' As Hazel gazed into the eyes of a large brown bear, she felt a peculiar twist in her stomach. 'But it's not all bad news,' the professor continued, watching her from the corner of his eye, 'sometimes you think something has gone – then it turns out it was just hiding.' A curious smile spread across his face. 'Hiding in plain sight.'

Before Hazel could ask what that meant, the professor cleared his throat.

'Please excuse me,' he said, 'I must get back to my research. Something fascinating has come my way.' Then he hurried up to his study and closed the door firmly behind him.

Five days after Hazel had arrived at the Keeper's Lodge, the professor brought back something else from the museum. Reaching into his pocket, he drew out a solid-looking object wrapped in a clean white handkerchief.

'I have something that might interest you,' he said with a smile. He sat down at the table, placed the small bundle in front of him, then pushed it towards her. The handkerchief fell away to reveal a chunk of greenish-grey stone. Hazel reached forward and picked it up. It was heavy and compact, its rough texture sparkling in the morning light. As she held it in her palm, she felt a cool tingling. Grinling folded his hands on his stomach and breathed a satisfied sigh. 'Cornish greenstone,' he said, 'from the Paleoproterozoic Era!'

She stared at him blankly.

'Very old rock, from the time the planet itself was formed. Rock like that has a long memory, you know. It contains the whole story of the Earth . . .'

As the professor spoke, the tingling intensified. A weird energy was building in her hand. Then it began to spread, flowing and pulsing up her arm towards her shoulder. It was a delicious sensation, cool and steady. She curled her fingers more tightly round the stone and, as she did so, the world around her seemed to flex. It only lasted an instant, but in that wafer of time the professor's tidy breakfast room shivered. She heard the polished wood of the table creak, the feathers in the cushions rustle. A flicker of movement drew her eye upwards to the bell-jar on top of the cabinet. She watched, astonished, as the stuffed owl glared at her with its great yellow eyes, then blinked.

Hazel dropped the stone with a clatter. At once, the room returned to its previous sedate appearance. The porridge steamed. The clock ticked. The professor was watching her through his round spectacles, an unreadable gleam in his eyes.

'Extraordinary, isn't it?' he whispered.

Hazel looked back at him, stunned.

'Mrs Plover needs me,' she mumbled, and bolted from the room.

It was Sunday afternoon when the telephone rang. Hazel was busy in the lodge's sunlit kitchen. A mushroom pie was on the menu and she was tasked with brushing and chopping a basketful of earthy fungi.

'Fetch some thyme from the garden, will you?' asked Mrs Plover. Hazel hurried out of the kitchen door and sniffed out the herbs in the flowerbed. She was just snipping off a bunch of stalks when the telephone shrilled indoors. The sound was coming from the window of the professor's study on the first floor which was cracked open by an inch or two. Her heart clenched. Was it the police? Was there news? She heard the click of the receiver, and the professor begin to speak. His voice was low and muffled and Hazel struggled to make out the words. Holding her breath, she moved closer and stood on the tips of her toes.

'It's a most exciting discovery,' said the professor, a thrill in his voice. 'Terribly rare.'

Museum business, she thought, heart sinking. She took a step back towards the kitchen door, but his next words stopped her in her tracks.

'I'm keeping a close eye on her,' he said. 'You can leave it to me.'

There was a low crackling from the other end of the line.

'Her friend?' the professor muttered. 'Unimportant . . . Of no interest to us.' He let out a long sigh. 'He was captured, no doubt. She thinks the police are looking for him. I'll give it a little longer, then tell her he couldn't be found.'

CHAPTER NINE

The Key

NUMB WITH SHOCK, HAZEL WALKED BACK INTO the kitchen and handed Mrs Plover the bunch of herbs. A large pile of mushrooms was waiting on her chopping board. Mechanically, she began slicing.

'Not too thin!' cautioned the housekeeper. 'Nice big chunks, please.' Hazel nodded absently, turning the professor's words over in her mind, not daring to believe what she had heard.

'Are you all right, love?' asked Mrs Plover, drying her hands on her apron. 'You look a bit peaky.'

'I'm fine,' said Hazel, forcing a smile. But, as she chopped and sliced, a film of fear settled over every surface in the room.

The first chance she got, Hazel ran up to her bedroom beneath the eaves and locked the door. Perched on the edge of the bed, she tried to unravel the questions that were growing wild in her mind: had the professor been lying to her all this time? Had there even *been* a police search? He must have found Pete's bag himself. She shook her head in disbelief. And what did he mean, Pete had been 'captured'? By whom?

All of a sudden, the bedroom, which until that moment had felt so safe and comfortable, began to waver like some hideous illusion. She imagined shadowy things moving in the depths of the mirror, sliding beneath the patterns of the wallpaper. A hollow panic rose in her chest, forcing the air from her lungs. Gripped by a sudden urge to escape, she kneeled up on the bed, flung open the window and took great gulps of the cold autumn air.

A strong wind was blowing. A burst of crows wheeled over the roof of the museum, tumbling and diving. As the wind whipped around her face it cooled her cheeks and cleared her head. She steadied herself against the windowsill and drew a slow breath. The professor knew what had happened to Pete. Perhaps he knew where he was. Her mind slid back to the locked study door, her fingertips prickling with the memory of that strange electricity in the air. If there was anything that could help her find Pete, it would be in that room. She drew herself back into the bedroom and closed the window, a plan forming in her mind.

The professor never left the door unlocked and kept the only key in the breast pocket of his jacket. She would need to find a way to steal it. But how? As she paced the bedroom, she remembered what Pete, a skilled pickpocket, had told her one night in the belfry. 'If you see an opportunity,' he'd said, 'grab it.' That opportunity came knocking the very next day.

It was a frosty Monday morning. The professor was taking his coffee by the living-room fire before going to the library. As Hazel passed him his cup and saucer she noticed his jacket, neatly folded on an ottoman next to the armchair. For a moment she wondered if she could lift the key there and then, but it was far too risky. She was just turning back to the kitchen when the professor reached out and caught her wrist in his soft white hand.

'Sit down, dear,' he said, gesturing to the armchair opposite. Hazel's heart missed a beat, but she sat, trying to act as normally as possible. He picked up a poker and prodded the embers in the fireplace. A burst of sparks reflected in the glass of his spectacles.

'I spoke to the inspector this morning,' he said. 'I'm afraid they haven't found a thing, and I have to tell you that hope is beginning to fade. They will keep up the search tomorrow, but if there is still no sign –' he looked at her with cloudy blue eyes – 'then we shall have to assume the worst.'

'Wolves?' she whispered.

He nodded sadly.

Hazel looked back at him in appalled fascination. How easily he lied. He knew that Pete hadn't been taken by wolves. He might even know where he was, yet he sat there with his watery eyes and crinkled brow, telling her Pete was probably dead.

She felt something ignite deep inside of her. A ball of anger began to burn and grow in her chest. At that moment, Mrs Plover bustled in and set down a tray of shortbread.

'Oh dear,' she said, sensing a weight in the room. She turned to the professor. 'Bad news?'

'No news,' he replied. 'But we'd need a miracle now.'

The housekeeper clutched her hands to her heart and blinked distraught eyes. Hazel glared at her. How much did *she* know? Was this all part of the act too? The ball of anger was white hot now and swelling fast within her ribcage.

'I'm so sorry, my love,' said Mrs Plover. Then, just as she reached down to touch Hazel's hunched shoulders, the embers, which had been cooling and blackening in the fireplace, blazed up with a roar, darting tongues of flame into the room.

The professor lurched backwards, spilling coffee and shortbread all over the rug. Mrs Plover shrieked and grabbed a vase of water.

And that's when Hazel saw her chance.

As the professor and Mrs Plover rushed about, stamping

on sparks, Hazel lunged towards the ottoman, fished the key out of the jacket pocket and ran up the stairs to her bedroom.

She slammed the door, slid the bolt and listened. The kerfuffle soon settled and before long Mrs Plover was climbing the staircase. Hazel bit her lip, wondering what she could say to make her leave. But there was no need.

'Leave her, Josephine,' the professor whispered after her. 'She's upset. We'll deal with it later.' Mrs Plover's footsteps faded back down the stairs and Hazel exhaled in relief.

She held the key up in front of her, barely suppressing a shout of triumph. Soon the professor would leave for the museum, then at three o'clock Mrs Plover would go to the butcher's. That would give her an hour before the housekeeper returned to prepare the professor's dinner – an hour to search the study then leave the key on the hearth rug as though it had simply fallen from the jacket pocket. It was a plan – a good one.

So, the moment she heard the housekeeper bustling out of the house with her shopping basket, Hazel rushed down the stairs to the locked study door. She hovered outside for a moment, the key cool and heavy between her fingers. There was that feeling again – a strange prickling running over her skin, a sense that there was somebody, or something, waiting for her on the other side. She knocked lightly on the oak panelling, but there was no reply.

So she slipped the key into the lock and turned it.

CHAPTER TEN

Fairykind

THERE WAS NOBODY THERE – THOUGH THE ROOM was filled with so much clutter she could hardly tell. While the rest of the house was spotless, the professor's study was completely ajumble with pictures, trinkets and curiosities of every kind. Cobwebs floated in the corners, stained teacups lay abandoned on every surface and large display cases hung on the walls, each stuffed with a medley of pinned insects, bottled starfish, and glass-eyed birds.

Hazel shuddered. This was not the tidy, trim-whiskered professor she thought she knew. The feeling of trespass grew so strong she was tempted to back away. But this was a chance she couldn't squander.

Coughing from the smell of mothballs and feathers, Hazel stepped further into the room. Her gaze settled on the professor's desk – a monstrous thing on bulbous legs carved with strange, grimacing faces. Its top was cut from thickly veined marble, and amongst the dirty teacups and pots of anchovy relish were piles of papers and notebooks. What was written there? Something that could help her find Pete?

Taking care to avoid the towers of books that mushroomed from the carpet, Hazel crept towards the desk. The papers lay inches thick and did not appear to be in any kind of order. She lifted a few away, wondering where to begin. Then, as her eyes flickered over the bewildering mess of notes and sketches, she glimpsed two familiar words: *Goblyn Wood*.

Pushing the papers aside, she discovered a large, creased map of the forest. Her eyes scanned the dips and rises of the landscape – its streams, rivers and lakes. The woods were bigger than she had ever imagined. She recognised Ditchmoor – a mere spot on the western edge – and traced the route that she had travelled with Pete.

But there was also something there that she did not understand. Ruled across the map in heavy pencil was a web of straight, criss-crossed lines. She followed one with her finger. It was radiating out from a great hill in the north-east. She studied the lines for a moment, then shook her head in puzzlement and turned her attention to the other scraps that littered the desk.

Sifting through the muddle, her hopes began to deflate. There were mysterious diagrams, long calculations and strange symbols that she couldn't decipher. As Grinling's ornate mantel clock ticked and whirred, her anxiety sharpened.

Then, beneath the wilderness of manuscripts, she uncovered a large notebook. The cover was marbled in green ink and the spine was bound in soft brown leather. Hazel opened it and saw what appeared to be the beginning of a book. She blinked in disbelief as she read the title. Scrawled in the professor's baroque handwriting were the words:

Fairykind: An Unnatural History

An image flashed through her mind: shrieking shadows in the woods, Pete lifted into the air. She glanced towards the half-open door. There was no movement in the house, not a sound. So she took a breath and began to read.

Introduction: What is a Fairy?

Do you believe in fairies? Not many do these days. We have little use for them, after all. Humans are comfortable in their modern towns and cities and prefer the company of dogs, horses and other tameable beasts.

Yet there was a time when humans not only believed in fairies, but worked, fought and lived alongside them. I can hear the murmurs of disapproval already: Fairies? Not a proper object of scientific enquiry! I beg you to remember, however, that the author is, himself, a man of science. I deal not in folklore and superstition, but in facts. If you will grant me a few moments of your time, I shall endeavour to prove not only the existence of fairykind, but the great benefits of getting to know our fairy neighbours once more. Indeed, the continued progress of the human race depends on it.

Fairies. Fairy tales. Hazel had come across a book of those in Ditchmoor's neglected library. She remembered snowy fairy godmothers who granted wishes, and vengeful fairies who cursed baby princesses. Baffled, she read further:

First, let us dispense with the myths: fairies are not flimsy little winged creatures that live in flowers or dance in sunbeams. This is the stuff of nursery tales and children's pantomimes.

Fairies are like us and, at the same time, they are not us. Like humans, they may be spiteful or generous, brave or cowardly, violent or peaceful, fickle or true. But unlike us, their life force is drawn from the deep energies of the earth and they may live for many hundreds of years, sometimes longer. Their lives, therefore, have a shape and colour that is entirely different from our own.

But not all fairies are alike. Indeed, there are two broad classes of the genus Faerie: Common and Uncommon. Let us begin with the Common variety.

A Common Fairy is what you and I would have become if we had never been born. If your father had not attended your great-aunt's tea party, he would never have met your mother, and you would not have been brought, howling, into the world you know. Instead, you would have had to have found somewhere else to be. Somewhere on the edges. You would have been a possible person — a fairy. And, as a fairy, you would have lived in those betwixt-and-between places where people hardly look, or do not look properly: inside the hills, below the ground, and under the roots of trees. It is a shadow-country, parallel to our own, and the fairies call it the Hollows.

When you have ventured, as I have, into the Hollows, you quickly appreciate the variety of fairy life. As in human society, the fairy world is divided up into different fairy peoples, each with their own habits, cultures and dwellings. There are the Seelies: fairy craftsmen and merchants who live in the deep root systems of our forests and woods. Then there are the Druics: musicians and storytellers who have no fixed abode but travel from place to place. And lastly there are the Arboreans, an aristocratic breed of fairy warrior who settle near the ley lines – the life force of the earth.

Hazel glanced over at the map – is that what the long, intersecting lines were? Ley lines? She imagined great underground channels of pulsing energy and felt a strange shiver pass through her. She read on:

However, not all fairies are the unborn. As well as Common Fairies, there are the Uncommon kind and these are quite different. There is only one type of Uncommon Fairy in our hills and they are known as the Fae. The Fae are the most elusive and the most powerful of our native fairies. But, above all else, they must be treated with extreme caution, for they are also the most dangerous . . .

There was no more written after this. Hazel let out a burst of nervous laughter. Is that what she'd seen in the forest?

Fairies? Yet, despite the laughter, a poisonous dread was spreading through her veins.

She slammed the book shut and checked the clock. Time was running out and she still hadn't found anything that would lead her to Pete. Hastily, she scanned the room. Her eyes settled on a tall, glass-fronted cabinet that stood behind the door. As she held it in her gaze, the curious feeling returned – the feeling that somebody else was present. There was a strange density in the air concentrated around the cabinet, and it was drawing her in. As if pulled by invisible threads, she stepped around the desk, walked towards it and touched the small brass key.

It turned easily and, as the doors rattled open, the resiny smell of the forest reached her nostrils. Before her was an odd assortment of objects, each carefully labelled, all stolen from the heart of the woods. There were twisting fragments of tree root, splintering pine cones, flat grey pebbles still clumped with moss. Each of these pebbles had a circular hole at its centre, large enough to peep through. But there were stranger things still.

Hazel's eyes wandered up to the top shelf where she found a small burnished goblet, engraved with the same curious signs she had discovered amongst the professor's notes. It looked ancient, as if it had been dredged from a shipwreck, yet the rim was still stained with a blackish juice. She searched through the professor's collection, moving objects aside to reach further in. Kneeling down, she found a deerskin satchel that clinked when she moved it. She pulled it out and peeked inside. It was stuffed with small glass vials, each of which was labelled and filled with a watery fluid. One was marked SMOKE, another MORROW, then there were other more mysterious words like EBBLE, OG and DUN.

Hazel frowned, but as she breathed in the deep green smell of the woods, something within her stirred – something from long ago. Without knowing why, she reached for the pendant on her necklace and held it for a moment, warm and heavy in her fist.

The mantel clock's grating chimes made her start. It was four o'clock and Mrs Plover would return any minute. Hurriedly, she stuffed the satchel back onto the shelf and got to her feet. She was about to close the glass doors when something moved.

A small rounded bottle of silvered glass was jittering about on the top shelf. At first Hazel thought she must have disturbed it, but it did not settle down. Instead, it shook more and more vigorously. She stepped back in alarm. It was the same rattling sound that had woken her on her first night in the house. The bottle paused for a moment, then tipped itself over and rolled straight off the edge. Hazel shot forward and caught it before it could hit the floor. She fumbled it back into the cabinet, but it was now shaking violently, as if something were trapped inside and bouncing angrily off the glass.

At that moment, a vicious hissing made Hazel jump clean

out of her skin. She spun round to see Purkiss, the professor's cat, in the doorway, spitting with fury. She closed up the cabinet as quickly as she could and fled the study, locking the door behind her.

CHAPTER ELEVEN

The Silvered Bottle

HAZEL SAT ON HER BED, HEART THUMPING AND mind racing. She'd refused Mrs Plover's offer of a pork chop and had retired to her room at the first opportunity.

As she stared, unseeing, at the patterns on the bedside rug, she tried to make sense of what she'd found in the study. Had she really seen *fairies* in the woods? It wasn't possible. Was it? She chewed her thumbnail. What would she do now? The professor couldn't be trusted, that much was certain. Should she go to the police herself? But what if they packed her off to rat-catcher Pike? She shook her head sharply. *No.* She'd have to look for Pete on her own – find a way back to the woods. But how would she get there? And what if there *were* fairies in that forest?

'That's ridiculous,' she said out loud. But something within her told her otherwise.

Outside the moon was rising, but her room felt stuffy

and hot. She went to the wash basin and splashed her face with water. As she dried her hands on her apron she noticed that it was heavier than usual. There was something in the pocket.

Reaching inside, her hand closed around a hard, round object. She took it out and stared. It was the silvered bottle from the professor's study. A sudden chill ran up her spine. How did it get there? She thought she'd put it back in the cabinet. Had it leaped into her pocket all by itself? There was a small tag around the bottle's neck. Written on it, in Professor Grinling's fussy handwriting, were the words *Seely juvenis: Common Imp, juvenile.*

At that moment, the bottle began to tremble then shake so vigorously that Hazel could barely keep hold of it. It jerked left and right, dragging her about the room. Then, with a sudden burst of energy it sprang out of her hands and smashed on the floor.

Instantly, an orb of light shot from the neck and darted madly around the bedroom. Hazel stifled a shriek and grabbed a hairbrush to defend herself. This only seemed to anger the tiny fireball, which shot suddenly towards her, sending her tumbling backwards onto the floor. Then in a bright flash of green, it transformed into the strangest child Hazel had ever laid eyes on.

The child was about the same size as Hazel but looked as though she were made from solid light. She flickered slightly around the edges and her tangled hair seemed to crackle

with electricity. Hazel noticed her large, delicate ears and bright, shining eyes. There was something wild in those eyes. And they were round with fury.

'Who are *you*?!' spat the child, clenching her small fists. 'And what is *that*?!' She seized Hazel's hairbrush, sniffed it disapprovingly, then tossed it away. Hazel was so astounded she could barely speak.

'I'm . . . I'm Hazel,' she whispered.

The child did not look satisfied.

'I'm . . . um . . . I work here.'

The child's eyes narrowed.

'As a housemaid,' Hazel continued. 'This is Professor Grinling's house.'

At that, the child gave an angry shriek. 'I knew it!' she shouted, stamping a bare foot on the floorboards. 'I knew it was him who bottled me! Always lurking about the woods with his traps and boxes.' As she grew angrier, she flared up like a torch. 'Oh, he's due some mischief, that one! I'll hide his shadow, see how he likes that! No, wait! I'll curdle the milk in his tea – it's an oldie, but a goody!' The child chattered to herself now, the light around her shimmering in greens and golds. 'I know! I'll make his hat stand sprout twigs. Ha!' By this time she was chortling with delight and seemed to have forgotten Hazel was there at all. Hazel slowly got to her feet.

'Are you . . .' she ventured, 'are you a *fairy*?'

'Certainly not.' The child sniffed. 'That's people-speak.

I am a Seely, and my name is Portuna.' Hazel remembered the notes in the professor's book. Seelies – they were the common sort, root-dwellers. 'But the real question,' Portuna continued, advancing towards her, 'is what are *you*?' With this, she reached forward and gave Hazel a hard pinch on the arm.

'Ow!' she yelped. 'That hurt!'

Portuna looked unmoved. Then she came right up close, so that their noses were almost touching. 'You *look* like a clayfoot . . .'

'A clayfoot?'

'Yes – an earthborn, a long-legs, a *person*.'

'I am,' Hazel stammered, 'I *am* a person.' Portuna ignored her. She peered closely into Hazel's eyes and, as Hazel looked back, she saw that the fairy's eyes were changing and flickering like fire opals – sea-green one moment, coppery bright the next. They were eyes just like her own.

Portuna stepped back with a satisfied smile.

'You're *not* a person,' she said conclusively. 'Or not a normal one anyway. You're also one of us.'

'A . . . a *fairy*?' said Hazel.

Portuna rolled her eyes. 'Well, if you must use that word, yes – a fairy. But you're the strangest sort of fairy I've ever seen.'

Hazel frowned. Coming from such an odd-looking creature that was a little rich.

'No, I'm not,' she said crossly. 'I'm not a fairy. I don't

fly about or ... or sit on toadstools. I do normal stuff like peeling potatoes and ... and getting stains out of the carpet.'

Portuna looked amused. 'You don't know anything about fairies, do you?'

'No, I don't,' Hazel replied, folding her arms.

Portuna peered at her slyly. 'So how do you know you're not one?'

This was a good point, and Hazel couldn't answer.

'In any case,' Portuna continued, glimmering a mischievous pink, 'you don't really think Grinling is keeping you here to peel potatoes, do you? He knows what you are.'

Hazel didn't reply. As the fairy stared at her expectantly, an eerie light dawned over the events of the previous days. It was true that the professor had been quick to invite her to stay. So generous, she'd thought at the time.

'He'll be watching you,' Portuna added, looking briskly around the room. 'You're a specimen!'

'A specimen?' Hazel thought of the boxed and bottled creatures in the study. Then she remembered the odd gleam in the professor's eyes and felt a slow thickening in her throat.

'He's a collector,' said Portuna. 'And a stinking nuisance! Oh, I bet he was thrilled to catch you! Did that cat sniff you out? It's a notorious fairy-hunter, you know.'

Hazel sat down on the edge of the bed, bewildered. She closed her eyes for a moment, wondering if she was dreaming. But when she opened them again, the fairy was still there – as real as the brass bedstead and the chest of drawers.

Hazel shook her head. 'But, *I'm* not ... I'm not like you.'

Portuna sat down next to her and gave her a sideways glance. 'Aren't you?'

Hazel said nothing.

The fairy sat a little closer. 'Don't you sometimes notice things,' she whispered, a glitter in her eye, 'things that other people don't?'

Hazel folded her arms and stared at her toes.

'Clayfeet are good at knowing stuff,' said Portuna, 'and making things. But in other ways they're as blunt as hammers.' She leaned in further, voice dropping to a whisper. 'They can't even see the grass grow!' At that, she burst out laughing – a bright, melodious laughter that made her edges sparkle. 'They just go clodding about all over the place, shouting and stomping and knocking things over.' She leaped to her feet and gave her best impression of a great clumsy clayfoot, puffing out her cheeks and swinging her fists. 'Let's bash that down! Let's build a thing! Heave-ho, laddies!' The fairy chortled at her own performance, then sat back down next to Hazel. 'But *us*,' she said, 'we're as sharp as needles. We *feel* it all, don't we?'

As Hazel listened to the strange luminous child, something inside her began to uncurl like a fern. Yes, she too had seen the grass grow. In the moments before Miss Fitch would pull her ears and tell her she was having a 'turn', she could hear the soft crackling of the soil, see each blade pushing upwards. She'd always thought there was something wrong with her, but here was somebody who – peculiar though she was – saw what she saw and felt what she felt.

Hazel gave a small nod.

'See!' said Portuna proudly. 'You know *exactly* what I mean!'

Hazel looked into the fairy's glimmering eyes, then walked over to the mirror to inspect her own. They shimmered from green, to blue, to fire-flecked brown. They were wild eyes. Fairy eyes?

'Right!' said Portuna, clapping her hands together. 'We need to go!'

'What, now?' asked Hazel, startled.

'Well, stay if you like,' said Portuna, 'but I'm off. I'm not getting sucked into a bottle again. I don't know what that professor's got planned for you, but if you've got any sense you won't stick around to find out.'

'But . . . where are we going?'

'Home, of course. To Goblyn Wood!'

'Oh!' Hope flared in Hazel's heart, and fear too. But before she had the chance to think, the fairy shrunk back down to an orb of light and darted towards the crack under the door.

'Wait!' cried Hazel. But Portuna wasn't waiting for anyone. Hazel hesitated a moment, but Professor Grinling's house now felt like a narrowing trap and, baffling though she was, Portuna seemed like her only way back to the woods, and her best chance of finding Pete. So she grabbed her coat and, taking care not to make a sound, followed the fairy down the stairs, along the hallway and out of the front door.

She was just closing the door behind her when a soft rustling made her hesitate. Glancing back, she saw the professor's old hat stand shivering in the hall, busily sprouting fresh shoots and leaves.

CHAPTER TWELVE

The Elfin Oak

I T WAS A CRISP, STAR-LITTERED NIGHT. HAZEL RAN
down the white-pillared avenues of Kensington, her eyes
fixed on the darting light ahead. The fairy shone more
dimly now and Hazel saw that she was not a ball of fire but
had simply shrunk down to a smaller size. What's more, she
wasn't flying so much as leaping and springing along the
pavement like a cricket.

Before long, they reached the high gates of Kensington
Gardens. Portuna slipped through the bars in a trice and
skipped away across the lawns. Hazel paused a moment to
study the size of the gap between the railings, then tried to
squeeze through after her.

'Wait!' she called out, as she tried to unwedge herself. The
fairy orb paused, flickered impatiently, then darted on again.
With a wrench, Hazel forced herself free, then stumbled on
after her. Once they were far from the glow of the streetlamps,
Portuna slowed down and grew back to her full size.

'Ahh!' she breathed, rolling her shoulders. 'That's better. I'd been scrunched up in that bottle for *ages!*'

'How do you shrink like that?' Hazel asked, struggling to catch her breath.

'I dunno.' Portuna shrugged. 'But I won't be able to do it much longer. I'm a hundred and two – nearly fully grown!'

'A hundred and two!' Hazel gasped.

Portuna grinned with pride. 'At least! How old are *you?*'

'I'm not sure,' Hazel murmured, counting on her fingers. 'Eleven . . . I think. What's that in fairy years?'

But Portuna's attention had wandered. She was balancing on the tips of her toes, large ears swivelling slightly.

All was quiet in the gardens. The playing children and strolling couples had gone home hours earlier but, as Hazel looked about her, she became aware of another population – the watchful, whispering company of trees.

The park was lightly wooded, giving each tree enough space to spread and grow into its natural shape. There were drooping mulberries, crooked old medlars and billowing chestnuts that tossed and tumbled high above.

'Listen!' whispered Portuna.

Hazel closed her eyes and let her ears search the night.

At first all she heard was the low murmur of the breeze – just waves and ripples of air stirring the leaves around her. But, as her ears attuned, she was able to tease out different threads and what she heard began to sound less like rustling and more like the hum of a conversation. The wind moved through the leaves like breath, giving each tree its own peculiar voice. Some whistled and chattered; others muttered, moaned, huffed or grumbled. Hazel laughed in astonishment.

'They're gossiping,' said Portuna. 'About you, probably.' Hazel frowned and listened again. The trees were indeed conferring in a bristling language, full of exclamations, questions and sighs. Then, rising up from below, came the deep groan of great branches swaying.

'What's that?!' gasped Hazel, alarmed.

'An Elfin Oak.'

'A what?'

'An Elfin Oak.' Portuna laughed. 'Flaming foxgloves! You don't know anything, do you?' She grasped Hazel's hand and led her purposefully towards the far edge of the park.

There, at the top of a bald slope, stood the most fearsome-looking tree Hazel had ever seen. It was a gnarly giant, almost as wide as it was tall, with strong boughs, a bulging belly and thick roots, heavily mossed with age. Standing in its dense shadow, Hazel couldn't help but feel afraid. Portuna, on the other hand, seemed completely at ease.

'Hello, old man,' she said with a smile. She approached the trunk and laid her small hand on its knobbly bark. At once, the oak softened and a happy rustle spread through its leaves. Hazel didn't understand what the tree was saying, but it was warm and affectionate, as if welcoming a friend. Then, with a great creaking and cracking, the thick ridges of the oak's bark pulled apart, opening a doorway into its massive trunk.

Hazel gasped and took a step back.

'Quick!' said Portuna, gesturing for her to follow. But the moment the fairy had stepped into the cavernous bole, the bark quickly closed, leaving Hazel behind. She rushed to the tree in a panic.

'Portuna?' she whispered. But there was no reply. The leaves around her crackled drily. The oak seemed to be waiting. Uncertainly, she placed her hand on the wrinkled bark. It felt surprisingly warm, as if it were blood, not sap, that flowed through its hoary veins.

At first, nothing happened. Hazel stood with her palm on the tree, feeling more and more anxious by the second. Then, from deep within the oak's belly, she heard a low muttering and grumbling. She glanced up the mighty trunk. Its great twists and burls were frowning and grimacing, as if the tree were puzzling over a fiendishly difficult problem.

'I'm ... I'm Hazel,' she stammered, and immediately felt foolish. Then, just as she was beginning to think that the tree would never decide what to do with her, a loud cracking made her leap away in alarm.

She made a dash backwards, half expecting to be crushed by a falling bough. But the oak's branches were not breaking. They were bending and slithering towards her like tentacles.

Long twiggy fingers poked her legs and tugged at her hair.

'Hey! Stop!' Hazel yelped. But the tree ignored her

protests. It prodded her stomach, spun her around and dangled her upside-down by her ankles. Then it huffed loudly through its leaves and let her go. Hazel fell to the ground and lay there, stunned, as the branches returned to their haughty stillness.

The murmur of the trees had died down now and the gardens were silent save for the chilly hoots of a tawny owl. She sat up and inspected her scratches and bruises. A bead of blood dribbled down her shin. Hazel watched it for a moment, trickling thick and red towards her ankle.

'A fairy!' she muttered to herself. 'Of course you're not a fairy!'

She scrubbed the blood away with her sleeve, then rose briskly to her feet and dusted off the leaf-litter that clung to her clothes. 'What were you *thinking*? How ridiculous. How *stupid*!'

The stars glittered coldly in the midnight sky. Somewhere in the distance, she could hear the noise of revellers lurching home – a jubilant shout, the smash of a bottle.

She turned her back on the oak and glanced around the park, hoping in vain for some sign of Portuna. But the gardens were empty and still. Even the trees, which moments before had chattered and gossiped, now stood lofty and indifferent.

Hazel hugged her coat around her, fighting back the tears. How would she get to the woods without Portuna? How would she ever find Pete?

The night was growing colder, seeping through her skin. She looked back across the gardens in the direction of the gates. If she snuck back to the professor's, he might not notice she'd been gone. She could bide her time, find out what she could and make another plan. It was risky, no doubt, but what choice did she have?

But she did no such thing. For the moment she stepped away from the oak, a thick branch whipped out, wrapped itself around her waist and dragged her backwards into the trunk's open hollow.

CHAPTER THIRTEEN

The Hollows

HAZEL FELT AS THOUGH SHE'D BEEN PULLED into a hurricane. High winds whistled in her ears, buffeting her this way and that, and it was so dark she couldn't even see her own body. Indeed, if it weren't for the fragments of leaves that dashed against her legs and face, she wouldn't have been sure that her body was there at all. She cried out, but the winds whipped her voice away before she'd even heard it.

Yet she was not falling, so much as being passed through the darkness by great living hands of air. Deft currents caught her, then swung her, then seized her again, sending her tumbling and cartwheeling through the gloom, downwards and downwards, tossed and tickled, until she was laughing and shrieking with delight.

Gradually, the darkness began to thin and, as Hazel spun through endless space, pulses of light streaked past her, dim at first, then flashing and blazing in bright greens, golds and fiery reds. Eventually the winds slowed, and she was settled onto a sandy floor, as lightly as a leaf.

Hazel found herself in a rooty underground cavern – the sort that might have been made by a badger, if that badger had stood ten-feet tall and had claws like scythes. It was earthy and warm and, high above her head, the soil was supported by strong, spreading tree roots. She scrambled to her feet and looked around in wonder. The glowing lights, she now realised, were dozens of copper lanterns strung up higgledy-piggledy around the cavern. But these lanterns were not lit by flames. Instead, each

one contained a gemstone the size of a fist. There were chunks of amethyst, pinkish quartz, blue agate and lumps of blood-red garnet, each glimmering with its own light. The lanterns continued down four round tunnels that led away from the cavern and appeared to have other, smaller tunnels branching off them.

Footsteps pattered swiftly behind her. She turned and Portuna pinched her nose playfully in greeting.

'You took your time!' she grinned. Hazel rubbed her nose and smiled back.

'Is this . . . ? Are we under London?'

'Is this what you'd expect to find under London?' Portuna scoffed. Hazel didn't think that was very fair. If the last few days had taught her anything it was that expectations didn't count for much. Portuna laughed and flung out her arms. 'We're under Goblyn Wood. In the Hollows!'

Hazel looked up at the dark, root-filled ceiling and shivered as she imagined the great weight of the forest, pressing down overhead.

'It's a bit of a trek to my village,' tutted Portuna. 'I *did* ask the oak to take us straight there, but you know what Elfin Oaks are like.'

Hazel shook her head.

'They're old, aren't they? Get muddled.' Portuna scratched her cheek and glanced around her. 'We'll have to find a burrow for the night.'

'A burrow?' asked Hazel, still trying to take it all in.

'What kind of . . . ?' But before she could finish her question, Portuna seized her hand and led her into one of the passages.

They entered a tangled labyrinth of tunnels, low and narrow with frequent forks and twists. Portuna seemed to know where she was going and, as the gemstone lanterns cast wavering shadows around them, Hazel stuck close to her fairy guide, grateful for the warm pressure of her hand.

Before long, they came to a crossways with a signpost sticking wonkily out of the ground. Hazel paused to read the names carved into its wooden arms: YARROW, WHISTLEDOWN, EBBLESIDE . . . Portuna took a turn in the direction of UNDERSTONE.

'Is that the name of your village?' asked Hazel. 'Where the Seelies live?'

'You're learning!' said Portuna.

Hazel smiled. 'And do you have a family?'

'Of course!' said Portuna. 'Don't you?'

She didn't reply.

Portuna chattered on, eyes brightening. 'There's my pa – he makes the finest goblets this side of Morrow River. Then there's my brother, Corrie, and all the tinies – too many of them to count. You'll meet Auntie Mag too. Mind you don't get on the wrong side of *her*, though. Pa says her tongue's as sharp as a thorn, and that's no lie!'

Hazel listened closely as Portuna chattered merrily about her uncles, aunts, cousins and neighbours. As she tried to keep track of their gossip, squabbles and centuries-long feuds, a worry began to form.

'And will . . . ?' Hazel didn't know how to ask. 'Will there be room for me?'

'Probably not.' Portuna shrugged.

'Oh . . .'

'But we'll squeeze you in!'

Hazel sighed with relief.

'Ah, this looks like a good spot for a snooze.' Portuna had stopped and was pointing at a round opening near the tunnel floor, just large enough to squeeze through. Hazel stooped to peer in. The burrow's mouth was laced with spiderwebs and it was pitch dark inside. She frowned uncertainly.

'Are you sure . . . ?' she began, but Portuna was already flat on her stomach, wriggling her way in backwards. Not wanting to be left alone in the gloomy passage, Hazel scrambled after her, feet first, down into the earthy chamber.

The moment her toes touched the floor, an amber lantern began to glow. Hazel dusted off her coat and gazed at her surroundings. She and Portuna were in a perfectly cosy little hole where all was arranged for the comfort of the weary traveller. There was a sturdy bunk made up with a blanket of what looked like matted dandelion down. A large map of the tunnels was pinned to the wall, and below that stood a table set with a bowl of walnuts and two wooden goblets, which to Hazel's astonishment were steaming with a fragrant tea.

'Lavender,' Portuna yawned, 'for sweet dreams.' She drained her goblet in one gulp then clambered into the bunk.

Hazel took the other and sniffed the sleepy brew. Sipping slowly, she studied the tattered map on the wall. Unlike the professor's above-ground map, this one sketched out the bewildering web of passages that branched like nerves beneath the forest floor. As she tried to make sense of it, her heart sank. Was Pete lost somewhere in this vast warren? How could she hope to find him?

'Portuna?' Hazel whispered. But the fairy was already fast asleep in the bunk, the blanket pulled over her ears.

CHAPTER FOURTEEN

Nettle Pie

AZEL NEVER DREAMED OF HER MOTHER. SHE often thought about her – a patchwork picture made of hopes and guesses – but she didn't have a single memory from which dreams might be woven. There were no photographs or bundles of letters and, however deeply she rummaged within herself, she never found a trace of her earliest years. In the place where those memories should have been, there was nothing but a gaping black hole.

But that night, as Hazel lay under the dandelion blanket, the pendant of her necklace in her fist, something came to her. Not a face or a voice, but an encircling warmth. It was as if she had been sinking like a stone, then suddenly scooped upwards by quick, strong arms. It was a feeling of being held. When she woke the next morning, all traces of the dream had vanished, but she felt strangely stronger, as if something had wrapped around her and was holding her together.

*

Once Portuna had woken, yawning and arching like a cat, they cracked some walnuts for breakfast. As they gobbled the crispy kernels, Hazel puzzled over the map on the wall. If anybody knew their way around the forest it was Portuna. Perhaps she knew who had taken Pete. Perhaps she knew where he was.

'Portuna,' said Hazel. 'I need your help. Please. There's somebody I need to find.'

The fairy's ears twitched with interest as Hazel told the story of Pete's disappearance. She described the wavering light, the circle of dead trees, the shrieking shadows.

'They carried him away,' she said. 'He called out for me. Then he was gone.'

Portuna chewed thoughtfully, the glow of her skin flickering a curious blue. 'This Pete. He's a clayfoot, is he?'

'A person, yes.'

'Hmm,' said Portuna, 'sounds like he got caught up in a hunt.'

'A hunt?!' Hazel gasped.

'Yes. They must be on the snatch again.'

'Who are?!'

'Shhhhh!' Portuna whispered fiercely. 'We can't talk about it. Not here. Not until we get back to Understone.'

But Hazel was wild with panic. 'Is he ... Is he ... ?' she stammered, unable to say it.

'Oh, he's not *dead* if that's what's worrying you,' said Portuna. 'Well, probably not.'

'That *is* what's worrying me, *yes*!'

At that, Portuna gripped Hazel's shoulders with her small, strong hands. 'Don't get all sparked up!' she hissed. 'I said I'd help you, didn't I?'

'You . . . you did?' Hazel stammered. 'You *will?*'

'Of course!' said Portuna, as if it were the most obvious thing in the world. She stood and dusted herself down. 'But first we need to get back to the village.'

Hazel couldn't speak for a moment. 'Thank you,' she babbled 'Thank you. Pete's like family to me . . . he . . .'

But Portuna was already wriggling headfirst out of the burrow.

As they continued their journey to Understone, Portuna skipped over roots and brushed cobwebs out of their path, humming lightly. In some places the tunnels were so low and narrow that Hazel had to crawl on her belly. Elsewhere, they blossomed into giant chambers of beaten earth. At each step, winking lanterns lit the way, casting bright blooms of light all around them.

'Not far now!' said Portuna as she hurried down a wide passageway glittering with topaz and opal. 'We should reach the village by supper. Oh, Pa's just going to burst when he sees me!'

As they rounded a corner, a small, crooked figure appeared up ahead. It was bent double under the weight of a large bundle and was shuffling quickly forwards with a knotty walking stick. Hazel slowed to a halt, but Portuna was up on her toes, waving furiously.

'Granny Webcap!' she shouted. The figure stopped in surprise and Portuna ran to greet her, Hazel a few steps behind.

Granny Webcap was a gnarled, sharp-eyed old Seely with long green hairs sprouting from the top of her speckled head, and a few more from her chin. The pack on her back was almost as big as she was, and out of its pockets wafted a pungent smell. On seeing Portuna, a delighted smile spread across her crinkled face.

'Portuna Babbage?' she cried. 'Is it really you? Oh, your pa will be as happy as a lark. He's been fussing and fretting – he thought that pesky clayfoot'd caught you!'

'He did – couldn't keep me, though!' Portuna said proudly. Granny Webcap gasped and tutted.

'If I were your pa, I'd keep you locked in a box. Tsk, tsk, you Babbages, always running about, getting yourselves into mischief.'

'And out of it.' Portuna smiled. Granny Webcap stretched out a knobbly hand and gave her an affectionate tweak on the nose. Then she turned her beady eyes on Hazel.

'And who's this?' she muttered, squinting at her with unabashed curiosity.

'I'm ... er ...' Hazel began. Granny Webcap's eyes narrowed and Hazel drew back, suddenly afraid that she was about to be exposed as a blundering clayfoot. Portuna seized Hazel's hand and pulled her close to her side.

'She's a friend,' said Portuna briskly. 'Now what have you got in that backpack, Granny? Smells good!'

To Hazel's relief, Granny Webcap slowly peeled her attention away.

'Always sniffing about for a spot of grub, aren't you, young Babbage? I'm taking these to Yarrow, so paws off!'

'Oh, go on, Granny!' Portuna smiled craftily. 'We've hardly had a peck to eat all day. And nobody makes a pie like a Webcap.'

'Well, that's true,' said Granny, arching an eyebrow. 'Even if you are a wicked flatterer. Hurry up, then. Help yourselves.'

Delighted, Portuna reached into a pocket of the backpack and drew out two round pies, each encased in thick golden pastry.

'Now be off with you,' said Granny, 'but take care. The Ley is sluggish under Rushy Beck.'

'Oh?' said Portuna.

'Folks are steering clear. So no loitering.' Granny shook her speckled head. 'It's getting worse by the day, I tell you, *worse by the day!*'

'Thanks, Granny,' said Portuna as the ancient fairy shuffled away down the tunnel. 'We'll be all right.'

'You're not immortal, Portuna Babbage!' Granny Webcap muttered, waggling a finger in the air. 'Locked in a box, you should be, locked in a box!' Then she disappeared into the gloom, leaving a bitter smell hanging in the air behind her.

'What was that about?' asked Hazel.

Portuna huffed through her nose.

'Ley lines are weak,' she said. Hazel remembered those words from the professor's book. Ley lines: the life force of the earth.

'Sounds bad,' said Hazel, worried.

'Pffft.' Portuna shrugged and took a bite of her pie. 'Don't pay any attention to her. The Webcaps are a bunch of doom-mongers, that's all.' Portuna was trying to sound casual, but there was a tightness in her voice. 'Luckily,' she continued, licking her lips, 'they're also the best bakers in the Hollows!'

She handed Hazel a large golden pie. It was wonderfully heavy in her hand and the smell of browned pastry made her mouth water. They found a thick root to rest on and sat down for their long-overdue lunch.

The crust was deliciously flaky and the green filling warm and rich. But, as Hazel chewed, she suddenly felt a painful prickling, as if she had swallowed a small swarm of bees. Instantly she spat it out, spraying a greenish mess across the tunnel.

'Ugh! What *is* it?' she choked. Portuna stared at her with a mix of horror and amusement.

'Nettle pie. What did you think?'

'But ... but the nettles are ... stinging!' Hazel cried, trying to wipe her tongue clean.

'Of course,' said Portuna, through snorting giggles. 'If you didn't want a sting-y one, you should have said!' She pointed at Hazel's pie. 'Now are you going to eat that or not?'

CHAPTER FIFTEEN

The Shade

'WHAT SORT OF FAIRY DO YOU THINK I AM?' asked Hazel as they walked on through the glimmering tunnels. She could hardly believe she was asking such a question. Portuna turned and gave her a quick up-and-down glance.

'You're only part fairy,' she replied decisively. Hazel couldn't help but feel a little hurt.

'The fairy part, then,' she said. 'What sort of fairy?'

'Well you're not an Arborean, that's for sure,' said Portuna, enjoying playing the expert. 'That's a good thing!'

'Why's that?'

'Oh, they're all high-and-mighties. Full of their own wind and importance.'

Hazel recalled Grinling's book. Arboreans – they were the warrior kind.

As they pressed on, deeper into the tunnels, Hazel

noticed that the way was growing darker, the temperature slowly dropping.

'Maybe you have some Druic in you.' Portuna shrugged. 'They're a wandering tribe. They come and they go. But if you can't see them, you can sometimes hear them. Druics are the best musicians in the woods. Or maybe you're part Seely.' She put a small skip in her step. 'Like me!'

'But not Fae?' said Hazel.

No sooner had the words left her mouth than Portuna whipped round and stared. The light that flickered around her had turned a silvery green and her eyes flashed uncertainly. There was anger there, but also fear.

'I thought you didn't know anything about fairies,' she snapped.

'I don't ... not really,' Hazel stammered, alarmed by Portuna's sudden turn. 'I saw the professor's book, that's all.' Portuna was silent for a moment, watching Hazel with sharp eyes, clicking her pointed nails together.

'No!' she said, suddenly satisfied. 'You can't be a Fae. It's not possible.' She turned and carried on walking up the gloomy passage. Hazel followed on, shaken. 'And if Grinling is trying to catch a Fae, well –' Portuna smiled grimly – 'he'll get what's coming to him!'

The gemstones cast only the palest light now. As they travelled on through the twisting burrows, the air felt drier and colder, slithering around Hazel's ankles and down the back of her neck. Further and further they trudged until the lanterns were completely extinguished and the only light was cast by Portuna herself. But the fairy's glow was much dimmer than before.

'Granny Webcap was right,' Portuna tutted, running her fingers along the dusty walls. 'Leys are running slow. And it's got worse, much worse.' Then, as they were rounding a corner, they heard a weak cry.

It was a frail, shuddering cry, and it was coming from near their feet. Hazel stopped and searched the darkness. At first she saw nothing. But slowly she was able to make out the faintest ghost of a creature. It looked like a fairy and was curled up near the wall of the tunnel. But its light was so faded that it was barely traceable.

Hazel stepped closer and the creature turned its face towards hers. It was a fairy boy who looked much like Portuna, only, while Portuna's eyes flickered and flashed, the boy's were as dark and empty as caves.

Portuna gasped sharply and kneeled at the boy's side. She stretched her hand towards his chest, but before she could touch him, the fragile form trembled like a bubble on water then vanished altogether.

Portuna let out an angry shriek and blazed up suddenly, allowing Hazel to see more clearly. The fairy had disappeared, but in his place was a black shadow on the earth.

'Who was that?' Hazel whispered, aghast. 'What happened?'

'A Druic,' Portuna replied flatly, getting to her feet. 'He died.'

'Died?'

'Yes,' said Portuna, pointing at the darkened ground. 'Can't you see his shade?' Hazel saw that Portuna's eyes had turned a deep grey. She looked away quickly, but not before Hazel had seen the glitter of tears. 'And we won't last long either, if we don't get a move on.' Portuna marched off down the tunnel, sniffing and muttering under her breath.

Paralyzed with shock, Hazel stayed where she was, watching the boy's shadow merge into the grainy darkness. He had looked so fragile, so afraid. What had happened to him? But there was no time to linger. As the shadows folded around her, she became aware of a heavy weakness in her muscles and a sickening in her stomach. This time she recognised it straight away. It was the chapel roof again; the same rushing darkness she had felt just before Pete was snatched.

Dizzy, she reached for something to hold onto and grasped an overhanging tree root. But no sooner had her fingers closed around the dry bark than the root crumbled to dust, sending her tumbling to her knees.

Fragments of earth and debris fell around her. The roots supporting the tunnel were disintegrating fast. A surge of terror propelled her back onto her feet, then she stumbled away as fast as she could. Chunks of dry soil and stone dropped from the ceiling, thudding down left and right.

Hands over her head, she ran, choking on the dirty air, until suddenly there was a thunderous blast behind her. She didn't need to look back to know the tunnel was collapsing. The roar of falling soil grew louder and louder. Her legs and lungs were burning. Then, just as she felt sure she'd be crushed by the collapsing earth, there was a burst of light and strong hands pulled her sharply into a narrow side-tunnel. She tumbled a short distance and lay dazed on the pebbly ground, blood pounding in her ears.

A sharp pinch on her arm brought her to her senses. Portuna was leaning over her looking worried.

'It's terrible!' she said, shaking her head. 'Much worse than I thought!' Hazel glanced behind her. The main tunnel was now entirely clogged with collapsed earth, some of which had spilled into the space behind them.

'What do you mean?' asked Hazel.

Portuna picked up a dusty clump of soil and crumbled it between her fingers. It was grey as ashes and, as it scattered onto the floor, Hazel noticed dead insects amongst the litter. Everything was leached and burned – stripped of life.

'This is the work of the Fae,' said Portuna. 'This is what they do.'

CHAPTER SIXTEEN

Understone

PORTUNA PULLED HAZEL TO HER FEET.

'Come on,' she said. 'We've got to keep moving. Can you run?'

Hazel nodded, though her legs felt like lead and she could hardly force herself to stand.

'We'll take the Understone Pass,' said Portuna, pointing down the tunnel. 'Here, hold my hand. We'll be home in no time!'

Portuna seized Hazel's hand then tugged her on at a run, zigzagging quickly through the parched hollows. The fairy seemed to know her way by instinct and, supporting the stumbling Hazel, urged her on through the bewildering maze.

Hazel could hardly feel her legs and her head was swimming, but she kept struggling forwards as fast as she could manage. On they ran, further and further, until at last their feet pounded firm soil. Hazel heard the sound of water flowing up ahead, then they burst into a high-domed chamber.

'Here!' gasped Portuna. 'We're safe.'

Huffing and panting, Hazel gazed around. The roots that girded the ceiling were thick and strong again, and the gemstone lanterns had recovered their brightness. On the other side of the chamber a narrow waterfall splashed down over some rounded rocks. Hazel doubled over, hands on her knees, hauling air into her lungs.

'What's going on, Portuna?' she gasped. 'What happened back there? Tell me!'

'Shh! Not so loud!' Portuna hissed sharply.

'Tell me!' Hazel hissed back.

The fairy tutted and looked around warily. 'All right, all right,' she huffed. 'Don't drop your petals!' She beckoned for Hazel to follow and led her to a flat rock near the falls. They sat down, close together, the water rushing down noisily beside them.

'The Hollows are in trouble,' Portuna whispered. 'Terrible trouble. Much worse than I knew.' She thumped her fists against the stone. 'Oh, if I hadn't been stuck in that stupid bottle . . . !'

'Trouble?' said Hazel. 'What sort of trouble?'

'The Fae.' Portuna glittered with anger. 'They've got these woods in their grip, and every fairy, beast and bird who lives here. It's *them* who control the flow of the Ley. It's *them* who drained those tunnels back there. They can leach the life from a place – just like that.' She snapped her fingers sharply.

'But why?' asked Hazel.

'Hoarding it for themselves, aren't they?' Portuna spat. 'While the rest of us fade and die.'

Hazel thought of the fairy in the tunnel: his transparent limbs, his empty eyes.

'And the boy?' she said.

'Must've got lost. Stayed too long in the faded places.' Portuna turned her head to wipe away tears.

Instinctively, Hazel took Portuna's hand and held it tight. For a long moment, the two of them sat side by side in silence. Hazel thought of the boy's frail cry, his black shade on the ground. Then, as the waterfall rushed and gurgled beside them, her mind turned once more to Pete. Her chest tightened.

'Do you think . . .' she whispered. 'Do you think the Fae took him? Took Pete?'

Portuna sighed. 'Their servants, probably. Goblyn is full of their spies and allies. Usually they're out to catch the Fae's enemies – anyone who stands up to them, that is – but if you're in the wrong part of the woods at the wrong time . . .' She clicked her tongue and shook her head.

'Oh!' Hazel gasped, close to despair.

Portuna's eyes flicked between the two tunnels that gave onto the chamber, then she leaned in closer.

'Listen,' she said, a conspiratorial gleam in her eye. 'I

know folks. Folks who can help. We'll find him. We will. Seely's honour!'

Hazel was taken aback by this sudden show of kindness. Portuna's eyes were a deep, tawny gold and, for the first time since Pete was taken, Hazel had the unmistakable feeling that she was in the presence of someone good. Infuriating, fickle and huffy, but good.

'We'll start asking around tomorrow,' said Portuna, getting up. She stretched out her hand and pulled Hazel to her feet. 'Come on,' she said with a smile. 'You have to try Pa's marrow bean stew. No nettles, I promise!'

They followed the path of the underground stream, splashing and gurgling over the mottled rock. Sensing the nearness of home, Portuna hurried on ahead, her mass of hair bouncing lightly behind her.

'We're almost there!' she called. 'Can you hear it?'

Hazel paused and listened. Amongst the clicking of beetles' wings and the steady stretching of tree roots, she detected the distant babble of voices.

Soon, the tunnel grew higher and wider and Hazel noticed that, set into the earthen walls, were windows and low doors each brightly painted in cornflower blues, ivy greens or berry reds. The pointed face of a young Seely child bobbed up from behind a windowsill, flashed with mischief, then vanished again. Portuna shrugged off her cloak and tossed it to Hazel.

'Here,' she said. 'Wear this.'

The cloak felt surprising light in her hands, as if it had been woven from mosses and thistledown. She wrapped it round her shoulders and pulled up the hood. It was as soft and warm as fur.

'And take off those clodhoppers,' said Portuna, pointing at Hazel's shoes. 'You don't need them.'

Hazel looked at Portuna's wide but nimble fairy feet – feet much like her own. She sat down and tugged off her clumpy shoes, along with her coarsely woven socks.

'Better, right?' Portuna grinned.

Hazel wiggled her free toes, then stood up again, glad to feel her soles pressing into the earth.

'Perfect!' Portuna announced, fixing the wooden clasp of the cape. 'That should stop those tongues wagging!' Then she took Hazel's hand and led her down the widening tunnel into the clamour and chatter of the Seely village.

Hazel's eyes stretched wide in amazement. When she had looked out at the forest from the chapel roof, she'd often wondered what life might be like in the treetops, but never had she imagined a busy world bubbling away beneath the forest floor. In fact, Understone was more of a hive or warren than a village. The huge, unevenly shaped chamber was buttressed with sturdy roots that snaked down on all sides, and amongst the knots and burls were dozens of windows and doorways leading back into earthen dwellings. From where she stood, she could see across the stream to what appeared to be a busy marketplace. Seely fairies swarmed

between stalls and barrels, carrying baskets of nuts, bundles of herbs and wriggling Seely infants. Hazel rubbed her eyes. It was all so hard to believe yet, at the same time, it was oddly familiar.

'Come on. Quick!' urged Portuna, tugging Hazel's hand. 'I want to get home before anyone corners me.'

They hurried over a dry-stone bridge into the hum and hustle of the market. The air was full of shouts and whistles as vendors hawked their wares. Somewhere in the crowd, a fiddle played a lively tune. While Portuna kept her head down, pushing quickly through the jostling throng, Hazel peered from under her hood at the crowded stalls. All around her were barrows and baskets loaded with the forest's autumn harvest: walnuts and dimpled apples; piles of bruised damsons, pears and blackberries.

'How ripe d'you want 'em?' a vendor asked his customer, a clutch of green plums in his hands. Hazel didn't hear the answer but watched wide-eyed as the vendor rolled the plums between his palms, bringing them quickly to a deep, ripe purple.

But the market was not only selling the fruits of the woods. There were also stinking cheeses, pitchers of cream and huge dusty sacks of flour. Hazel noticed a milk churn marked with the name of a dairy and quickly realised that the produce had been pilfered from nearby farms. And it had been put to good use too. At the next stall were baskets of crusty loaves, seed cakes and round fruity puddings dripping with a syrupy glaze. Hazel recognised Granny Webcap's nettle pies, stacked high on the counter, and spluttered with disgust as the bitter taste returned to her mouth.

The fiddle music grew louder, spooling into the air like long, colourful ribbons. Through the crowds, Hazel could see the fiddler, sitting high on a barrel, foot tapping the air, elbow jigging quickly back and forth. He was a scruff-haired lad of about her age, with beautiful blue tattoos over one side of his face: circles, swirls and dots climbing right up to his hairline. As she gazed at the intricate patterns, he leaned his head back and looked her in the eye. Hazel started, embarrassed to have been caught staring, but the boy just smiled at her – an open, generous smile that dimpled his cheeks. It was a smile you had to return. But before she had the chance, a small hand tugged her own sharply and dragged her away.

'Hurry up, slow-worm!' said Portuna, voice bubbling with excitement. 'I can smell Pa's stew already!'

CHAPTER SEVENTEEN

The Fading

THE MOMENT PA BABBAGE SAW HIS DAUGHTER he dropped his ladle and scooped her into his arms. Portuna's father was a small, round-bellied fairy with tufts of grey hair that sprouted on either side of his head, giving him the appearance of a friendly squirrel.

'My little acorn!' he blustered, looking at her in disbelief. He hugged her again and, for a second, father and daughter fused together in a warm pulse of light.

As far as Pa was concerned, Hazel was part of the family the moment she walked through their rickety front door. It was a large family, too. A litter of small Seely children leaped and sparked like firecrackers, while an ancient-looking fairy sat in a rocking chair by a warm lump of glowing amber. One flash of her glittering black eyes told Hazel that this must be spiky Aunt Mag. She was chewing on a thistlehead and playing cards with Portuna's brother, Corrie, who was plainly delighted to see his sister but too shy to show it. He greeted her with a pinch on the arm then went back to losing to his quick-fingered auntie.

Before long, supper was ready. To Hazel's relief there was not a nettle pie in sight, but a herby bean stew and hot potatoes served with slabs of melting yellow butter. The Babbage children climbed onto stools around the low cherrywood table and attacked their supper with greedy little spoons. As the family listened to Portuna tell an exaggerated account of their escape from Grinling, Hazel looked around at the Babbages' comfortable dwelling – the low, curved ceiling, the whistling kettle, the carved applewood goblets. Above ground she had always been so small. Clothes were always too big, tabletops too high. But here, in this snug little burrow, everything was just the right size. Then, rising up within her, came a feeling that was as warm and steady as the glow of the amber – the strangely certain feeling that she had been in Understone before.

'Gracious *me*!' Portuna was all puffed up, acting out Grinling's imagined outrage on discovering his sprouting hat stand. Auntie Mag hooted with laughter, rocking forwards in her chair. But when Portuna came to the story of the collapsing tunnel, the mood in the burrow darkened. Pa Babbage shook his head with a bewildered sadness.

'It's the Fading,' he said. 'It's got so much worse!'

'The Fading?' Hazel asked.

Portuna caught her breath and explained.

'Like I told you. It's when the ley lines are drained of energy. The Fading makes everything die.'

Corrie, who until then had been sulking over his lost game of cards, now looked up at Hazel with a wary eye.

'How come you don't know what a Fading is?' he asked suspiciously.

Hazel felt the blood rush to her cheeks.

'She's not from round here,' Portuna replied sharply.

'Then where *is* she from?' Corrie lashed back, stung by Portuna's tone.

'Manners, Corrie,' Pa intervened. 'A friend of Portuna's is a friend of ours.' The boy returned moodily to his plate and Pa picked up where Portuna had left off.

'The Ley used to be strong in Goblyn. The ferns were thick, the streams flowed quickly, but now –' he raised his hands in puzzled despair – 'the pulse is terribly weak. It's worrying, yes, very worrying indeed.'

Pa was interrupted by a rasping, throaty sound. Auntie Mag spat out a thistle-head.

'Hogweed!' she croaked, waggling a dismissive finger. 'We've seen it all before. In my nine hundred years, I've seen the Ley ebb and flow, ebb and flow. It runs weakly now, yes, but give it time and it'll be back to full force.' She plucked a prickle out of her tongue. 'It's just the way of things.'

'That's not true,' Portuna said, looking annoyed. 'This time is different. The Fading is much quicker, and far more dangerous.'

111

Pa Babbage nodded in agreement.

'She's right, Auntie,' he said, 'and it's unpredictable too. If you fall asleep in the wrong part of the forest, you'll be nothing but a shade by morning.'

Auntie Mag huffed loudly. 'The Fae will protect us,' she muttered, pulling her patchwork over her knees.

At this, Portuna flared up hotly. 'The Fae are the *problem*, Auntie!' she cried in exasperation.

Immediately, Pa Babbage sprang to his feet and hurried to shutter the windows.

'Hush, hush!' he fretted. But Portuna would not be silenced.

'It's the Fae who are behind the Fading!' she insisted, waving a finger in the air. 'The Fae and their Arborean henchmen. I don't see any Fading in Arborean territory, do you?! I don't see any Arborean shades in the tunnels! They do the Fae's dirty work for them and get plenty of Ley in return. It's as plain as the ears on my head!'

'No need to shout, Portuna,' Pa urged, comforting a wailing infant against his shoulder. 'Now, settle down and eat your blackberries.'

Corrie was watching his sister with a look of weary irritation. 'She's been listening to those crackpots again,' he grumbled. 'She reads all their stupid pamphlets.'

Portuna turned and fixed him with a narrow stare. 'And I suppose *you've* been listening to the Webcap boy,' she snarled. 'I bet *he* thinks it's all the Druics' fault.'

Corrie flamed a deep red. 'They take our Ley!' he growled. 'And don't say they don't, cos they do!'

'It's not *our* Ley, Corrie!' Brother and sister were both burning fiercely now and Hazel began to worry they'd explode in a shower of sparks. 'Clouds above!' Portuna cried. 'You really do have mud for brains!' At this, Corrie shrank into a fist-sized fireball and launched himself at his sister.

Auntie Mag screeched with glee as the two Babbage siblings hurtled about the room, knocking pots and pans from the shelves and tangling in the strings of onions hanging from the ceiling. Pa groaned and fetched a net in which he tried to catch one or other of his children without tripping over the younger ones who were tumbling around his feet, some dancing with joy, others howling with fright. Hazel had never known such a rumpus and felt something between horror and exhilaration as Corrie and Portuna sprang from the walls shrieking, clashing and striking sparks off one another.

After knocking the kettle off the stove and accidently netting Auntie's head, Pa trapped Portuna on the rug. Immediately she sprang back up to her normal size, fists clenched and gasping for breath.

'CORRIGAN!' Pa Babbage roared in a voice much bigger than himself. Corrie too appeared before them. His teeth were clenched, but there was a glimmer of tears in his eyes.

'Enough now, enough,' said Pa, drawing them both into his arms. 'We're all together again. That's what matters. Now kiss and make up. We're late for the revels.'

CHAPTER EIGHTEEN

Nautilus Strike

HAZEL WAS ASTONISHED BY HOW QUICKLY THE siblings' fury switched to a playful teasing. One moment they had been spinning through the air in a wild rage and the next they were chortling together, conspiring to put a thistle on Auntie's rocking chair.

After supper, Pa poured Hazel a hot bath in a large copper tub. After years of shivering scrub-downs, she marvelled at the feel of being suspended in warmth, the wonderful weight of clean water running through her hair. She was joined by three of the little Babbages, who dipped and dived like ducklings and squabbled over the soap. Before long, Hazel was laughing and splashing with them till the stony floor was awash with giant puddles.

'What's a revel?' she asked as she pulled on some clothes Portuna had given her.

'You'll see,' said Portuna mischievously. She tied the belt

then stepped back to admire Hazel's transformation. 'There!' She grinned. 'You're a proper Seely now!'

Hazel turned to look at her reflection in a large black-spotted mirror. Staring back at her was the girl she had always known: those large ears, that brambled hedge of hair, those flickering, opaline eyes. But now, dressed in her fairy garb, she saw herself anew. She was wearing a mushroom-brown tunic with small embroidered pockets, and a pair of soft green leggings that moulded perfectly to her legs. Clothes had never fitted her so comfortably. She was as snug as a rabbit inside its own fur.

'Oh,' she whispered, astonished. And, for the first time in as long as she could remember, she smiled at her own reflection.

Once everyone was scrubbed and dressed, the Babbage clan hurried out of their burrow and walked together up an uneven stairway that spiralled upwards into the open bole of a hornbeam tree. Then, one by one, they climbed out of the trunk into the green of Goblyn Wood.

It was dusk and the light was low, but, after so many hours underground, it took Hazel's eyes a moment to adjust. Dozens of Seelies, old and young, clambered and hopped out of nearby trees. The whole village was present, it seemed, and there was a giddy excitement in the air.

They had emerged into a large grassy glade. At the centre of the glade, poking crookedly from the earth like the finger of a buried giant, was a tall, narrow stone. It looked as though it had been there forever, long before even the most ancient trees in the forest, perhaps before the forest itself.

'Hurry up!' said Portuna, grabbing Hazel's hand. The Seelies were forming circles round the standing stone, one inside the other, like ripples on water. Hazel and Portuna joined one of the innermost rings where the other Babbages had gathered. As shrieking children dashed between legs and raced in and out of the circles, Hazel kept her eyes on the huge stone. Closer up, she could see that its lichen-patched surface was covered with worn engravings. Though many of the marks had been blurred by time, she could still make out the twining images of animals, birds and insects. Wolves, rabbits, moths, hawks – each creature seemed to grow into the next, as if they were all part of the same living substance. Hazel followed a sinuous line towards a heavily weathered figure halfway up the stone. Straining her eyes through the thickening gloom, she was able to identify the outline of a hand, the curve of a face. It was a human form. Or was it a fairy? Hazel wasn't sure but, for a few moments, she was utterly absorbed in the image, as if it were an impossible knot that she had to untangle.

The last flush of sunlight left the sky and a hush rippled through the crowd. Squawking children were seized and dragged back into their family groups, and all present joined hands and looked towards the giant stone. Hazel found herself between Portuna and Corrie, her hands tingling in theirs.

Then, from somewhere nearby, one strong, smooth voice soared up towards the gradually emerging stars. The other Seelies hummed a low, melodic response and Hazel felt the circles begin to sway. As she moved along with them, the chorus around her grew fuller, the melody separating into different strands that twisted upwards into the cool night air. To Hazel's delight, she found that she was able to sing along in a light, clear voice that she never knew she had. The song was rising up within her from some long-forgotten place, and with it came a breath-snatching rush of joy.

The swaying turned to stamping. Dozens of bare feet pounded the ground in a steady rhythm and Hazel found herself moving easily in time, the grass damp and cool between her toes. Then, as the pace quickened, she felt something awakening, deep in the earth below. In the moment before Pete had been captured, and again in the parched tunnels, she had felt the life leached from her body, sucked down into the ground. But now she felt the opposite – a powerful, living force surging up beneath her: the Ley.

She looked at the Seelies and saw that, as they sang and stamped, their bodies were all flickering more brightly, shimmering with that changing, opaline light. Then Hazel felt it too – an electricity in her toes that spread up her legs, and up her spine, right to the roots of her hair. It was the same delicious fire that she had felt in the presence of the professor's greenstone. As the bright energy raced through her she saw that the skin on her arms glowed with a soft rainbow sheen.

Suddenly the stamping stopped and a wild, twirling music struck up. Perched high on top of the stone was the tattooed boy from the marketplace, playing his fiddle faster than the thrum of a cricket's legs. Hooting and hollering with glee, the rings of Seelies began to turn. Still holding tightly onto each other's hands, they danced and flew through the air like fireflies, feet barely skimming the ground. Hazel found herself yelling and whooping with them, her heart blazing with a joy so fierce it almost frightened her.

She didn't know how long she had been dancing when, feet burning and sides aching, she collapsed onto the grass, howling with laughter. Portuna flopped down beside her and the two new friends lay still for a moment. A sharp sickle moon dangled in the night sky and Hazel was sure she could hear the chilly tinkle of the stars. The revels were winding down now and the Seely folk were slipping back into the hollows of the trees, exhausted infants dangling over their shoulders.

'It's funny,' Hazel whispered, feeling the throb of the Ley in the earth below her. 'All this is so new. So *strange*. But at the same time it's like everything makes more sense here. I don't know how to explain it, but it's like . . . I don't know . . . like I fit together better.'

Portuna yawned. 'It's like you've come home?'

'Right!' A smile spread across Hazel's face. 'Maybe that's what it is. Like I've come *home*.'

As Portuna hummed the fiddler's tune, Hazel felt a sudden urge to talk to Pete, to tell him all about this strange but familiar world. Then, with a pang, she remembered she couldn't.

The two girls got to their feet and walked arm in arm towards the open trunk of the hornbeam. They were just a few feet away when Hazel saw something that made her reel back with shock.

Scratched into the scaly surface of the bark was a familiar symbol. It was swirled like a snail shell, with a line struck through its centre. Hazel put her hand to her collarbone and felt for her necklace. The symbol was exactly the same as the engraving on her pendant.

'What's that?' she said, pointing to the carving on the tree. 'What does it mean?' Portuna took one look at it, then grinned widely.

'The Nautilus Strike!' she whispered. 'It's the sign of the "conspirators", the "crackpots" that Corrie was talking about.'

'Who?' said Hazel, puzzled.

'Our best hope.' Portuna smiled. 'The rebels!'

CHAPTER NINETEEN

Arboreans

THE BABBAGE CHILDREN SLEPT IN HAMMOCKS slung haphazardly around their bedroom like giant cobwebs. Portuna's was large enough for two and Hazel had squeezed in beside her, beneath a thick thistledown blanket. For hours now, Portuna had been snoring gently in an infuriating cycle of grunts and whistles, but Hazel couldn't sleep.

She tugged her pendant from her collar and ran her thumb over its coiled engraving. Her necklace was her only link to the life she had forgotten, and she treasured it. But now it seemed to glow with other meanings. It was no longer a simple gift from her mother, meant only for her, but a mysterious object that belonged to another world – one that others understood better than she did.

Hazel sighed uneasily. Her patched-together image of her mother was pulling apart at the seams, and a question that, until then, had only been hovering at the edges of her thoughts now pulled into focus: Had her mother also been a fairy?

One of the tiny Babbages whimpered then sent up a pitiful wailing. Rubbing his eyes, Pa shuffled through the door, scooped the unhappy child out of his hammock and carried him out of the room, patting his back and whispering promises of warm milk and honey. As Hazel listened to the gurgling of the comforted infant, she reached deep into her memory, searching for some trace of her own parents. But, as usual, there was nothing there – nothing for her to stand on, just an endless treading of water. She felt a heavy ache in her chest and, pendant slipping between her fingers, lapsed wearily into sleep.

Breakfast next morning was chaos. Pa had gone to his workshop to carve some bowls for market, so Corrie and Portuna were in charge of getting everyone fed and dressed. Before long, the smell of burned oats filled the room and toddlers were hiding under tables and chairs, wearing no more than undershirts and the odd hat. Hazel helped Corrie wrangle them into their tunics and trousers and, after his tetchiness the day before, she was glad to receive a friendly smile.

It was while they were sitting round the table picking charred clots out of their porridge that they heard a commotion outside. Corrie sat up, his skin sparkling with excitement. But Portuna had turned a wary silver and was glaring at the door, eyes flashing suspiciously. There was a sudden rush of footsteps. Dozens of fairies were clattering past. Within seconds, the whole Babbage clan had dashed outside to join them. Hazel followed and quickly found herself caught up in the flow of hurrying Seelies. Everyone was pushing and jostling along the narrow stairway that led down to the market square. But as they reached a turn, Portuna seized Hazel's hand and steered her out of the crowds.

'Come with me!' she whispered. She dragged Hazel up some steps to a high balcony hidden amongst some knotted roots. From here they could see over the rambling roofs of the dwellings and stalls, all the way down to the stream.

Four riders were crossing the bridge on green-eyed fairy horses. As Hazel watched them approach, she felt a horrid crawling under her skin, like the stirrings of a forgotten nightmare.

'Arboreans!' Portuna hissed.

Crowds of Seely fairies were leaving their dwellings and hurrying towards the riders. High on their dazzling white steeds, the Arboreans appeared taller, or at least better fed, than most of the gathering Seelies. They were dressed in dark-green tunics embroidered with fine silver thread, and slung across their backs were thick sheaves of arrows.

Hazel's eye was drawn to the leader. He was powerfully built, with pale green hair tied in a high knot. On his left hand he wore the three-fingered glove of an archer, while his right was heavy with amethyst rings. He was gazing down at the clustering Seelies, his face as smooth as marble.

'Who's that?' she whispered.

'Ruis,' Portuna replied with a snort of disgust. 'All Arboreans are thugs, but Ruis is the worst.' Hazel didn't find that hard to believe. In the set of his mouth was the unmistakable curve of cruelty.

At Ruis's command, the horses came to a halt. He cast an imperious eye over the waiting Seelies, many of whom were taking off their hats and bowing their heads.

'Where is she?' he asked in a dry, almost rattling, voice.

After a hushed moment, there was movement in the crowd and a Seely mother stepped forward carrying a young child in her arms. The child looked faded and weak, her head lolling heavily against her mother's shoulder. With a shock, Hazel remembered the fading shape of the boy in the tunnel.

'It's Pip Crabfoot,' gasped Portuna. 'Her ma's always telling her not to wander off. Looks like she strayed too far.' The mother held the girl up towards Ruis and, with an empty smile, the Arborean leaned forward and placed his jewelled hand on the girl's forehead. His fingers, Hazel noticed, were long and sinewy, each ending in a sharply pointed nail. A hush rippled through the anxious crowd then Ruis breathed in deeply and closed his eyes.

There was a pulse of light and the Arborean's body was bathed in a shimmering iridescence. Hazel gasped at the colours that billowed around him – blues, pinks, golds and greens. It was as if all the colours of the dawn were swelling and cresting in a mesmerising dance. Enchanted, the crowd looked on as the glimmering waves of Ley gathered in the Arborean's fingertips then began to flow into little Pip's body.

After a few moments, the light wavered and faded, and Ruis lifted his hand away. Pip's mother drew her daughter to her chest, stroking her still-drooping head. Everyone held their breath, including Hazel. But soon a soft glow returned to the child's limbs, and she appeared denser and stronger. Then her eyes blinked open and she cried mightily, wriggling and kicking her stout little legs.

The Seelies cheered and whistled, kissing Ruis's hands and stirruped feet while the mother hugged her screaming daughter, weeping with relief. Amongst the jubilant crowd, Hazel spied Corrie. He was smiling broadly, a look of bashful admiration in his eyes.

She turned to Portuna, puzzled. 'Did he just save her?'

'Yes,' Portuna muttered. 'But don't be fooled. It's all for show.'

'For show?'

'It stops people asking questions. You heard Auntie Mag. She thinks Arboreans fell from the sun itself!'

Hazel watched as several frail-looking Seelies stepped shakily forward, hoping for the same treatment. But the Arboreans had clearly finished their business in Understone and did not give them so much as a glance. Ruis whisked a finger in the air and the horses turned smartly back towards the bridge, flicking their smooth white tails. As the Arboreans departed, they looked slyly at one another as if they were sharing a joke. Then, as their shadows disappeared down a wide passage, Hazel heard a sound that seized her heart and squeezed it still.

Rattling down the tunnel came a hollow shriek of laughter. It was icy, inhuman. Hazel gripped Portuna's arm in horror.

'It was ... it was them!' she stammered. 'They took him. They took Pete!'

CHAPTER TWENTY

Fen

HAZEL SAT DOWN SHAKILY ON THE TREE ROOT behind her, sick to the stomach.

Portuna whistled through her teeth. 'Thought it might have been them,' she said. 'Worse luck!' She plumped herself down next to Hazel and peered closely at her face. 'Don't get your turnips in a tangle,' she said. 'I said we'd find him, didn't I?'

Hazel stared at her, not knowing whether to be appalled or reassured by Portuna's matter-of-factness.

'I'll, y'know, put my ear to the ground.' Portuna shrugged. 'See what I can find out. I expect somebody knows *something.*'

Hazel frowned. She didn't like how vague this all sounded. 'You said you know folks,' she said. 'Folks who can help us.'

'I do . . . sort of.'

'What do you mean, *sort of?*'

'Weeeell . . .' Portuna replied. 'I haven't actually *met* them yet.'

'You haven't *met* them?' said Hazel. 'But you told me—!'

'Not so loud!'

Hazel gave an exasperated growl but fell silent.

'Look –' Portuna glanced around for twitching ears – 'I'm not supposed to tell anybody, but . . . I've been in touch with the *rebels*.' Hazel detected pride in her friend's voice. 'I was supposed to join them, you see. They sent me instructions and everything. But I got lost and wandered into the wrong part of the forest – that's when Grinling trapped me.'

'The rebels?' said Hazel. 'They're the ones who can help us?'

'If anyone knows what's going on in this forest, *they* do.'

Hazel felt a flurry of hope, but something told her there was a catch.

'Of course,' said Portuna, looking uncomfortable, 'we'll have to help *them* in return.'

'How?'

'I dunno . . .' Portuna scratched the back of her neck. 'Do a bit of fighting, something like that.'

'Fighting?! But you never said—!'

'Look,' Portuna snapped. 'Do you want to find Pete or not?'

Hazel sighed in frustration then nodded. 'All right. So how do we find them?'

'I've still got their instructions,' said Portuna. 'But . . .'

'What?'

'We can't tell Pa we're leaving.'

Hazel narrowed her eyes suspiciously. 'Why not?'

'Cos he'll try to stop us, won't he? You heard Granny Webcap. I go missing for a few days and he's all a-jitter. If he knows we're going to join the rebels, he'll have a fit.'

Hazel thought of Pa's beaming face when he saw Portuna walk through the door. She frowned and shook her head. 'No,' she said. 'We can't just sneak off. You have to tell him.'

'Why?'

'*Because*,' said Hazel, amazed that she had to explain such a thing. 'If we just creep away, he'll be even more worried. You need to say goodbye at least.'

Portuna rolled her eyes. 'Goodbyes are horrible things,' she sniffed, 'I don't know why you clayfeet insist on them.'

'Because if somebody just vanishes and you don't know why,' said Hazel, her voice rising in urgency, 'and you don't know where they are, or what happened to them . . . there's nothing worse. Nothing worse in the world.' Hazel folded her arms. 'I'm not sneaking off. You have to tell him.'

Portuna stared back at her, stunned. 'All right,' she said, 'I will.' Then she leaped to her feet and scurried off.

Hazel found herself alone on the rooty balcony. She peered down over the village and saw Portuna skipping through the maze of dwellings to find Pa in his workshop. Immediately, she was gripped with regret. She hadn't thought this through. What if Pa talked Portuna out of it? She chewed anxiously on a thumbnail and was just wondering whether or not to chase after her friend, when she heard somebody coming up the steps towards her.

It was the boy from the market. He didn't have his fiddle with him and was walking with his head down, hands stuffed loosely in the pockets of his too-short trousers. As he neared, he looked up and smiled. Hazel moved back to let him pass through, but he stayed where he was, looking at her with unblushing curiosity.

'You're not from round here, are you?' he said.

A knot tightened in Hazel's stomach. 'No,' she said, 'I'm not.'

'So where you from, then?' asked the boy, eyes crinkling.

'I ... uh ...' Hazel cast about for the right answer. 'I'm from ... from Ditchmoor,' she said, then immediately regretted it.

The boy wrinkled his nose in puzzlement. 'Ditchmoor? That in the Hollows?'

'No, it's, er ... er ...'

'Sorry,' said the boy. 'Didn't mean to spook you. I'm not from Understone either, y'know.'

'No?' said Hazel, with a sigh of relief.

'Nah, I'm not from anywhere, really.' The boy's smile

folded his tattoos into lovely new waves of pattern. 'I get funny looks all the time.'

They both laughed and Hazel felt suddenly glad of his presence – simple, and welcoming. She wanted to say something to keep him there a bit longer.

'I liked your playing,' she said, '. . . the fiddle.'

'Thanks,' said the boy. 'I prefer the flute, but Seelies love a bit of fiddle music!'

Hazel thought of the leaping, revelling Seelies and laughed.

At that moment, a gang of Seely children rushed by. One bumped roughly into the boy as she passed. 'Ley-sucker!' she jeered, then ran off.

'What was that about?' Hazel frowned.

The boy shrugged. 'Think we steal their Ley, don't they?'

Hazel remembered Corrie's argument with Portuna. 'I didn't think the Ley belonged to anyone.'

'Too right it doesn't!' he said with a grin.

There was a scurrying on the steps, and a big-eyed girl who looked around eight in human years appeared at the boy's side. She also had blue tattoos curling up her neck and face.

'There you are, Fen!' she said. 'Ma's been looking all over. We're leaving now.'

'All right then, Merrin,' said the boy, putting his arm round her shoulder. 'I'm coming.' The boy gave Hazel a big, sweeping wave, then turned and followed his sister back down the steps.

Hazel watched until they had both disappeared into the narrow alleys of Understone, her heart beating a little faster than before.

CHAPTER TWENTY-ONE

Nightjar

'THE FOREST IS GROWING MORE DANGEROUS BY the day,' said Pa, wrapping chestnut dumplings in sheets of beeswax. 'You've got to look after each other. Stay out of the faded places and move quickly. Eyes sharp, ears a-prick!'

It was the next morning. The other Babbage children were still asleep in their hammocks, but Pa had risen early to prepare food parcels for Portuna and Hazel's journey.

'I'm a hundred and two, Pa!' groaned Portuna. 'I know how to look after myself.'

'Perhaps,' he replied, packing the parcels into his daughter's knapsack. 'But you're still my little acorn.' Pa was smiling but his voice was strained. He wagged his finger. 'And don't you forget it!'

'I won't.' Portuna smiled. 'Don't worry, Pa. We'll be back before Auntie finishes her next batch of thistles, you'll see.'

At that Pa gathered Hazel and Portuna into his arms and kissed them both firmly on the cheek.

'I hope you find your friend, my dear,' he said to Hazel. 'Now go, both of you, before I change my mind.' Portuna gave her father one last hug then headed for the door, tugging Hazel behind her.

'How did you talk him round?' asked Hazel as they scampered up the snaking stairway towards the forest floor. 'I didn't think he'd let you go.'

'You won't believe it,' Portuna whispered, 'but Pa told me that, when he was my age, he used to be with the rebels too.'

'Really?' gasped Hazel, struggling to imagine mild-mannered Pa scrapping with Arboreans.

'He didn't fight,' Portuna continued, 'but he gave them shelter when they needed it. Said he's always believed in the Cause.' That, Hazel could believe. From the moment she had set foot in the Babbages' burrow it had felt like a circle of safety, its flimsy door a barricade against evil.

Portuna clicked her tongue in thought. 'I never thought of Pa doing stuff before I was born,' she said. 'He was always just Pa. Now he's, I dunno – somebody else too.' She wrinkled her nose. 'It's funny.'

'It's *great!*' said Hazel.

Portuna thought for a moment longer, then glowed a happy yellow. 'It is, isn't it?' She put a skip in her step. 'My Pa. A rebel!'

'Why'd he stop?' asked Hazel.

'Well, there was Ma, then us kids. Got too risky. Anyway, he said I'm old enough to make my own mistakes and that, in any case –' Portuna sniffed proudly – 'he knew he couldn't stop me!'

'If I had a family like yours,' said Hazel, 'I don't think I'd ever want to leave.'

'Oh, I wouldn't bet on it,' Portuna scoffed. 'You haven't met Aunt Prim – daisies *literally* wilt in her presence.' Then she broke away and sprinted up the coiling stairway. 'Race you to the top!'

It was a glorious autumn morning – all russets and greens and golds. Arrows of sunlight pierced the thinning canopy, and the air hung cool and dewy. Though Hazel and Portuna both knew that a darkness gnawed at the forest, in that moment the world seemed so full of hope that it was impossible to believe.

Hazel glanced up at the sky. She thought of Pete, somewhere beneath the same sharp blue, and felt a flash of courage. 'All right, then,' she said. 'Which way do we go?'

'Oh, that's easy!' said Portuna, tugging a small bundle out of her pocket. 'This thing'll tell us!' She held up a dull pebble on the end of a looped string.

Hazel wrinkled her nose. 'What is it?'

'The rebels sent it to me,' Portuna whispered. 'Look, you

dangle it like this and wait to see which direction it tugs you in. It'll take us straight to them!' She stretched out her arm, dangled the stone by its string and closed her eyes. Hazel watched the pebble carefully. It circled then came to a trembling rest. She held her breath and waited, but the stone did not do anything unusual.

'I think . . .' Portuna squinted in concentration. 'I think it's telling us to go this way!' She pointed towards a gap between two ivy-laced elms. Hazel shrugged and they set off, Portuna swinging the stone out in front of her.

The way was clear and bright. Coppery leaves shimmered above them, bracken crisped at their feet, and all around was the chatter of squirrels jealously hiding nuts.

'Portuna?' Hazel asked as they leaped over a ditch. 'Who's Fen?'

'Fen?'

'Yes, the fiddler at the revels. The one with the blue markings on his face.'

Portuna shrugged. 'Must be a Druic.'

Hazel waited for more, but Portuna was concentrating on her pebble. 'So you don't know him?' she prompted.

Portuna shook her head. 'Druics never stay long.'

'Oh.' Hazel felt a pang of disappointment.

After a while, the route grew clumped and snarled and they found themselves hacking through deep briar and brambles. Thorns snagged Hazel's skin, leaving stinging red lines on her arms and the backs of her hands. Every now and again Portuna would stop, dangle her pebble, then after a moment's head-scratching call, 'This way! This way!' and lead them straight into another tangle of gorse.

By the time they stopped to unwrap Pa's food parcels neither of them would have been able to find their way back to Understone.

'Are you sure that thing works?' asked Hazel, pointing at the pebble.

'Course it does!' said Portuna, looking offended but sounding uncertain. 'I've used it before, remember.'

'Yes, but . . .' Hazel muttered. 'You got *lost*.'

After they'd finished their dumplings, they pushed on through the trackless woods. On and on they went until the sun had crossed the sky and was sinking slowly in the west.

Hazel paused by a rotting stump to stretch her cramping legs and gazed around at the darkening shadows. Dusk was falling swiftly now, and it wouldn't be long before night closed in. Once again Portuna swung the stone out in front of her, scowling and muttering.

'Can I try?' asked Hazel. Portuna tossed it towards her and sat down on the stump, arms folded. Hazel sighed and picked the stone out of the dirt.

It was unremarkable to look at, smooth and grey with a clean white stripe across its middle, but when she turned it between her fingers she noticed that the pebble had two small holes bored into it, one at either end. Moving into a patch of fading light, she was able to study it more closely. There was something embedded deep inside.

Hazel plucked a long needle off a pine and teased it out. It was a tightly rolled scrap of paper.

'Portuna, look!'

Portuna sniffed moodily but slid off the stump and sloped towards her. Hazel unrolled the scrap and saw a message scrawled in a childlike script:

Just blow and you'll know which way you must go!

She burst out laughing.

'It's a whistle! A whistle!'

Portuna grabbed the stone and stared at it angrily, as if it had played the most dreadful trick on her. 'Fine, yes, it's a whistle,' she huffed, shoving it back into Hazel's hands. 'Go on, then. Blow!' Hazel put the stone to her lips and puffed lightly. The little grey pebble gave out a melodious trill. She blew again, longer this time, and a delicate song skipped lightly through the evening air.

Portuna's face lit up. 'Let me try!' She blew hard, and full, bright notes rose high into the trees, sending a family of birds into a frenzy of warbling. After a few more puffs others came flocking: blackbirds, sparrows, finches and wrens all twittering and carolling in reply to the whistle's fluting calls.

Dancing with glee, the girls took it in turns to blow

and, before long, the surrounding trees were bristling with birdsong. They were having so much fun that it was a long time before they noticed the strange, ragged creature that had settled on a nearby branch.

It was a large bird with a flattish head and a tiny, sharp bill. Its dry feathers were mottled greys and browns, giving it the appearance of a clutch of dead leaves, and it was watching them intently. Hazel was the first to spot it and, as soon as its cryptic eye met hers, she knew that the bird had come to find them. She also knew that they were drawing far too much attention to themselves.

'Shhh, Portuna!' she murmured. The fairy stopped her whistling and looked to where Hazel was pointing. She gasped and scurried to Hazel's side.

'A nightjar!' Portuna whispered. 'Strange to see one at this time of year.' The bird shook out its gritty mess of feathers then swooped silently to another branch. It turned and gave a low, rattling cry. Hazel and Portuna crept towards it, but as soon as they came close, the bird flew on again, settling in the branches of the next tree.

'I think he wants us to follow him,' said Hazel. The nightjar churred briefly then flew on, winging swiftly from branch to branch.

As the light faded, the two girls hurried behind the curious bird. To Hazel's relief, the thorny undergrowth thinned out and soon they were running easily between widely-spaced pillars of birch. A thin mist was rising from the forest floor, but despite the gathering dusk, she could now see further down the long alleys of trees. The blue shadow of a deer darted across the path ahead and, with a shiver, she realised that they too could more easily be seen.

Before long, the nightjar's mottled plumage mingled with the shadows and they had to rely on its whirring call.

'People say nightjars are bad luck,' Portuna whispered as they waited for the bird's next signal. 'They call them death-bringers.'

Hazel stared at her in horror. 'What?' she gasped. 'Why didn't you say so earlier? What makes you think we can trust it?'

'Well, people talk all kinds of rubbish!' Portuna retorted. 'If we believed everything that people said we'd never—' But Portuna did not finish her sentence, for at that moment they both heard the snap of a twig underfoot.

They grasped each other's hands and stared into the darkness between the trees. The shadows were wavering, shapeless, impossible to decipher. But a prickling at the nape of her neck told Hazel they were being watched. There was another faint rustle. The girls startled and looked wildly around them. Something was there. And it was creeping closer.

'Where's that bird gone?' Portuna whispered. But the woods were utterly silent. She raised the whistle to her lips and, in a flash, Hazel knocked it clean out of her hand.

'No!' she whispered, shards of panic in her voice. 'It's a trap!'

Then a hiss split the air and she felt a stab of pain.

CHAPTER TWENTY-TWO

The Earth Wizard

'WHAT ABOUT "DEFENDERS OF THE LEY"?'

'Too long.'

'All right, well how about "the Green Mist"?'

'Don't get it.'

'"Silver Hand?"'

'That's just weird!'

Hazel stirred from a heavy slumber. She opened her eyes to see who was talking, but her vision was dim and blurred. Her cheek was pressed against a dry, planked floor and slowly she became conscious of a deep stinging in her shoulder. She remembered the nightjar, the sound of something whistling through the air. She tried to move but her whole body felt as if it had been filled with molten iron.

The bickering continued.

'Well, have you got any better ideas?'

'I told you, I like "the Outlanders".' The voices belonged

to two children. 'Or what about "the Brotherhood". The Brotherhood of . . . um . . . um . . .'

'Hey!' came an older, female voice from further away, 'we're not all *brothers* here.'

'Well what's *your* favourite, then?'

'Urgh, it doesn't matter, does it? What's wrong with "the Rebels"?'

'BORING!' chorused the two younger voices.

Hazel felt a flood of relief. So, they'd been captured by the *rebels*. They'd made it!

'Hello?' she ventured. Chair legs scraped and footsteps hurried towards her. She was hauled upright, dragged a few feet, then sat brusquely on a hard surface. She tried to steady herself but her hands were tightly tied. Once she'd regained her balance, she squinted and strained her eyes, trying to sharpen her vision. She made out three dim shapes crowding around her.

'Who are you? What are you? What are you doing in our territory?!' said the older, female voice. The questions rapped painfully against Hazel's sore head.

'I'm . . . My name is Hazel Quince. And I thought I was a person, but I might be a fairy . . . I think . . . but I don't know what sort . . . and . . . Sorry, what was the last question?'

There was some muttering, and an impatient intake of breath.

'What are you doing in *our* territory?'

Hazel hesitated, unnerved by the questioner's hostility.

144

'We were looking for you,' she replied, squinting at the shapes. 'We think you can help us.'

There was a snort of laughter, then one of the younger voices cut in. 'Help you? Why should we help *you?*'

Hazel back-pedalled quickly. 'No, I mean, we want to *join* you. We're on your side!'

There was more laughter and Hazel felt a twinge of panic.

'All right,' the voice continued, amused, 'but how do *we* know you're on our side?'

'Prove it!' said the other, with some swagger in his voice.

Hazel was stumped. She thought of showing them her necklace, but she was afraid that it would raise more questions than it answered. Besides, she was beginning to wonder if *she* should trust *them*.

'Where's Portuna?' she asked.

There was a pause.

'Portuna?'

'Yes, she was with me. Portuna Babbage. Where is she?'

The laughter turned to a low mumbling. As the three conferred, Hazel's eyes cleared well enough for her to see that she was in a clumsily built wooden cabin. The door was closed and the windows shuttered, but daylight seeped between the planks, allowing her a look at her captors. There were two identical gap-toothed boys who, to her surprise, did not appear to be fairies but human children. With them was a grave-looking girl with short blue-black hair. She could have been seventeen in human years, but,

145

unlike the boys, her skin had the flickering glow of a fairy. After a lot of whispering and nodding, the atmosphere started to loosen and, eventually, the fairy girl turned to face Hazel.

'We've been expecting Portuna,' she said gruffly. 'Took her long enough.' She nodded to the twins. 'Wake her up, will you?' The boys hurried to a dark corner where Portuna lay curled up like a leaf, fast asleep. Seizing her under the arms, they hoisted her to her feet, hauled her across the room and plonked her down on a stool beside Hazel.

Portuna swayed and groaned as the boys undid the bonds on her wrists.

'Ow, ow,' she whined, twisting in discomfort. 'My shoulder!'

Hazel noticed a small puncture mark in Portuna's tunic, just above her shoulder blade. Once her own hands had been untied, she reached round to her upper back and felt a similar wound, tender and sticky.

'Just a dart,' said the girl coolly, pulling up a stool in front of them. 'We needed to make sure you were allies.' She produced a pot of ointment from her cloak. 'Here,' she said. 'Rub this in. It'll heal fast.' Hazel dabbed her finger into the waxy balm and, reaching under her tunic, rubbed it gingerly onto her shoulder blade. It stung like a hornet, but the pain soon began to melt to a tingling numbness.

Portuna gazed groggily around her.

'Where . . . ?' she mumbled. 'Who . . . ?' Then, as she looked up at her captors, her eyes slowly widened, first in shock, then delight.

'Wait . . .' She gasped. 'Are you . . . ?'

'We are!' cried one of the boys, thrusting a fist in the air. 'We are the Outlanders!'

Instantly his twin cuffed him on the back of the head. 'No, we're not!' he shouted crossly. 'We haven't voted yet! Arden, tell him!'

'Quiet!' said the girl, flashing the boys a look of such ferocity that they both fell silent. At the mention of the girl's name, Portuna turned to look at her, flickering brightly in admiration.

'Arden?' she said. 'Arden Silverthorne?' The girl looked embarrassed. 'Oh, I can't believe it's you! I've read *The Arborean Ally*, twice!' The girl shifted awkwardly and, with a jolt of alarm, Hazel saw that beneath her cloak she was dressed in dark green. The silver embroidery was half unpicked and grey with grime, but she was wearing the distinctive livery of the Arboreans.

Portuna leaned towards Hazel. 'It's all right,' she whispered loudly. 'She's not like the others. She *defected*!'

'Defected?'

'She left her folks to join the rebels.'

Arden pretended not to hear. She gestured towards the twin boys. 'This is Spud and Sprout,' she said. 'You know who we are. Welcome.'

It had started to rain outside. Cold droplets slid through

the timbers and splashed onto the back of Hazel's neck. The twins filled cups with water from a barrel and offered them to the new arrivals. Portuna was dizzy with excitement and pestering Arden about her book, but Hazel's hopes were beginning to wilt.

She hadn't really known what to expect from a rebel group, but as she looked around the broken-down cabin with its grimy cooking stove, untidy bunks and patched-up roof, she couldn't help but feel a creeping disappointment. Was this really her best hope of finding Pete? She took a sip of her water. It was gritty with dirt and tasted of rotting leaves.

'Is this . . . all of you?' she ventured. Then, as if to answer her question, the door swung open.

The last member of the group was so large he had to squeeze himself through the doorframe. His hood was pulled up against the rain and a dark, scruffy cloak hung from his shoulders, giving him the appearance of a giant bedraggled crow. Around his middle was a wide belt, loaded with ropes of rough-hewn crystals that swung and struck each other as he moved.

'Who's that?' Hazel whispered.

'Perig! Perig Tumblestone!' Portuna replied, her voice tinged with excitement. 'He's a geomancer.'

'A what?'

'An earth wizard. He knows stone magic.'

Perig pulled back his hood. He was as bald as a boulder with features that looked as if they had been carved with a blunt axe. His head, throat and entire face were inked with the swirling tattoos of the Druics and beneath his bent nose was a mossy green moustache, twisted into two thick plaits. Were it not for the merry spark in his eye, he would have looked fearsome indeed.

'Raining cats and cows out there!' he boomed in a voice that made the pots rattle. He shrugged off his mud-caked cloak and hung it on a peg. 'Heard the trees gossiping. Told me we had visitors.'

'Portuna Babbage is here,' said Arden. On hearing Portuna's name, Perig's tattoos creased happily.

'Ah! Young Babbage!' he roared. Portuna shimmered with delight. 'Welcome, welcome!' He gave Portuna a broad smile. Then his gaze came to rest on Hazel.

As the wizard's bright black eyes took in her presence, Hazel thought she saw a look of astonished recognition cross his face. It was the briefest shimmer – a wink of sunlight behind a craggy peak – then it was gone.

The twins came bundling across the room and threw themselves at Perig's massive frame.

'Lunch!' yelled Spud, grabbing a dirty sack from Perig's hands and spilling the earthy contents on the floor. Quick as a trick, the wizard grabbed the boys by their ankles and hoisted them into the air, wriggling like fish on a line.

'Where's your manners?' he growled playfully, as the boys twisted and shrieked with glee. 'Now behave and make a nice fry-up for our guests!'

Once the stove was lit and the frying pan was hissing merrily, the rebels' tumbledown shack began to feel more like a home. Hazel and Portuna warmed themselves by the flickering bronze grate as Spud and Sprout scrubbed potatoes, sliced cabbage and tossed salted perch into the pan. Perig, meanwhile, filled six clay cups with a golden brew, while Arden fixed the leaking roof. To Hazel's astonishment, she didn't use a hammer or nails, but ran her fingers over the cracks. As she did so, the wood seemed to soften then knit together, sealing the gaps.

As their hosts busied about, Hazel and Portuna took a moment to study their surroundings. Besides the bunks and cooking equipment there were fishing rods, buckets and nets, a wooden tub for washing and – hanging from hooks near the door – a quiver full of arrows and several grubby slingshots.

'Look!' said Portuna, tugging on Hazel's sleeve and

pointing behind them. Hazel turned to see a wide worktable and, above it, three shelves, each crammed full of books. Curious, she swivelled round on her stool to peer at their faded spines. Amongst the titles were: *The Old Wars: An Unfinished Story*; *Speaking with Trees: A Beginner's Guide*; *The Earth Wizard's Almanac* and, at the end of the row, *The Little Book of Big Rocks*. Below the shelves, on the table itself, was a collection of dusty stones and crystals, along with a pick, a chisel and a magnifying glass.

'Geomancer tools,' Portuna whispered excitedly. 'I wonder what he's cooking up!' She was about to reach for a rose-coloured crystal when a thick shadow fell across them.

'Now, then,' said a booming voice. They both started and turned. The wizard was looming over them with steaming cups of brew. He chuckled, balanced his enormous mass on a creaking stool and eyed his new recruits.

'Portuna Babbage,' he said, passing them their cups. 'Good to meet you at last. I know your pa from back in the day.' Portuna glowed pink with pride. 'And *his* pa too.'

'Grampy Babbage?!' gasped Portuna, astonished.

Perig nodded. 'Sturdy stock, the Babbages – always welcome here.' He took a sip of his brew, then turned his attention to Hazel. 'Now, who's your friend?' he asked, though, for some reason, Hazel suspected that he already knew the answer.

Portuna cleared her throat. 'I found her at the professor's,' she said, then began to reel off the tale of how she'd been

151

captured by Grinling but had made a daring escape, rescuing Hazel in the process. As she chattered on, Hazel noticed that Arden had stopped sealing up the roof and was listening to every word.

'And you, Hazel?' Perig observed her from beneath tangled green eyebrows. 'You must be all a-muddle.'

'Yes,' she said uncertainly, 'and no. I mean ... I don't know.' Perig nodded, as though he knew exactly how she was feeling. It was unsettling and reassuring, all at the same time.

Before long, the twins served up heaped dishes of fried potatoes and buttery cabbage, and plates of crispy-skinned perch. Then they all huddled round a low, wobbling table to eat.

'Your pa's a good'un,' Perig told Portuna as he refilled outstretched cups with the golden, honeyed brew. 'Nimble brain, stout heart. Made Understone a safe port in a storm.'

'He never told me,' said Portuna.

'Course not!' said Perig. 'He wouldn't have told anyone. Aldo keeps secrets safer than magpie loot.'

Portuna puffed up with delight as the wizard shared tales of Pa's distant youth.

'One time,' Perig chortled, 'he hid four of us in his pantry overnight. Next morning there wasn't a crumb left in there. Clouds above, was he cross!' He roared with laughter and thumped the table so hard it cracked. 'And now here you are, young Babbage.' He wiped his streaming eyes. 'The apple don't fall far from the tree.'

As the conversation meandered merrily on, Hazel noticed that Arden hadn't said a word since she'd heard the story of their escape from Grinling and, though she did not cast a single glance in Hazel's direction, Hazel had the distinct feeling that she was being watched.

After the dishes had been scraped clean and the last of the brew had been shared, Arden cleared her throat. 'What brings you here, Hazel?' she asked. 'Why do you want to join us?' She gazed at her steadily with serious brown eyes. Caught off guard, Hazel took a moment to find her words.

'The Arboreans,' she began, 'they took my friend.'

At that, the room fell silent. Everyone turned to look at her. Perig was frowning, deep lines furrowing his heavy brow.

'They did, did they?' he growled. 'Tell us everything.'

CHAPTER TWENTY-THREE

The Den

THE WIND RATTLED THROUGH A BROKEN shutter, flustering the candle flames, as Hazel told the story of Pete's capture. She spoke of their journey to Goblyn Wood, the beckoning light, the moon-bleached trees. By now the tale was starting to feel unreal, almost as if it had happened to somebody else. And, though the words came more easily, they brought a new kind of ache, as if her friend were slipping further and further away, fading to a distant memory. By the time she had finished, the atmosphere in the room had darkened.

The company sat silently as the rain trampled the roof. Eventually Perig tapped his cup on the table and scratched his tattooed cheek.

'That's Ruis and his gang all right,' he muttered. 'They're mostly after us rebels. Several of us were taken just this summer, weren't they, Arden?' Arden nodded briefly.

'They got Midge.' Spud frowned, wrinkling his nose.

'Pan too,' added Sprout. For a moment he looked like he might cry, but he sniffed the tears away.

Hazel swallowed hard. 'And what . . .' she said, uncertain that she wanted to hear the answer to her question, 'what happens to them?'

Perig sighed. 'Nobody knows for sure. But remember –' he wagged a large finger – 'Arboreans do what the Fae tell 'em to. Nothing but a bunch of spineless, weaselling—'

'Hey!' Arden snapped.

Perig immediately reined in his temper. 'Except our Arden, of course. She's not like the rest of them.'

'There are Seelies that support the Fae,' said Arden crossly. 'Some Druics too.'

'True, true,' Perig agreed. 'The Fae spread clever lies, no doubt. Folks don't know up from down.'

Arden nodded, appeased.

Outside, the storm was building, the wind whistling between the cracks in the shutters.

Perig swilled the now-cold brew in his cup. 'Your Pete will be in the Knoll, I expect.'

'The Knoll?' asked Hazel.

He nodded. 'A hollow hill in the north-east of the forest. Where the leylines cross.' Suddenly, Hazel remembered the map of Goblyn Wood that she had discovered in the professor's study – the ruled lines radiating from a great rise in the corner. Knowing where Pete might be gave her a burst of hope.

'And how do I get there?'

At that, Arden gave a short, dry laugh. 'Getting there is not so difficult,' she said. 'It's getting *in* that's the problem.'

'What do you mean?' Hazel asked, frowning.

'The Knoll is the Fae's dominion,' Arden replied. 'You can't just wander in. It's protected by a wreath of Fae magic.'

Perig nodded. 'The Wildermist,' he said. 'Those who approach it, quickly lose their way. Most never come back and even if they do, they've usually lost their minds.'

'Gets you all befuddled,' Spud mumbled through a mouthful of blackcurrants.

'That it does,' Perig agreed. 'Mirage, shadow, vapour. That's the stuff of the Fae.'

Hazel felt a cold dread branching through her veins. She pulled her cloak tightly around her but felt no warmer.

'Like my nan used to say,' Perig murmured, 'the Fae aren't like other fairy folk.' The company muttered grimly in agreement. Hazel remembered what she'd read in the professor's unfinished manuscript.

'Are they ... *uncommon* fairies?' she asked.

Perig raised his eyebrows. 'Where d'you hear that?'

'Professor Grinling's book,' Hazel explained. 'It said that there are common fairies, like you, and "uncommon" fairies, like the Fae.'

There was a moment of puzzled silence then Perig erupted into laughter. 'That's what he wrote, did he?' he roared. '*Common* fairies – ruddy cheek! Nothing but a pest, that professor!'

The others laughed too, but it was a nervous laughter, full of wild energy.

'So ...' Hazel persisted. 'What are they, then? Who *are* the Fae?'

The company settled down and Perig cleared his throat.

'The question,' he replied, 'isn't so much who *are* the Fae, but who *were* they.'

Hazel frowned, perplexed.

'Us lot –' Perig gestured to Portuna and Arden – 'we are the unborn – possible people who never were. But the Fae are different. They were born human.'

Hazel's stomach turned. She didn't dare think long about her next question: 'Like ... like me?' she stuttered. Perig raised his mossy eyebrows in surprise.

'Clouds above! There's no Fae in you, Hazel! Not a bit!' Hazel breathed a sigh of relief. 'No, no, don't worry yourself about that.'

Perig knotted his fingers around his cup and, as the thunder rolled overhead, his face began to darken. 'The Fae lived and loved as humans, that much is true, but they died before their time was up. Young men and women in all the fullness of life, struck down by disaster.' The wizard slowly shook his head. 'Their lives were unfinished, you see, so death didn't open its doors to them. Once they'd left their broken bodies, they had nowhere to go.'

The rain was now lashing at the roof; the wind rattling the shutters.

'Oh,' Hazel whispered. 'That's terrible.' She looked up at the wizard, bewildered.

'Yes indeed,' Perig replied, 'the grief of the Fae is terrible. And their anger is more terrible still. They were robbed of life, see. And they are hungry for it.'

Hazel glanced round at the others. All were listening to Perig, faces flickering in the candlelight.

'For a while they wandered,' Perig continued, 'shut out of life, refused by death. Then the hills sheltered them and they became guardians of the Ley, life force of the earth.'

'Guardians, pshhh,' Portuna muttered. 'We all know they're hoarding Ley and draining it from everyone else!'

'Perhaps.' Perig nodded. 'But we don't think that's all there is to it.'

At that moment, a fierce gust of wind burst the shutter open, scattering leaves and twigs all around. It took both twins to close the panel against the roaring rain, then Arden set to work, fusing the wood with her fingers, sealing it shut.

Hazel felt a thickening despair. She thought of Pete, imprisoned in an empty hill, guarded by a strange, impenetrable magic. Perig pulled his stool closer to hers and rested a heavy hand on her back.

'Sounds like a good lad, your Pete,' he said. Hazel nodded, blinking back tears. 'Take heart.' He smiled. 'You're one of us now. We'll help you.'

'You will?' said Hazel. 'Thank you, thank you! I won't let you down, I promise!'

Perig laughed. 'I know it,' he said. 'And there is reason to be hopeful.' He nodded towards his table, littered with pebbles and tools. 'I'm working up a charm.'

'A charm?'

'I've been travelling all over, collecting stones from across the Isles. Powerful stones. Good counter-magic. Once the charm is ready, it'll get us through the Wildermist, right to the heart of the Knoll. Never fear, Hazel. We'll rescue our friends.' He leaned closer. 'And we'll save this forest!'

Perig squeezed the last dregs of brew from a leather pouch and shared it between everyone's cups.

'Now that's enough talk of snatchings and such,' he said. 'We have new friends, new allies! We grow stronger!' He raised his cup in the air. 'Welcome, Portuna and Hazel!' The new arrivals were toasted with a clashing of cups, then the conversation turned to robbing a troupe of patrolling Arboreans.

Before long, the wind dropped, the rain thinned and shafts of sunlight streamed through gaps in the cabin walls. The twins were showing Portuna and Hazel how to load a slingshot when there was a shout from just outside, then many voices, calling and shrieking.

Portuna leaped to her feet, fists clenched and blazing. At the sight of her, tense and ready for battle, the twins burst out laughing.

'Settle down!' said Sprout. 'Come outside and see!' He ran to the cabin door and flung it open.

Hazel followed the others outside and instantly lurched back with shock. The cabin was not, as she had imagined, on the forest floor, but high in the treetops, wedged tightly between the trunk and branches of a giant beech. They were standing on a platform and sprawling out before them was a rambling treetop village.

Wooden huts perched between the glistening, rain-darkened boughs, and each was strung with dozens of colourful paper lanterns. On top of the huts, small windmills turned quickly in the breeze, and between them – stretching from tree to tree – hung a web of rope bridges sparkling with fresh rain. Everywhere, human children were streaming out of the huts, racing along the bridges and swinging down rope ladders to skid about on the mulchy earth below.

'The Wild Children!' Hazel whispered. 'They're *real!*'

'Course we are!' said Spud and Sprout in unison. 'And this is the Den – our home.'

The children were running and shrieking, stuffing fistfuls of wet leaves down each other's backs. The youngest were barely older than babies while the eldest looked no more than fifteen. There was not an adult in sight. Hazel gazed down at the scene, astonished.

'Are there really only children here?' she asked.

'No grown-ups allowed, that's the rule,' said Sprout. 'Can't be trusted. Human grown-ups, that is.' Hazel nodded. She'd never known a human adult she could trust.

'But . . . how do you survive out here, on your own?'

Spud whistled sharply between his teeth. 'Don't have much faith in children, do you?' He laughed. 'We look after the forest, the forest looks after us.'

'And the Arboreans?'

'Ha! We're not scared of them!' said Spud, with a bit too much swagger to convince. 'Anyway, Perig and Arden help us out. We give 'em shelter, they help us fight.'

Hazel watched silently as the children leaped and ran on their tough bare feet. 'Pete was right,' she whispered to herself in amazement. 'Oh, he would have loved this place!'

That night, Hazel lay in her narrow bunk, tossing and turning. Her mind was whirling, and the more tired she felt, the faster it whirled, till all her thoughts were knotted together like wool. She slid out of bed, pulled her grubby blanket around her shoulders and crept out of the cabin.

Amongst the thinning leaves of the canopy, the air was damp and sweet. The village was dark now, save for the coloured lanterns, and the only sound was the whirr of the windmills.

For a while, she wandered silently across the rope bridges. She thought of Pete and remembered the plans they had made on their way to the woods: acorn cakes and autumn bonfires, gooseberry jam and fishing rods. *If only we hadn't*

161

followed that light, she thought. *If only we'd made it here instead.* She paused on a bridge and imagined herself and Pete sitting on the porch of the opposite treehouse, swinging their legs in the cool forest air. How fine it would have been.

Eventually, her thoughts began to turn more slowly. Then, limbs heavy, eyelids drooping, she made her way back to the cabin.

She was so sleepy she didn't see the two dark shapes hidden in the nearby branches. As soon as she had passed, they stepped out of the shadows and continued their conversation out of earshot.

'Lucky we found her first,' said a low, rumbling voice. It was Perig. 'She's safe with us.'

'I didn't think there were any of her kind left,' said Arden. 'Are you really sure?'

'Never been more sure of anything in my life.'

Arden frowned. 'Can we trust her?'

Perig nodded. 'She'll draw danger, no doubt about it. But she also brings hope. Our *greatest* hope.'

CHAPTER TWENTY-FOUR

The Mist

Folk of the Forest!
The Fae and their Arborean servants are no
friends of Goblyn!
Remember Riverton!
Change is coming! Be ready!
Ley for all. Forever.

The rebels and their new recruits had been out since the first wink of dawn, plastering the forest with their handmade notices. Three days had passed since Hazel and Portuna had arrived at the Den. This was their first job and they were keen to impress.

'They won't stay up long,' said Arden, 'but some will see them, and they'll tell others.'

The morning light was grey and watery, the trees wreathed in a chilly mist. Hazel and Portuna found a large sycamore tree and smoothed a poster against its silvery trunk.

'What's Riverton?' Hazel asked as she brushed a resiny glue over the paper.

Portuna frowned. 'A Seely village. Not far from Morrow River. There was a Fading there, years ago.' The glow of her skin shuddered. 'It came overnight. Very bad, very sudden. Half the village were dead by morning.'

Hazel gasped.

'The Arboreans put word out that it was a natural catastrophe,' Portuna continued, 'a kink in the flow of the Ley. But everyone knew that was hogweed.'

'Why?'

Portuna looked her in the eye. 'Riverton folk were known to harbour rebels.'

'Do you mean ...?' A ghastly thought formed in Hazel's mind.

'Of course,' said Portuna. 'It was punishment.'

The clouds turned a pearly grey as an invisible sun floated above the horizon. Perig glanced skywards.

'Almost time we got back,' he called. 'Let's split up. Get these last ones done.' The group dispersed and Hazel found herself alone in the shrouded forest. Portuna's story had left a sick feeling in her gut. She remembered the dying boy in the tunnel and imagined a whole village, leached dry, blackened with the shades of Seely folk – old and young, emptied of life as they slept. She clutched her brush tighter and slid to the bottom of a boulder-strewn slope. There, she got swiftly back to work, gluing the rebels' posters prominently to the surrounding trees.

She was about to put up the last one when there was a sudden rushing in the undergrowth behind her. She turned to see a small deer springing through the ferns. The creature swerved sharply to avoid her then dashed away between the trees. Hazel stared after it. As its white tail bobbed into the mist, her nostrils caught a thin trail of scent – bitter and acrid. It was the unmistakable reek of fear.

Skin stippling to goosebumps, she turned and looked back to where the deer had run from. The mist hung dense and white, thinning the trees to a host of slim, grey shadows. She held her breath, straining her ears. The forest was oddly still, as if every living thing had fled back to its burrow or nest and was waiting in trembling silence. She noticed a ripple in the air. Then, before her eyes, the mists began to swirl, then billow and boil. Something was moving, gliding towards her. She heard the huff of animal breath and, from deep in the vapours, three tall figures emerged.

Arboreans. They were mounted on their luminous white horses, eyes fastening upon her. At the centre of the group was Ruis.

The riders brought their strange green-eyed beasts to a halt and peered down at Hazel with chilly curiosity.

'What *is* it?' sniffed one of Ruis's companions, clicking her nails together. The other leaned forward in his saddle and stared.

'Clayfoot. A wild one.' He grinned. 'Look at its thick skin! Look at its clumsy little fingers!'

As the riders tittered, Hazel's eyes flashed from left to right, searching for some opportunity to escape, but she could see the sheaves of silver arrows strapped to their backs. Even if she ran, she would be felled in an instant.

Ruis said nothing but made a sharp clicking sound with his tongue. The horses fanned around Hazel on silent, silvery hooves. She stepped away in fright but quickly found herself backed up against the rocky slope. Instinctively, she raised her brush in the air, as if to strike. There was a surprised pause, then two of the riders spluttered with laughter.

Ruis remained silent, his lips curling. Keeping his gaze fixed upon her, he gestured to the rolled-up poster in her hand.

'Don't let us stop you,' he rasped in his strange, dry voice. She stared up at him blankly, unsure that she had understood. The Arborean captain waited a second, then flicked a pointed fingernail at the tree trunk next to her.

Not knowing what else to do, she slowly approached the tree and unrolled the poster. Her hands were shaking

so violently she could barely hold it steady and, as she brushed on the glue, sniggers of contempt curdled the air behind her.

Once the poster had been awkwardly stuck to the bark, Ruis approached on his horse. As his eyes slid over the bold declamations his thin brows arched in amusement.

'Change is coming, is it?' he said. 'How exciting. When?' He looked at her round-eyed, as if expecting a reply, but Hazel's throat was too clogged with fear to speak.

'I hate to disappoint you,' Ruis continued with feigned concern, 'but the trouble with change is that – how can I put this? – nobody *wants* it.' His companions scoffed and Ruis suppressed a smile. 'Those Seelies are perfectly snug in their little warrens, you see. And they're not fond of vagrant Druics leaching off their Ley. It's *bothersome* and, truth be told –' he leaned forward in his saddle as if he were about to share a secret – 'it *disgusts* them.' Ruis's mouth flicked into a grin, then he pulled back and laughed his hollow, rattling laugh. It was the same terrible laughter that tore through Hazel's nightmares and, as it resounded in the vaults of the trees, she felt a shiver spread over her back and down her arms.

Ruis's face twisted into a look of acute disdain.

'You could stick a poster to every tree in Goblyn,' he sneered. 'Nobody would answer your call.'

The rider to his left straightened in his saddle.

'Capture or kill, sir?' he asked, plainly bored. Ruis sniffed and drew his horse nearer, near enough for Hazel to feel the creature's breath, to see the weird green fire in its eyes. Then he pulled an arrow from his quiver and lifted Hazel's chin with its silver tip. Up close, the Arborean captain had the scentless presence of a reptile and, as he stared at her, unblinking, Hazel feared she might be swallowed whole.

'Capture or kill, sir?' the rider repeated.

But Ruis did not reply. Hazel saw a thrill of astonished revulsion ripple through him.

'Wait,' he said. 'This isn't a clayfoot.'

He bent down from his saddle and, with extraordinary strength, grasped Hazel's throat with one hand and wrenched her off the ground. She gasped in fright, legs pedalling the air.

'Look at the eyes,' he said, dangling her like a rabbit. 'There's fire there, and yet . . .' His hand constricted round her throat. 'Not clayfoot, not fairy . . .' As the Arboreans puzzled over her, Hazel plucked helplessly at Ruis's fingers. Her limbs were weakening, her head swimming. Then, as her terror thickened, she felt a strange prickling beneath her skin.

It began between her shoulder blades and spread quickly over her back, shoulders and arms. Sharper and sharper it grew, as if the points of needles were pressing against her skin from the inside, piercing it, pushing through.

Suddenly, the female rider cawed in alarm. 'Look at its skin!' she cried. 'Look at its arms!'

Ruis's face fell. Instantly, he dropped Hazel and reached for an arrow. Hazel landed hard on the ground and fell backwards. She rolled over, heaving breath into her starved lungs. As she struggled to her knees, she saw what they had seen.

All over her arms and the backs of her hands, long, sharp spines were growing out through her skin – dark brown shafts with white tips, pointed and bristling. Hazel stared at herself, wide-eyed with horror.

'Kill it! Kill it!' hollered the rider. Instinctively, Hazel covered her head with her hands. Then, just as she felt sure she would be struck by a dozen arrows, she heard the twang of a slingshot.

A shout followed, and the male rider clutched the side of his head, cursing in pain. The other swung her horse around and stared into the trees.

'Ambush!' she called. Ruis drew his bow and, with terrifying speed, the three Arboreans sent a hail of arrows whistling into the ferns.

All at once, the forest shattered into a cacophony of shouts and orders. Hazel crouched on the earth, as shots and arrows streaked the air above her. Glancing up, she saw Spud dash between tree trunks, slingshot in hand, then heard a howl as an arrow grazed him. The horses were whinnying and stamping. Hazel scrambled backwards to avoid their sharp hooves, then turned to climb the slope behind her. She had only gone a short distance when a heavy thud shook the earth. Up above her, standing high on the ridge, was Perig.

The earth wizard stood tall as an oak, a long staff clutched tightly in his burled fist. His hood was drawn about his face and all was bathed in a billowing green light. Raising his staff in both hands, he thumped the ground twice more. Ruis wheeled his horse around and, on seeing Perig, reached quickly for another arrow. But before he could shoot there was an ominous creak, then a shuddering crack, and the earth lurched beneath them.

The horses skittered backwards, eyes rolling. Hazel heard a rumbling crescendo of noise, then a flood of rock and boulder came crashing through the trees. Clouds of dirt burst skywards as the deadly wave hurtled down the slope. Giant boulders bounced past her; chunks of flint whirled above. The horses were wheeling and shrieking, the Arboreans shouting and fleeing. The earth was travelling at such speed that even the smallest pebble could have knocked Hazel cold. She curled into a ball, sure she would be buried alive, but to her astonishment nothing touched her. By some strange magnetism, each rock and stone swerved around her bunched body and crashed ferociously towards the riders.

After seconds that felt like hours, the thunder died away. Hazel uncurled and cautiously opened her dirt-filled eyes. All around was shattered stone and smashed trees, but she lay safe on an undisturbed island. She sat up, bewildered. The river of rock had parted around her.

'Hazel!' Portuna appeared from the undergrowth, and ran towards her followed by Arden and the twins. 'Are you all right?'

Hazel looked down at her arms. They were covered with nothing but her usual downy hair. The strange spines had disappeared, as if they had never been there at all.

'Did you see the look on his face?!' Spud beamed, bandaging the gash on his upper arm. 'Didn't see that coming, did he?' He imitated the stunned stare of the Arborean captain as Perig's rockfall thundered towards him. Portuna and Sprout spluttered with laughter.

The rebels were back at the cabin. Perig was making parsnip stew and Arden watched with a wry smile as the others gleefully restaged their victory. Perig stirred the pot slowly, deep in thought.

'It troubles me,' he muttered, shaking the thick green plaits of his moustache. 'Shouldn't've been Arboreans in that part of the woods. If Portuna here hadn't given early warning, it could've been a different story!' Portuna shrugged, but Hazel could see that she was brimming with pride.

Hazel listened quietly as the group celebrated, utterly miserable. While the others had fought bravely and swiftly, she had been paralyzed with terror, barely able to speak, let alone fight. And what had *happened* to her? What were those strange spines that had bristled over her skin?

She ran a hand down the back of her arm, now perfectly smooth. Had she imagined it all? But the Arboreans – it had frightened them.

Night had fallen and moonbeams were sliding through the shutters. Outside, a group of Wild Children were gossiping and giggling in the treetops. Perig ambled over to Hazel and pulled up a stool beside her. He said nothing, but the weight of his presence was an invitation to speak.

'I think ...' Hazel whispered. 'I think something happened. Out there. In the forest.'

Perig sat stone still, listening.

'It was like I was ...' Hazel continued. 'Like I was ... *changing*. Ruis was squeezing my throat, and I was scared. Just terrified. Then I felt a prickling under my skin and ...' She flushed red with shame. 'Sorry,' she said. 'I'm sorry.'

'For what?' said Perig.

'I let you down, didn't I? You all fought back, but ...' She shook her head. 'I *want* to help. I *want* to fight, but ...'

'But what?'

'What if I ... what if I can't? What if I don't have it in me?'

Perig stared at her in amused astonishment.

'You do, Hazel,' he said firmly. 'More than you know.'

She looked up at him, confused. 'What do you mean?'

He drummed his fingers on his knees and pressed his lips together in thought. Then he heaved himself to his feet, looked under his worktable and dragged out a large muddy trunk.

'Your trouble, Hazel,' he said, 'is that you don't know what you are.' He set the box down and opened the lid. 'It's time you learned.'

CHAPTER TWENTY-FIVE

Slipskin

THE LID OF THE BATTERED OLD TRUNK CREAKED rustily as it opened. Inside was a glittering heap of rocks, stones and crystals of every shape and colour. As the wizard rummaged inside, Portuna and the others pulled their stools closer, curious. Amongst the collection were gritty pink crystals, egg-smooth pebbles and stones of striped amber that glinted like cat's eyes. Eventually, Perig pulled out a grey-green lump the size of an apple, and weighed it in his hand.

'Greenstone.' He smiled, eyes crinkling. 'Just what we need.'

Hazel remembered the rock the professor had showed her. 'From the Paleo- ... the Paleo-something Era?'

'Eh?' said Perig.

'The professor,' Hazel replied. 'He showed me some. It made my arm tingle.'

'Course it did,' chuckled the wizard. 'Ley runs strongest

in greenstone. There's no rock more magical. Especially when I wake it up.'

Closing his eyes, Perig cupped the stone in his hands and drummed his fingertips briskly over it, muttering under his breath. For a moment Hazel saw a dim pulse of light beneath the stone's rough surface. Perig gave a nod of satisfaction and passed it to her.

The stone tingled between her palms. It was strangely heavy, as if it held far more than its size suggested. Perig closed the trunk and gestured for her to set the stone on its lid, then he reached into the folds of his cloak and pulled out a small hammer with a sharpened head.

'Split it,' he said, passing her the tool.

Hazel hesitated, unsure.

'I'll do it!' Portuna cried, reaching for the hammer.

'No,' said Perig firmly. 'It has to be Hazel.'

Hazel took a breath then, holding the rock with one hand, struck it sharply. The hammer bounced off the stone's surface and clattered noisily to the floor.

'Ouch!' she yelped. The rock was unscratched, but the bones of her hand buzzed unpleasantly from the impact.

Perig laughed. 'Harder than that! You've got to give it some welly! Look, I'll hold it for you.'

Arden picked up the hammer and passed it back.

'Come on now.' Perig winked. 'Really put your back into it.'

'Go on, Hazel!' said Sprout. 'Whack it!'

Hazel rose to her feet and, using both hands, raised the hammer above her head, balanced a moment, then swung it down with all her might. The sharp end struck squarely and, with a deep crack, the rock split open.

The two halves shone brightly, washing the whole cabin in waves of meandering light – greens, blues, indigos and golds. As the shock of the blow juddered through her body, Hazel felt as though her whole being and everything she knew was cracking apart, crumbling to bits, then whirling through the air in broken pieces, before slowing and settling into a strange new constellation. Her limbs felt looser, stronger, as if, all her life, she had been bound by invisible ties which had suddenly been severed. A surge of pure happiness rushed through her.

Perig picked up one half of the stone and polished it on his sleeve.

'Take a look,' he said, and passed it to Hazel. She sat back down and, holding the rock in both hands, gazed at the smoothly cut surface. The colours clouded and flashed like a stormy sky.

'What's it doing?' she whispered.

'Keep looking,' said Perig, 'and let your thoughts wander.' Hazel frowned in concentration. 'Don't follow them,' he added, 'just let 'em float past.'

This was more difficult than it sounded but, after a while, Hazel was able to let her thoughts travel by untroubled. When she did, the clouds in the cut stone began to thin and part, and she saw the contours of a face looking back at her.

It felt as though she were looking in a mirror, only the face reflected there was not her own. It was not human, or even fairy. Deep in the black glass she saw the glint of small bright eyes, whiskers sprouting from a furred nose and, all around the tiny face, a halo of white-tipped prickles.

'What do you see?' said Perig.

'A . . . a hedgehog?' said Hazel, confused. 'What does that mean? I'm not . . . a *hedgehog*.'

The wizard gave a low laugh. 'Yes, you are . . . sort of. But that's not all you are.'

Hazel breathed an anxious sigh, struggling to follow.

'Now, close your eyes,' said Perig, 'and think of something that makes you mad. Mad as a wasp!' She nodded and shut her eyes tight. Before long, her mind drifted back to Ditchmoor, so distant now. She thought of Elsie Pocket shoving Pete to the ground; she heard him coughing and spluttering in the mud. A pressure was building in her chest, a rising heat.

'Now look again,' said Perig. Hazel opened her eyes and peered into the dark surface of the stone. The hedgehog had vanished and, looking back at her, eyes burning like coals, was a snarling hound. So ferocious was the dog's glare that Hazel dropped the stone in alarm.

'I . . . I don't understand,' she cried, heart racing. 'What am I really? A hedgehog? A dog?'

'Both!' said Perig. 'And much more.' He shifted on his stool and cleared his throat. 'Tell me,' he said, 'what d'you know of your parents?'

Hazel felt her cheeks begin to burn. She swallowed hard. 'Nothing,' she whispered.

The wizard nodded gently. 'Well, I can tell you this much. One of them was human, and the other fairy.'

Portuna nudged Hazel in the ribs. 'I said you were a funny sort of fairy!' she whispered. 'I knew it!'

'So what does that make me?' Hazel asked.

'Rare!' said Perig. 'The mingling of humans and fairies has been forbidden since the Old Wars. You, Hazel Quince, are a slipskin.'

Spud stopped fidgeting with a chunk of amethyst and stared. 'A slip-what?'

'Slipskin,' Perig repeated, a low thrill in his voice. 'A slipskin is solid flesh, like a human, but has all the fire of a fairy. Ah, the things you can do, Hazel, you don't know the half of it. *I* don't know the half of it!'

Hazel shook her head. It was all too much, too quickly.

'I don't understand,' she said with a frown. 'Why did the stone show me a hedgehog, then a dog?'

The candlelight flickered over the crags and hollows of Perig's face. 'Your kind,' he replied, 'they can take the shape of other living things: feathers, scales, fleece or fur. Hazel, you contain the whole world. Every living creature; every bird, every beast. They've slept soundly in you since

179

before you were born. But now they are waking. You've felt it, haven't you?' The company listened closely as the trees rustled softly outside. Hazel remembered the sudden violence that had bolted through her when she sprang at Elsie's throat; she remembered Miss Fitch's panicked words: *Eyes flashing, snapping and snarling like a wild beast!* A wild beast. Is that what she'd become? Then she remembered what Pete had said on Ditchmoor's doorstep: *It's the thing, isn't it? You've always had it.* The way she could hear a sparrow's breath, or see raindrops form in the sky – now this strange, wild magic. It was all part of the same thing. It was who she was.

The greenstone flickered dimly at her feet. She picked it up and cupped it between her hands. Behind the cut surface, the depths of the stone seemed bottomless: a dark, churning ocean. She cast her mind free and gazed down into the depths. And, as she gazed deeper and deeper, the world around her peeled away, the walls of the cabin, her new friends, the glow of the candle, until the rock in her hands seemed the only thing with any weight and density. She curled over it, an oyster around a black pearl, waiting. And then she saw.

Out of the dark magma, forms appeared. Hazel couldn't make them out at first, but then she saw the shapes of moving limbs, wings and fins, some swift and agile, others slow and creeping. The forms flowed into one another as if they were all part of one great animal. Then slowly they pulled apart: beasts and birds prowling, slithering, galloping and crawling in a swirling cacophony of hoots and roars. Hazel remembered the time-blurred engravings on the standing stone at the revels and, at once, her nerves pulsed with fire and all her joy and strength came rushing back.

But the stone had not yet shown her everything. As if startled by sudden thunder, the creatures in the reflection fell silent and still. Then they turned and fled, vanishing into the swirling gloom. Hazel watched as the stone emptied and darkened until she was staring down into a dizzying black hole. Her spine prickled but she could not tear her eyes away. Then, in a series of lightning flashes, she saw other things: dead white trees shivering, splitting and crumbling to dust; ravens circling in a purple sky; rain falling upwards into billowing thunderheads; three women watching as a green hill cracked open; and bodies, many bodies, trapped in crystal. As the visions shuddered past, Hazel finally saw, with a thrill of horror, a great black star falling, falling, fiercely burning with a reverse light that swallowed and destroyed, turning everything to nothing.

'Hazel! Hazel!' She was being shaken violently. She clutched for the rock, but her hands were empty.

'Hazel! Are you all right? What's wrong?' Perig was gripping her shoulders, staring anxiously into her eyes. The rock was in bits on the cabin floor, smashed to pieces, its light extinguished. Hazel steadied herself on her wooden stool as objects and people settled around her.

181

'What is it?' Perig repeated. She tried to hang onto the visions, but they were slipping quickly from her mind.

'Animals ...' she said shakily. 'Birds ...' But there was nothing more, only a hollow feeling in the pit of her stomach, the residue of a nightmare.

Panic bolted through her. She wanted to push everything away, to return to the safer place, just minutes earlier, when these strange powers were little more than a collection of odd feelings, easily denied.

Perig took her hand firmly in his fist and looked at her from beneath his heavy brow.

'It's all right,' he said. 'Don't be afraid.'

'But I am,' she gasped.

Somewhere, deep in the forest, an owl called out, and another answered.

'Your magic is young now,' said Perig. 'A seedling. Since you were born, it's been deep underground, spreading its roots. But now that you're here in Goblyn, now that you are needed, it is breaking the surface, feeling the air. It's new, Hazel – it doesn't know where it's going, but soon enough it will thicken and strengthen. Then it'll grow quickly towards the light.'

'How?' Hazel whispered. She thought again of the wild force with which she had attacked Elsie. She thought of the strange spines that had suddenly bristled over her skin. 'What if I can't control it?'

'You can't,' said Perig. 'Not really. But you'll come to

accept it, and it will accept you. Takes learning, that's all. Like any magic, it takes practice. Then, more often than not, it comes as easy as breathing.' He turned to the others who had been listening silently, mouths agape. 'We believe in her, don't we?'

'Course we do!' Spud grinned.

'She's one of us!' added Sprout. As her new friends nodded and nudged her in encouragement, Hazel's spirits began to lift.

'And when your magic is full, Hazel,' Perig continued, eyes shining. 'When your magic is full, you will know it. And then you will have such terrible power. All the strength of the forest, flowing through you. The Fae, they fear it. It's not for nothing they hunted your kind down. And they *will* hunt you, make no mistake. Ruis saw what you are, and he will tell them. But have no fear. We will help you. You may not know it yet, but your coming to Goblyn – it changes everything.' His voice was rising now, swelling with hope. 'With you at our side, Hazel, we will free the captured and restore the balance of the world.' He beamed happily down at her. 'And we will find your friend.'

Suddenly there was a bitter taste in the air. The room was filling with black smoke.

'Dinner!' gasped Perig and lunged at the burning pot.

CHAPTER TWENTY-SIX

The Weald

'GO ON! TRY IT!'

'A bear! Try a bear!'

'No, an eagle! I want to see an eagle!' The twins danced around Hazel tugging at her sleeves. The sun was not long up, and the birds chippered gaily overhead as the band of rebels followed Perig through the forest.

'I don't know how!' said Hazel, laughing.

'Don't *think* about it,' said Portuna. 'It's magic! You've just got to . . . I dunno . . . do it!'

'Almost there,' said Perig.

Hazel felt a thrill of nervous excitement. They were walking to an ancient part of the forest where she could try out her powers.

'Magic runs deep in the Weald,' said the wizard. 'It'll help you.'

As they walked on, the trees became more slumped and gnarled, trunks grimacing with the weight of thickly jointed limbs. Perig stopped and tugged his mossy moustache in thought. Then he took his staff in both hands and thudded it down on the earth. He paused as if listening for a reply from below.

'Strong!' he said, pleased. 'Very strong. Wait here.' He wandered away into the woods, muttering and bashing his staff on the ground.

As they waited, Portuna plucked some horse chestnuts from a branch and, to the twins' delight, made them swell and burst their satiny cases. Arden rolled her eyes, then took herself off to a nearby stump and began sharpening an arrowhead. Hazel sniffed the woody autumn air and listened to the mutter and rustle of the leaves around her. She could tell this part of the forest was different. It was older. It knew more.

She scanned the trees, impatient for Perig to return. Soon enough, she saw his burly form approaching.

'Now look,' he said, crouching down to Hazel's height. 'See those crocuses?' For as far as she could see, purple-petalled heads were poking between the fallen leaves. 'If there are crocuses, you're safe. I've made a protected area, see. So you can practise in peace. Nothing can harm you here.'

'But you're going to show me, aren't you?' she said. 'Show me what I need to do?'

Perig smiled. 'Wish I could! But slipskin powers are a lost magic. You'll have to find them on your own.'

'Oh!' She realised he was about to leave. 'You mean, you won't . . . you can't . . . ?'

185

He gripped her shoulders. 'You'll find your way. It'll take time, but you'll find it. I've faith in you!'

She gave a small nod.

'Now, stay alert,' said Perig. 'Don't stray from the crocuses, and there'll be nothing to fear.' He stood and called to the others. 'The White Elm tells me there's Arboreans travelling near Tinker's Tump. Got big trunks and boxes, he says. What say we take 'em?!' The twins and Portuna cheered and punched the air, Arden slung her bow across her back and, moments later, Hazel was left alone in the Weald.

Yellow sunlight filtered through the canopy and all was quiet save for the rattle of a woodpecker, and the occasional scrabble of claws on bark. Hazel gathered herself together and looked around at the crooked trunks.

'Right,' she whispered, rallying herself. 'You can do it, Hazel.' She wandered further in, amongst the mangled trees. 'I don't know *how* you're going to do it, but you can *definitely* do it! For the forest! For Pete!'

She came to a patch where the crocuses sprouted thickly between tree roots. Yes, the magic was strong there. She felt it. A tingling on her skin; a sense of her body brimming with possibilities she couldn't yet grasp.

Muttering encouragements to herself, she made her way to where a stream ran quickly over rounded stones. There, she crouched on the pebbled bank and collected her thoughts. How did this strange magic work? Did she only need to *imagine* the creature she wished to become? Could she just *make* it happen?

A sudden angry chattering snapped her concentration. On a nearby bough, clutching a nut and flouncing its pretty brush, was a small red squirrel. *Squirrel it is*, she thought, and squeezed her eyes shut.

Hazel held the image of the creature firmly in her mind – saw its little white vest and feathery ears. And, as she focused upon each detail of the animal's form, she imagined her own limbs changing and stretching, her face shrinking and sharpening, as if she were redrawing her whole—

'Ow!' Something small and hard struck her forehead. She opened her eyes and saw the squirrel spiralling up the tree trunk, chuckling wickedly. 'Very funny,' she muttered, picking up the cracked nut and tossing it aside.

As the day meandered on, Hazel tried to magic herself into a rabbit, a heron, even a snail. She studied them, pictured them, tried to mimic their shape and movement. But every hair on her head stayed exactly the same and, worse, she sensed that the trees were smirking at her efforts. By the time the sun had rolled across the sky, she hadn't managed to change so much as a fingernail.

'The longer you spend in the Weald, the quicker it'll come,' said Perig that evening. He was sitting at his worktable, peering at a lump of jasper through his magnifying glass. 'You can't rush it. It'll meet you when it's ready.'

Hazel nodded, but she couldn't suppress a growing anxiety.

'What if I can't do it?' she whispered to Portuna as they were tucked up in their bunk later that night.

'You worry too much.' Portuna yawned. 'Go to sleep.'

'They're all counting on me,' said Hazel, eyes bright in the darkness. 'They think I've got some special magic that'll help them. But what if I'm not who they think I am? What then?' She waited for a reply, but Portuna was already sound asleep and snoring earnestly.

At the first flush of dawn, Perig guided Hazel back to the Weald. All morning she wandered the ancient woodland, trying and failing to unlock her magic. By lunchtime she was utterly disheartened.

'Just a clayfoot, aren't I?' she muttered to herself. 'A clumsy clayfoot.' A fine rain was needling down, forming muddy rivers between the trees. Miserable, she flumped down in the shelter of an ash tree and drew her knees up to her chest.

As she sat on the soggy ground, cold and alone, she gazed at the forest around her, thick and strong, bristling with shoots and buds. Then ghastly thoughts crowded in: bulbs shrivelling in the soil, trees withering from the roots up, the whole forest crumbling away and Pete, still lost in an empty hill. She covered her head with her hands. It all felt utterly hopeless.

Pressing her forehead to her knees, she squeezed her eyes shut. She imagined herself back in the dusty old belfry with its squashed cushions, chess set and squeaking roost of bats. In that moment, she didn't want to turn herself into a hawk or a rabbit or a snake, or any other creature. She only wanted to be her old self again, sitting on the rooftops with Pete, sipping bottles of stolen lemonade.

Then, just as she felt tears rising, a warm, woody scent stung her nostrils. At once her senses sharpened, alert. She sprang to her feet and sniffed the air. Smoke. Treading softly through the crocuses, she followed the smell down a slope. The rain had thinned. Up ahead she saw grey coils rising from a hollow. Stealthily, she approached the ridge and peered down.

At the bottom of the hollow, a figure sat on a stump stoking a freshly lit fire. Nearby lay a large sack, spilling over with fruits, nuts and mushrooms. The figure turned to pick up what looked like a short stick resting on the stump, and Hazel caught sight of a face in profile, swirled with inky blue tattoos. Her heart leaped.

'Fen!'

The boy startled and dropped the stick in alarm.

'Oh!' he cried. 'You gave me a turn!'

'Sorry!' she said, sliding down the bank. As Fen recognised Hazel, his face relaxed into a welcoming smile.

He gestured to the stump. 'Warm up, won't you? Before you catch a chill.' Gratefully, she sat down and stretched her bare feet towards the bright orange flames. The warmth toasted her soles and softened her toes. Fen took a sip from a leather flask and offered it to her.

'Honeysuckle tea,' he said. It was sweetish and hot, and as it slipped down her throat a tingling warmth spread through her.

'So, what you doing all the way out here?' asked Fen, settling down beside her.

She hesitated a moment. 'Walking?'

Fen raised his eyebrows. 'It's a fair trek from Understone.' Hazel wasn't sure how to reply, but before she got into a muddle, he gave a broad laugh.

'You're a funny one, you are,' he said, tossing some kindling on the blaze. 'Look, I'm not going to poke my nose in. There's enough trouble these days without stirring up more.'

Hazel breathed a sigh of relief. 'And you?' she said. 'What are you doing in the Weald?'

'Foraging,' said Fen, pointing to the overstuffed sack. 'Been camping out for a few days. I'll soon have a good haul to take back to the family.'

'Big family?' she asked.

'No,' he laughed. 'Just hungry!'

The rain had stopped now and a pale sun winked through the dripping leaves. Fen picked the stick out of the leaf litter and Hazel saw that it was not a stick at all, but a wooden flute carved with twisting patterns of leaves and birds.

He cleaned it on his sleeve and turned the instrument between nimble fingers. 'Want to hear me play?'

Hazel hesitated. She'd have to get back to her practising soon, but in that moment she was so happy for the warmth, and the company.

She nodded and his face lit up.

'All right, what's this?' He wet his lips then played a few long, high whistles, followed by a quick run of low, trembling notes.

'That's a robin!' She smiled.

Fen bobbed his head, pleased, then played a new tune: this one mellow and fluting, softening to a twitter.

'Blackbird!'

'Right you are!' he laughed. 'Took me ages to learn it.'

Next came the hollow coos of a wood pigeon, the trill of a mistle thrush and the rippling song of the nightingale.

'Can you show me how to play?' asked Hazel.

'Course,' said Fen. He put the flute to his lips and demonstrated how to make the low seesaw call of the cuckoo. Then it was her turn. After much spluttering and puffing, she got the hang of it and, to her delight, a bluish bird landed clumsily on a branch above them and glared down with a fierce yellow eye.

'Ha! You're on his territory!' Fen laughed. 'Watch out!'

The afternoon slipped past quickly and merrily. By the time the fire had dwindled to embers, the day was tipping into night.

'Oh! I have to go,' Hazel said, flustered. Perig would soon come to meet her and she hadn't made an inch of progress all day.

'See you tomorrow, then?' Fen smiled, squinting into the last rays of sun.

'Tomorrow!' she called back to him as she dashed away between the trees.

CHAPTER TWENTY-SEVEN

The Changing

I T WAS A BRIGHT, COPPERY MORNING AND THE rebels were eating breakfast on the cabin's porch. Hazel sat with Perig and Arden while Portuna and the twins loudly reenacted the robbery at Tinker's Tump.

'How's the magic coming?' said Perig through a mouthful of porridge.

Hazel frowned. 'It's not.'

'It will,' the wizard replied. 'Don't lose hope.'

She felt a pang of guilt. She couldn't tell him she'd spent half the previous afternoon despairing, and the other half playing the flute. She kept her eyes fixed on her bowl, but could feel Arden silently watching her.

Perig leaned in close. 'Want to hear some good news?' he whispered.

Hazel nodded.

'I've been working with the amethyst,' he said. 'Makes a good little charm.'

She stared at him, eyes wide. He was grinning broadly, tattoos creasing into fanning patterns.

'Really?' she said. 'Strong enough to get us through the Wildermist? Strong enough to get us to the Knoll?'

The wizard nodded. 'There's still work to do. Might have to pair it with some jasper, or agate. But it could be ready in days.'

Hazel felt like a door had opened, with Pete on the other side of it.

'Magic's a tough job.' Perig smiled. 'But you mustn't lose hope, Hazel. There's always hope.'

Hazel ran all the way to the Weald. As soon as she was back amongst the crocuses, she felt its magic, old and strong, flowing through the roots and boughs. She kept running, dashing through the ferns and leaping over tree stumps. As she ran and ran, the air grew brighter, sweeter. She thought of Pete and for the first time since he'd been snatched, she dared to imagine finding him again.

Hazel didn't feel herself change, only the world around her. Some colours glowed more brightly while others faded away. Edges dissolved and new ones formed, like patterns in a kaleidoscope. But she did not see this re-patterning so much as sense it, through every fingertip and every pinch of her skin. Then, all of a sudden, her body fell away from her completely and she was tumbling through the air, and high over the ferns, like a butterfly. A *butterfly*.

As soon as the word entered Hazel's mind she dropped to the ground with a thud. She tumbled a short distance then sat up dizzily in the long grass. Her hip was bruised and her knees grazed, but she was too stunned to feel any pain. Breathless, she gazed down at her limbs.

'I did it!' she gasped. She didn't know how, but she had. For a moment her body felt scattered and weak, then it drew itself together again, stronger than before. Not wanting to lose momentum, she leaped back onto her feet, sprinted through the ferns and again floated up through the green air, spinning lightly on velvety wings. This time she risked climbing higher, flitting between the branches, the scent of ivy blossom tickling her feathery limbs.

All morning, Hazel practised moving in and out of this strange new body. There was no special trick or spell. Rather, she had the powerful sense that something inside her had woken from a deep sleep, and that there was no going back. Not ever.

Hazel tumbled from her butterfly form and lay gasping on a carpet of crocuses. She gazed up at the clouds – pulling apart like cotton, then gathering into new shapes – and a smile spread across her face.

'Did you just . . . ?' A shadow fell over her. It was Fen. 'I didn't know you could . . .' He looked puzzled, frightened even.

She sat up in alarm. 'What? I didn't do anything,' she babbled.

Fen's face softened. 'I'm sorry. I was surprised, that's all. Never met a fairy who could do that sort of magic.'

Hazel stared at him, wracking her brains for an explanation.

'Don't worry, I won't tell anyone!' he laughed.

'You mustn't!' she said, suddenly worried.

'I won't! Promise!' He stretched out his hand and pulled her to her feet. 'Like I told you. I'm not one for trouble.'

'Thank you,' Hazel sighed.

They began to walk together, following a winding path down to a stream. Fen was silent for a while, then piped up.

'So, if you don't mind my asking,' he said, 'what else can you change into?'

'Nothing! Not yet anyway. I'm just learning,' Hazel replied. 'But one day, I'll be able to become anything. Any living thing.'

Fen's eyes widened and she felt a flicker of pride.

'What I'd give to be a bird!' he chuckled as they ducked under a low branch. 'My feet'd never touch the ground again!'

Hazel felt suddenly bold. 'Shall I try?'

'What?'

'To become a bird.'

Fen stopped and grinned. 'Let's see it, then!'

'All right.' She took a few steps back and felt the air around her. 'But don't look!' Fen closed his eyes. Moments later, she was flittering up to a low-hanging bough on newly sprouted feathers.

'Is that you, Hazel?' he gasped, cautiously approaching the branch. The wren flew down on small, rounded wings and landed smartly on the edge of his hand. 'Stars above,' he said, shaking his head. 'You see the strangest things in this forest, no doubt about it.'

The rebels were delighted by her news.

'We'll have a job for you soon,' said Arden as they sat on the porch of the cabin, mending their weapons.

'That we will,' agreed Perig, rubbing his eyes. They were red and sore from a day spent poring over his stones. 'I told you it'd come. And the magic's taking root now, isn't it? I can tell.'

It was late afternoon. The winter light was dwindling fast and there was merriment in the air. The smell of stewing apples wafted from the cabins and, all around, the Den tinkled with laughter. Hazel glanced down towards the forest floor and saw some of the Wild Children looping strings of coloured flags around the tree trunks, while others built a bonfire. Somewhere down below, a playful drumming started up.

'What's going on?' asked Portuna. 'Bit early for Midwinter Revels, isn't it?'

'It's a Parting Ceremony,' Spud replied. 'For the older ones.' He pointed to a group of taller children chattering amongst themselves, large patchwork bags at their feet. 'They're leaving the forest. Off to grown-up land!'

'Come on,' said Sprout, getting to his feet and dusting his palms together. 'It'll start soon!'

Curious, Hazel followed Portuna and the twins down the swinging rope ladders. Soft ribbons of light were streaming through the canopy and children hurried back and forth, setting up long tables and benches beneath the lantern-hung trees. Hazel spotted the drummer, dreamily pattering out a rhythm, while the boy next to her tuned a guitar twice his size. Nearby, in the shelter of an oak, a circle of cross-legged children wound lengths of ivy and dried flowers around slim, fallen branches.

Then, with a crackle and flare, the bonfire was lit. The blaze swelled quickly, spitting and roaring like a beast, and the children who moments before had been peacefully occupied erupted into a frenzy of whoops and whistles. The excitement was infectious and Portuna and Hazel found themselves jigging up and down, fizzing with anticipation.

As the flames of the bonfire danced higher, the drumming grew louder and more purposeful. The circle of children gathered up their decorated branches and hurriedly passed them round. Everyone was arranging themselves into two long lines and holding their branches aloft. Caught up in the whirl, Hazel and Portuna joined the end of the lines and faced one another, branches crossed above them, unable to stop grinning.

The drumbeats built to a peak, then stopped abruptly. A breath of silence, then everyone began to sing at the tops of their voices, full and clear:

'Out of the forest, Away you go!
Out of the forest, Away you go!'

Eyes shining, the leavers shrugged their bags onto their backs and paired up, hand in hand.

'No leaves above you, no moss below,
Out in the sun, and the wind and the snow,
Out of the forest, Away you go!'

As the lines of Wild Children hollered and shook their flowered branches, the leavers squeezed each other's hands and raced breathlessly down the tunnel, shouting their last goodbyes. Then away they went, dashing and skidding towards the open world beyond, the trees showering them with golden leaves as they passed.

Hazel watched, round-eyed, as they disappeared down the track. 'Where will they go?' she asked Spud.

'Oh, they'll find others who left before them,' he said. 'Big caravans of 'em, travelling from place to place.'

Dusk folded in and the alley of children broke apart. The branches were tossed on the bonfire, then everyone made their way to the tables beneath the twinkling trees.

'Grub's up!' Sprout smiled, rubbing his hands together.

They took their seats at the end of a table and Hazel cast her eyes over the spread. On large wooden platters were puddings of all varieties: slabs of fruitcake and sticky piles of buns, autumn trifles and slices of blackberry crumble sprinkled with brown sugar. Everyone was helping themselves and pouring cups of spiced apple punch.

'Try this,' said Spud, handing Hazel a slice of pear cake. 'Made it myself!'

'Ooh, pears!' said Hazel. 'My favourite!'

She was about to take a bite when a shout resounded through the treetops.

They looked up in alarm. Another cry shook the canopy and, with a shock, Hazel realised that it had come from their cabin in the beech tree. Moments later, Perig and Arden rushed out of the cabin and onto the porch, then clambered quickly down the rope ladder.

'What's going on?' Portuna frowned, flickering warily as the pair came running towards them. But as they drew closer, and the bonfire illuminated their faces, Hazel saw that they were both grinning madly.

'He did it!' gasped Arden, thumping Perig heartily on the back.

'A little more onyx,' said Perig, 'then –' he paused a moment to catch his breath – 'then, my friends, we're on our way to the Knoll!'

Everyone stopped chewing and stared at the wizard.

'What, really?' gasped Hazel. 'You finished the charm?'

Perig wiped his brow, black and grimy with rock-dust, then nodded.

At that, the group leaped to their feet, whooping and whistling for joy.

'Steady now, steady!' Perig chuckled as the twins wrapped themselves round his waist. But there was no containing the rebels' glee. Arden punched the air with delight while Portuna yelped and hooted, firing shots from an imaginary sling,

'They'd better be ready for us!' she cried. 'Change is coming!'

'That it is,' said Perig. He seized a mug of apple punch and raised it high in the air. 'Change is coming!'

A guitarist struck up a twangy riff. Portuna seized Hazel's hands and pulled her into a whirling dance. Round and round they turned, the sparks of the bonfire streaking by.

'Change is coming!' they shouted together. 'CHANGE IS COMING!' Then, as they whirled and whirled, hearts pounding in their chests, Hazel realised that her feet had left the ground.

'Woohoo!' Portuna called up from below. 'Fly, Hazel, fly!'

Hazel beat her outspread wings, rising almost vertically through the dark patterns of the branches. Up and up she rose, till she was high above the canopy, hovering in the midnight sky.

The cool air riffled her feathers and filled her small lungs.

And, as she hung and swooped above the sprawling forest, a liquid song rippled through her heart and poured upwards, melodic and rolling, towards the chiming stars.

CHAPTER TWENTY-EIGHT

Merrin

OVER THE NEXT TWO DAYS, PERIG SAT HUNCHED at his workbench, muttering spells over his stones and threading them into six heavy bracelets. While he perfected his charm, Hazel spent every moment she could in the Weald, trying to strengthen her powers ahead of their journey to the Knoll.

Her skills were rapidly unfurling. She slipped skin after skin and lived, for a moment, within a deer's taut hide or a rabbit's downy fur. It was as if, one by one, each creature stirred within her, awakened from a long hibernation, then dashed free. She saw through eyes that bent the world around her or shattered it into a mosaic of colour. She smelled the shapes of the forest with damp, delicate nostrils and felt the touch of the wind with trembling whiskers. But although she could easily muster the smaller, nimbler creatures of the woods, there were many others that escaped her. Goshawk, wolf, bear; all the beasts and birds of prey refused her call.

203

'I don't understand it,' she told Fen as he gathered clutches of sweet chestnuts.

He looked up at her with a faint frown. 'Sorry . . . what?' All morning he had seemed distracted, hard to reach.

'The power to turn myself into this or that,' said Hazel. 'I can become a mouse in a blink. But a hawk? A fox?' She sighed in frustration. 'It's just not happening.' The day was cold as a knife. Only a few leaves now clung to the trees and silvery branches shivered in the wintry air. Hazel tucked her frozen hands into her armpits. Fen slung his bag over his shoulder and smiled.

'You're hungry,' he said. 'That's all. Can't work on an empty stomach.' Hazel nodded. She hadn't eaten since breakfast and her belly was growling. 'Come on,' he said, 'I've found a good spot for a fire and a peck of lunch.'

They walked together between the twisted trunks of the Weald, their feet leaving dark patches on the frosty ground.

Fen was quieter than usual, his eyes set deeper in his face.

'Are you all right?' Hazel asked. She sensed him startle slightly, but he quickly pulled himself together.

'Not really,' he said. 'There's trouble. In the family.'

'Oh!'

Fen's mouth twisted into an anxious smile. 'Sorry. I can't really talk about it.'

Hazel nodded, but her mind began to simmer with worry.

After a short while, they found the sheltered patch Fen had been looking for and built a spluttering fire. The sweet chestnuts were tossed into a pan and roasted until their skins split and a heavy aroma rose from their meaty insides. Fen clowned about as he juggled the hot chestnuts into their bowls, but his laughter seemed forced.

After they'd finished the chestnuts, Fen reached into his pack and drew out a purple-stained pouch.

'Bit squashed, these,' he said, tipping some overripe berries into his palm, 'but sweet as honey. Have some.' He passed the pouch to Hazel and she took a handful. They were soft and melted to syrup on the tongue.

'Thanks,' she said with a smile. They sat for a while, watching sparks spiral in the smoke. Hazel searched for something to say, but she didn't want to pry, and Fen was avoiding her gaze. To her relief, he spoke first.

'It's Merrin,' he said, tossing a twig into the flames, 'my sister.' Hazel remembered the big-eyed girl she'd seen in Understone. 'They took her.'

'What?' she gasped. 'Who took her?'

'Arboreans,' he snarled. 'She was out playing in the copse and they snatched her.'

'Oh no!'

As Fen stared into the flames, his eyes filled with tears. 'Nobody knows why. And there's nothing we can do about it. There's nothing *anyone* can do about it!' He stifled a sob. 'Wicked beasts,' he growled. 'Wicked.'

'They are,' she whispered, shaking her head. 'I'm so sorry, Fen. They've got my best friend too, you know.'

'They have?'

Hazel nodded.

Fen hissed in disgust and wiped his eyes with his palm. The firelight flickered up the trunks of the surrounding trees, throwing long shadows – shadows that seemed too dark for the time of day.

'But you know what?' said Hazel, taking his hand. 'We *can* do something about it. We can. And we will.'

Fen glanced across at her. 'Who's *we*?'

Hazel hesitated, worried she'd said too much.

Fen raised his eyebrows. 'The rebels? You're in with the rebels?'

'No, I meant ...' She searched for a way out, but Fen just shrugged.

'It's all right,' he said. 'I suspected as much.'

'You did?'

Fen nodded and poked at the fire. 'I've got nothing but respect for Perig and the crew, but it's no good. Ruis has got this place in a stranglehold.' His voice cracked. 'And now Merrin's gone. And it's my fault, I was supposed to watch her, but ...' Tears began to roll over the dots and circles of his tattooed cheeks.

Hazel searched for something she could say to comfort him. The woods were still and quiet. She glanced over her shoulder to make sure they were alone, then leaned in closer.

'Listen,' she said, voice dropping to a whisper, 'there's a plan.'

Fen turned to look at her. His face was half shaded in the light of the fire and, in that moment, Hazel felt a vague misgiving, the slightest pricking at her fingertips. She knew she shouldn't say any more, but he looked so desperate. He'd lost his sister, hadn't he? They were on the same side.

'Perig's made a charm,' she said. 'A counter-magic against Fae illusions. It'll get us through the Wildermist and into the Knoll, where the Fae are. We're going to free the captured, Fen!'

Fen swallowed hard. 'A charm?'

She nodded. 'Yes! Yes! There's hope, you see, there really is!'

Fen said nothing, but there was something in his gaze that she couldn't read. Suddenly he looked more distant, as if he were withdrawing, folding in on himself.

The flames were twining high and hot. As the shadows wavered around them, Hazel felt a drowsy weakness seeping into her limbs, then a swilling in the pit of her stomach. She looked down at the pouch of berries in her lap.

'What are these?' she asked, picking one up and crushing it between her fingers. The juice trickled down her hand, inky black.

'Fen? What are these?' she asked again, but he didn't reply. She looked up and saw that he was on his feet, backing away.

'I'm sorry,' he stammered. 'I'm really sorry.'

Hazel stared back at him, aghast.

'I had to!' he said, gulping back sobs. 'They told me I had to, or we'd never see Merrin again!'

Fear folded round her, thick and sudden. Hazel glanced wildly to her right and left. Not a crocus in sight. They had wandered far beyond Perig's protective charms.

'Fen!' she choked, as the juice of the berries turned bitter on her tongue. But he was already gone. She tried to run after him but her limbs were numb and heavy. She fell and began to crawl, dragging herself across the forest floor.

Then, before she could take a breath, she was wrenched up into the air and set twisting and turning as if her skin were a glove worn by an invisible hand. Hazel felt her body stretching and splitting. Feathers sprouted, bent and clotted; claws curled out of her hands and feet; her joints snapped backwards, bones hollowed out. And all the time, a terrible, unearthly sound screeched in her ears. She felt as if she were being pulled to pieces, her limbs disintegrating into writhing swarms.

And then nothing.

Nothing except the pendant of her necklace, burning fiercely over her heart.

CHAPTER TWENTY-NINE

Boggart Hole

A CURRENT OF DARKNESS DRAGGED HER downwards, downwards. All around, formless things twisted and slid; hungry shadows swarming like hagfish, slithering and sucking, leaching away all warmth and life.

Occasionally she would sense a cloudy light, hear a muffled cry. Then a rushing sense of surfacing would take hold, as if somebody had seized her and was pulling with all their strength. She would try to speak, or hold on, but her limbs would not respond, and soon she was being dragged under again, down into the suffocating deep.

Was it minutes or days before the voices came? 'Over here! She's here! Stars above, she's cold ... !' Bulky arms lifted her and carried her at a run, through the invisible forest.

Later, as she rose and fell on tides of darkness, she heard whispers and mutterings. Some close, some far away. She felt damp cloth on her forehead; caught a comforting whiff of honey brew. At moments she would feel a tingle of warmth spreading from her necklace, through her chest, and down to the tips of her fingers and toes. Then, just when she thought she might be able to open her eyes, she would be seized by electrifying nightmares: trees drawing back, shivering, as green riders approached; flaming arrows whistling into the canopy; and the acrid heat of smoke filling her lungs, burning and burning into blackness.

At last, Hazel's eyes blinked foggily open. The air was warm and sticky and her limbs lay heavy on a thinly matted stone floor. As she came to, she heard weak moans echoing around her. Many others lay nearby, some squirming or shivering, others motionless. They looked like fairies, but their light was faded, some barely more than flickering outlines in the darkness. Hazel tried to move but her muscles began to tremble and twitch. Instinctively, she cried out. Moments later, a familiar figure hurried to her side.

'There you are!' said Perig, taking her hand. 'Stars above, you had us worried!'

'Where am I?' Hazel whispered. Her tongue felt thick and dry in her mouth. Perig hoisted her to sitting and brought a cup of tepid water to her lips.

'You're safe,' he said. 'That's the main thing.'

Once she'd managed a few sips, he settled her back down again and started fussing with some stones. They were flat and smooth and had large holes bored through their middles.

'These'll help draw out the enchantment,' he muttered, arranging them around her. 'So stay where you are a while.' Hazel's thoughts were still tangled in shadow and she was struggling to understand.

'Enchantment?'

'Yes, indeed. Lucky the trees told me when they did, or you'd have been lost to us, no doubt about it.' He rubbed one of the strange pebbles on the hem of his cloak then placed it carefully next to her. The trembling subsided and her muscles softened, drawing her back into the depths of sleep.

For days, Hazel swam in and out of consciousness. When eventually the darkness receded and her mind began to clear, she took in her surroundings. She was in a gloomy, echoing chamber mined out of solid stone. It was uncomfortably hot and the walls were sweating with grime. Murmurs, voices and cries floated on the stagnant air, and all around her lay fairies of every size and age, strewn limply on the damp floor, faint as cobwebs. Most had the curving blue markings of the Druics etched on their necks and faces.

Nearby, on a makeshift bench, sat Perig. Arden was next to him, flipping one of the holed stones between restless fingers.

'What happened?' Hazel murmured, head thumping painfully.

Perig ripped a chunk of bread from a loaf and offered it to her. 'There's time for that,' he said. 'Just eat, will you?'

Arden looked up sharply. 'Tell her,' she said. 'If *you* won't, I will.'

Perig raised his palms in a gesture of peace. 'She's tired now. Later.'

Arden cursed under her breath and threw down the stone with a clatter. 'She's ruined *everything*!' she shouted, then stormed away.

Hazel stared at Perig, aghast.

He sighed and rubbed the top of his head. 'All right, I'll tell you, but don't go blaming yourself.'

'What . . . what do you mean?' Hazel stammered.

'I don't know what happened out there in the Weald,' Perig continued, 'but, one way or the other, the Fae almost had you.'

Hazel pressed a clammy palm to her forehead as shreds of memory came floating to the surface. She remembered the darkening shadows, the black juice dripping from her fingers.

'Oh!' she gasped. 'Fen! The berries!'

Perig nodded. 'Arboreans put him up to it,' he said. 'Ah, it's a terrible story. They snatched young Merrin. Told Fen that if he gave you those wicked berries, he'd get her back.' The wizard shook his head. 'He didn't, of course. No point bargaining with Arboreans.'

It was all pouring back now – Fen backing away, his face in the firelight, twisted with horror.

'You're safe here,' said Perig, 'but the Fae are hunting you, no doubt about it, and they'll come reaching for you any way they know how.'

Hazel remembered the trill of Fen's flute and felt as if tiny insects were crawling just beneath the surface of her skin. How could she have been so stupid?

Perig put his arm round her bunched shoulders. 'Eat now,' he said, holding up the bread. 'You have to eat.' But Hazel couldn't swallow a thing.

The tunnel outside the chamber fluttered with movement. A Druic child had arrived with an infant. Both were badly faded and the little one hung over his brother's shoulder, limp as a rag. Some stronger fairies hurried towards them and one scooped the infant into her arms.

'The Seam,' said another quickly. 'Take them to the Seam!'

'What's going on?' Hazel asked. 'Where are we?'

'Boggart Hole caves,' said Perig. 'Half a mile underground. There's a thick seam of greenstone here. Ley running through it. For now, at least.' Perig looked round the crowded chamber and ran large fingers over his tattooed scalp. 'Folks are travelling from all over – fleeing the Fading. It's terrible, Hazel. Never seen anything like it. Just this morning there was a little lad and his pa ...' He broke off and hung his head. Two bright tears splashed to the floor. 'Ah, it gets my blood a-roiling! We're all fairies, aren't we? This old Earth don't love one more than another!'

Hazel looked around at the faded fairies in fright and dismay. 'Where are the others?' she asked.

'Twins are back in Goblyn,' said Perig.

'And Portuna?'

Perig shifted uncomfortably and glanced sideways.

'She'll come right,' he said. There was a quiver of uncertainty in his voice. 'I'm looking after her.'

Hazel's heart lurched. 'What do you mean?' she said. 'Where is she? Is she here?'

Perig sighed and nodded towards the translucent shape lying next to her on the chamber floor.

Portuna was so faded that she was barely recognisable. Her fiery glow had dwindled to a bluish glimmer, and her eyes sat deep in their hollows. Hazel kneeled beside her friend and took her hand. It was as frail and skeletal as a leaf in winter.

'What happened?' she whispered.

Perig knotted his fingers together and breathed a shuddering sigh. 'Not long after we found you, Arboreans attacked the Den. They got wind of my working up a charm, see. So they came in the night; destroyed our cabin; destroyed my stones.'

The green riders, the flaming arrows – the nightmare visions swam back into Hazel's mind. 'No!' she gasped. 'Oh no!'

'All gone,' said Perig. 'Portuna tried to stop them. When they came for us, she was onto them in a flash – snapping their bowstrings, spooking the horses. But Ruis caught her. Drained the life out of her.' Hazel could still make out the black fingermarks striping her friend's neck. A shiver passed through her as she remembered the chill of Ruis's fingers around her throat.

'How . . . ?' she began, but before she finished her question, a terrible realisation dawned on her. *Fen* – she'd told him about Perig's charm. He hadn't even asked, but she'd told him. She could see it now – Fen bargaining for his sister's release, handing over whatever scraps of information he had.

'Oh, Perig,' Hazel whispered. 'I . . .' She could barely look at him. 'It was me.'

Perig's mouth twisted into a tired smile. 'We know,' he said calmly. 'Fen told us everything.' Hazel covered her face with her hands. 'The enemy is wily,' sighed Perig. 'There's no use blaming yourself, Hazel.'

But Hazel didn't know who else to blame. In the moments before she let the secret slip, she had sensed a flicker of danger, she'd caught its bitter scent. Then she'd wafted it away.

'I thought I could trust him,' she whispered. 'I really wanted to trust him.'

Perig tutted softly. 'Ah, but what we *want* to be true, that's not the same as the truth now, is it?'

Hazel hung her head.

'Muddling the two is a dangerous business,' said the wizard. 'You've got good instincts, Hazel. Listen to 'em.'

She felt a tightening in her chest. Arden was right. She'd ruined everything. She looked at Portuna's wavering shape and remembered the boy in the tunnel, his black shade on the earth.

It was too much.

Before Perig could stop her, Hazel rose to her feet and ran out of the chamber into the dismal stone labyrinth. Through the caves she stumbled, her legs weak, a heavy sickness in her heart. Faded Druics lay curled on the floor, or in makeshift hammocks, while those whose light was still strong rushed back and forth with blankets and baskets of food. The air was filled with a tense murmuring, broken occasionally by urgent shouts or a child's cry. Somewhere, a flute was playing and a small host of voices was rising to the tune. It was a lovely song, full of sadness and hope, but Hazel couldn't stand to hear it. She pressed her hands to her ears and wandered on, directionless, through the tunnels. If she could have turned herself into a worm and burrowed deeper into the ground she would have done so, but she felt as empty as an abandoned shell, and she knew her powers had left her. Eventually she found a narrow stairway that wound deep into the earth. Downwards she went, hoping at every step that the darkness and silence would swallow her whole.

The sound of swift-running water echoed in the gloom as the stairway opened onto a cramped chamber. A narrow stream carved a path beneath a pale lantern, hung crookedly from the cavern wall. Hazel sat down on a ledge above the water and watched the light tremble over its surface. Instinctively, she tugged the pendant of her necklace from her collar. It was what she had always done. It was her comfort – turning the glassy black stone between her fingers, imagining her mother sat beside her. But her little dream of the warming fire, the rosehip tea – it seemed absurd. Portuna was faded to a wisp, Perig's charm was destroyed and, with it, all her hopes of finding Pete again. She could hardly bear to think about it. Her Pete, waiting in a lonely hill, with no one coming to get him.

The stream gurgled mockingly below her feet. Hazel seized the pendant in her fist and tried to snap it off. It held fast. She pulled at it with all her might, but the fine silvery thread was stronger than steel. Defeated, she kicked her heels against the ledge and let out a miserable wail.

For a long time, she sat alone in the gloomy chamber, thoughts zigzagging like exhausted birds. Then there were footsteps.

'Black onyx, that is.'

Hazel turned to see Perig, stooped beneath the dripping ceiling. He gestured to her necklace and sat down beside her. 'Powerful protection against dark magic. If you hadn't been wearing that stone, you'd never have made it through.' Hazel gazed at the wizard, weary and bewildered. The patterns on his face wavered in the grainy shadows but his eyes were bright and steady. 'Make no mistake about it,' he said. 'The person who gave that to you loved you very much.'

At that, something inside Hazel buckled.

'No, she didn't,' she choked, shaking her head. 'She didn't.' Then, before her thoughts could catch up with her, she began to speak from the deepest hollows of her heart.

'I thought she'd come back,' she gasped. 'I told Pete she'd take us both; that we'd go and live somewhere with a fireplace, and a teapot, you know ... like in the books. I believed it, I really thought she'd come back. But she never did, did she? And she never *meant* to!'

Then the sobs she had been fighting back forced their way to the surface. Hazel hugged her knees to her chest and let them come, one after the other, tears flowing faster than she could wipe them away.

Perig put his arm round her hunched shoulders. The water slipped glassily below, casting a pale web of reflected light all around them. Eventually, Hazel rubbed her eyes with her cuffs and took a long, shuddering breath.

Then Perig spoke.

'There's something you need to know,' he said. 'I saw it when I first laid eyes on you, Hazel. I should've told you before, but I didn't know how.' He turned to look at her, eyes crinkling into a sad smile. 'You're Erith's girl.'

CHAPTER THIRTY

Erith

HAZEL STARED AT PERIG BLANKLY, UNABLE TO absorb his words.

'You knew my mum?' she whispered.

'That I did,' said Perig. 'I knew Erith.'

It was the first time Hazel had heard her mother's name. It sounded unreal.

'There's much to tell you,' said Perig, 'but we can't be mouldering in this cave forever.' He hauled himself upright and helped her to her feet. 'Come with me.'

Hazel followed the wizard out of the airless chamber and up through long, climbing passages, hardly feeling the steps beneath her bare soles. As they approached the earth's surface, the curdling odour of the deep caves began to clear and the atmosphere dried and cooled. At last, Perig rolled aside a boulder and they stepped out of the darkness into the dusky mauves of evening.

They were no longer in the woods, but on a heathered

hillside, far beyond the forest edge. Before them, the hill rolled downwards into a misted valley, then rose again to the horizon, where Goblyn Wood lay thick as a reef.

Perig led Hazel to a slab of mossy rock.

'Sit yourself down,' he said. Hazel sat, and Perig wrapped his heavy, moth-eaten cloak round her shoulders. She gathered the folds beneath her chin and waited, half dazed, as Perig unscrewed the top of a tarnished copper flask and took a long swig. Then he began.

'Your ma was a Seely,' he said, 'and an aquamancer – a water witch. I work with stones, but Erith, she worked the magic of rivers, rains and clouds.'

Hazel gazed into the white mists of the valley below, boiling and smouldering like a cauldron.

'Most Seelies never leave the forest,' Perig continued. 'They're homebodies at heart. But your ma was different. She'd go trekking upriver to lakes and mountains, or downstream all the way to the seas. Each river or spring has its own story, you see, and its own powers. Erith was always slinging her bag over her shoulder and going out collecting. That's how she met Calder – your pa.'

Hazel glanced across at Perig.

'And he . . . he was human?'

'He was,' Perig replied. 'Lovely lad, Cal. One day, he was down at Morrow River looking for kingfishers, but he found your ma instead. They fell in love faster than the apple drops from the tree. After that, your ma couldn't learn enough about the human world. Most fairy folk keep clear of clayfeet – 'never trust a long-legs', they say. But Erith wasn't like that. She thought fairies and humans should live together again, like it used to be. Each was poorer without the other, and sadder. The Old Wars, she'd say, left a big hole in the hearts of humans and fairies alike.'

Hazel squinted into the swollen sun as it sank behind the woods. She listened closely to Perig's words, understanding them but not quite taking them in.

'It wasn't long before you showed up.' Perig smiled. 'Ah, you were a sweet pea. Your ma and pa couldn't keep their eyes off you. But your family couldn't stay in Understone.'

Hazel felt a nudge of realisation. She *knew* she had been in Understone before. Of course – she had *lived* there.

'Why not?' she asked. 'Why couldn't we stay?'

'Forbidden!' said Perig. 'Since the wars, the mingling of humans and fairies has been absolutely forbidden. Like I said, the Fae fear slipskins. Fear 'em more than anything.'

Perig paused for a moment, his breath curling in the winter air.

'So your family were hunted. The Fae soon got to your pa – sent him mad with their poisonous magic. Erith tried everything to save him. Every day, she'd bundle you onto her back and walk miles to dredge waters from healing wells, or melt snowdrifts. But it was no good.' Perig rubbed the top of his head with his knuckle and frowned.

'After Cal died, she knew she couldn't protect you either.

That's why she left you with the clayfeet – beyond the reach of the Fae and their servants. That necklace, she worked on it for weeks, tumbled it in the waters of the Morrow – all to keep you safe.' Hazel touched the pendant at her throat. Despite the evening chill it felt warm, almost soft.

She didn't know how to ask her next question and, when she did, it was like somebody else spoke it for her. 'So . . . why didn't she come back for me?'

Perig clasped his hands tightly together.

'There was nothing she wanted more,' he replied. 'Leaving you there broke her to bits, but she had to wait for danger to pass. Once you were safe with the clayfeet, she joined us rebels. Never did we see such heart. She threw everything into the fight.'

Hazel listened silently as a new image of her mother began to form in her mind's eye.

'Erith had it all worked out, see,' Perig continued. 'Fae, Arboreans, they were lying about the Fadings and setting the peoples of the Hollows against each other – Seely against Druic, Druic against Seely. If we were busy blaming each other for our problems, she said, we'd never look to the Knoll. So she made it her mission to enter the Fae's dominion and find proof that the Fae were behind the Fadings. And, with that proof in hand, she meant to unite the Hollows against the Fae, and restore the balance of the earth. Oh, she was as brave as a bear!'

Hazel's eyes stayed fixed on the darkening sun.

'Erith was working up a water charm,' Perig went on, 'that would see her through the Wildermist and clear her path to the Knoll. She came *so* close! But she needed one last ingredient – a few drops from a waterfall, deep in Arborean territory. We didn't want her to go, but nobody could stop her. A few days later we got news that she'd made it there safely and had blended her charm. She was on her way.'

Hazel held her breath and waited to be told what she already knew.

'She never got there,' said Perig. 'The elms told me she'd been captured by Arboreans, and killed. We found her shade a few days later.'

CHAPTER THIRTY-ONE

New Hope

I N THE DAYS THAT FOLLOWED, HAZEL SPOKE LITTLE. She helped Perig with his healing stones, and fetched chamomile and garlic for the faded. At night, she curled up close to Portuna and held her hand tightly in her own. Portuna remained as frail as a curl of smoke, but her glow had shifted from wavering blue to a steady green.

As she went about her chores, Hazel's mind kept running through everything Perig had told her, turning each word over and over.

'It's strange,' she whispered to the sleeping Portuna one night. 'I used to find it so hard to believe she was real. Now I can't believe she's gone.' She pulled the edge of the blanket over her friend's shoulders. 'Her name was Erith. I think it's a nice name, don't you?' She searched Portuna's face for some response and, with astonished relief, saw a brief shimmer behind her closed eyelids.

The next day, Hazel was up on the frosty hillside trying

in vain to rekindle her lost powers, when she heard the tramping of heavy footsteps behind her.

'Hazel! Come in!' It was Perig, puffing and beaming. 'She's up! She's awake!'

Quick as a flash, Hazel scrambled to the mouth of the cave and flew down the stone steps, two at a time, until she was at her friend's side.

Portuna's glow was soft but steady. She was sitting up cross-legged, eyes wide, hair sticking out in all directions. Hazel rushed towards her and wrapped her in a tight hug. She was warm again, and solid.

'Portuna!' Hazel blurted. 'You're all right!'

'Course I am.' Portuna grinned. Her face was pinched but her eyes were flickering brightly. 'You missed a good fight!'

'Good fight?!' Hazel spluttered. 'You almost died!'

'Didn't, though, did I?' She twirled a holed stone on her finger. 'I'm hard to kill.'

Hazel laughed and hugged her again.

'Oh! You should be resting!' Perig scolded, wagging a finger at his unruly patient. 'And don't fiddle about with my hagstones!' He snatched back the pebble and, muttering, laid it by her side.

Portuna rolled her eyes. 'Anyway!' she said to Hazel. 'You should've seen it. There were at least ten of them, plus Ruis. Came rushing out of the trees on their horses, firing blazing arrows up at the cabin . . . *Pshew! Pshew!*'

Portuna recounted the rebels' assault on the attackers,

and as she glowed brighter and brighter with each detail, tears of relief slid down Hazel's cheeks.

Over the following days, Portuna grew stronger and was moved further from the Seam to a chamber near the surface. Every morning, dozens more fairies were arriving from desiccated swathes of woodlands – old and young, Druics and Seelies – and the air of the caves was thickening with sickness and despair. As she worked alongside Perig, Hazel sometimes thought she would collapse with exhaustion. Then she'd think of her mother, brave as a bear, and keep going.

Yet there was something in Perig's tale that snagged in Hazel's mind – something that seemed strangely familiar. As she washed blankets in scalding water or mashed up herbs for a salve, she combed through every detail; her father seeking kingfishers by the Morrow; her mother slinging her satchel over her shoulder, trudging uphill and down. Something in the story was calling out to her, but however many times she repeated it to herself, she could not see what it was.

It was almost midwinter before, finally, she understood.

She and Perig had toiled through the night, carrying limp and fading fairies closer to the Seam, working the healing magic of the hagstones. Now they sat, exhausted, on the green rock beyond the entrance to Boggart Hole, Portuna by their side. They were not alone. Clusters of other fairies rested in the heathers, escaping the crowding and heat of the caves. A little further down the slope, a family of Seelies huddled together trying to revive a dying fire.

The watery light of early morning washed over the crags of Perig's face.

'Ah, it's nothing but a drop in the sea,' he growled. 'Not enough hagstones in the world to keep the tide at bay.'

Hazel squinted wearily into the sun, now winking above the horizon. He was right. The caves were overflowing with fairies and, with every passing day, it felt more hopeless.

'We need to dig deeper,' Perig continued. 'Pull this evil out by its roots. It's time we went home.'

Hazel looked across the valley to the forest. 'The Den?'

'No, no. Ruis'll come looking for us there.'

'Where, then?' asked Portuna.

'Spud and Sprout are fixing up a new hideout, but it's not ready yet,' said Perig. 'We might have to call in on your pa, Portuna. Just like the old days!'

Portuna glowed pink with pleasure.

The sun was floating higher, ghostly white. In the far distance, Hazel could make out the shadow of a hill, rising like a sea creature beyond the line of the forest.

'Where's Arden?' she asked. Hazel hadn't seen her since she'd stalked angrily out of the caves.

'Fetching some stones,' said Perig. 'Jasper, a bit of quartz ...'

'For the charm?'

Perig nodded. 'That's right. Time to start again.'

Hazel felt a wave of despair. They had been so close. Now it all seemed impossible, and Pete more distant than ever. She pressed her lips together to stop herself from crying.

Perig nudged her shoulder. 'Don't lose hope now,' he said. 'Remember, there's always hope.'

Portuna sat closer and took Hazel's hand. 'And friends!'

Hazel bit back the tears. 'If it wasn't for me we'd never—'

'Pffff!' Portuna interrupted. 'If it wasn't for you I'd still be bouncing around in that bottle, wouldn't I?'

Hazel wiped her eyes and gave a small smile. She remembered the rattling that had woken her in the night, the silvered bottle shaking furiously in the professor's cabinet.

Then, like the sun burning through cloud, the answer she had been looking for appeared with shining clarity. She gasped.

'What is it?' said Perig. 'What's wrong?'

'Erith's charm,' she said. 'I know where it is!'

Perig and Portuna stared at her, speechless.

'The cabinet!' said Hazel. 'The satchel!'

'What satchel? Slow down now,' said Perig.

Hazel took a breath. 'In Professor Grinling's study, there was a cabinet stuffed with things he'd stolen from the Hollows, and from the forest. There was a satchel there, full of tiny bottles. It looked like they had water in them.

And they were labelled. They had weird names: EBBLE, OG, DUN . . .'

'Names of rivers,' said Perig.

'And there was one bottle,' Hazel continued breathlessly, 'that said "Morrow".'

A smile began to dawn on Perig's face. 'Morrow River.'

'Yes!' said Hazel. 'Where my parents met. Do you think . . . ? Could the satchel be my mum's? Could the charm still be inside it?'

Perig gave a gusty laugh. 'Well, scratch my back with a buckthorn! It might be, Hazel. It might very well be. There were reports of Grinling lurking in the forest round that time. He could've found Erith's belongings. It's not certain now, but it's possible.'

Portuna was looking from Perig to Hazel and back again, the tips of her ears glittering brightly.

'So, are you saying that the charm we need – the one that can get us through the Wildermist – it's been at the professor's all along?!'

Hazel nodded, unable to stop grinning.

'Perhaps,' said Perig, 'and if it is . . .' He shook his head in amazement. 'Well, that changes everything!'

Portuna blazed up like a torch and sprang to her feet. 'What are we waiting for?' she cried, seizing Hazel's hands and pulling her off the rock. 'Let's go get it. You and me, Hazel! Oh, I'd like to see the look on that old clayfoot's face when he—'

'Hang on, hang on!' growled Perig, straightening in alarm. 'If Grinling catches you, Portuna, he'll bottle you up like a firefly. And you, Hazel, he knows what you are. He lost you once, he's not going to take any chances next time.' The wizard shook his head fiercely. 'If you end up in a specimen box, you'll be no good to nobody.'

But as Portuna's hand squeezed her own, Hazel felt only a rising excitement. 'I think we can do it, Perig,' she said. 'We know where the satchel is, and Grinling won't see me, will he? Not if I'm a mouse, or a moth.'

Perig raised his eyebrows. 'I didn't know your magic'd come back.'

'Not yet,' she replied, 'but it will soon. I'm sure it will. Then we'll be ready!'

But Hazel was not in the least bit sure. For days she had waited for the wilderness within her to stir and hadn't felt so much as a flicker. As soon as she had the chance, she found a quiet spot on the hillside and tried to summon her powers. But nothing stirred. Traces of the Fae's enchantment still lurked in her veins and the creatures that lived within her kept still and silent. Then, early one frost-covered morning, as she stood amongst the heathers, reaching with all her senses, she heard a cry.

At first, she thought it was the shriek of a distant raven, but then she heard it again, louder this time. She paused, motionless. Several voices, fierce and billowing with violence, were coming from a spinney of silver birches further down the hill. Another cry followed, this one of pain.

It was a voice she knew.

Heart thundering in her chest, she rushed down the frosty slope, slipping and skidding towards the trees.

There were four of them – brawny and bedraggled, inked with the markings of the Druics. On the ground, shaking and clutching bloody fingers to her head, was Arden. One of the four had seized her bow and was dancing about with it, firing off pretend arrows, as the others howled with laughter.

'Give it here!' said the tallest of the gang, snatching it off his friend. He weighed the bow in his hand and fingered its finely carved grip. 'Very nice,' he chuckled. 'Real Arborean craftsmanship.' He glanced down at the wounded Arden with a lopsided grin. 'And look at that fancy livery. Got to dress fine for the Fae, eh? Got to look your best when you're hunting folks down!'

Arden glared up at him, bright red rivers branching down her face.

'I never . . .' she began, but the Druic was not in a listening mood. Quick as a cricket, he plucked an arrow from Arden's quiver, mounted it on the rest and aimed directly at her heart. She stared back at him, eyes unblinking.

'I don't serve the Fae,' she said. 'I'm with Perig.'

The Druic paused a moment, puzzled. 'Our Perig?'

Arden nodded.

The Druic frowned and relaxed the bow a little, but one of the others snorted in disbelief.

'Hogweed!' she snapped, waggling a wizened finger. 'She's just tryin' to daddle you, Sorrel. Don't listen to a word of it.' She leaned in close to him, hissing in his ear, 'Go on! Do us all a favour. One less Arborean Ley-sucker.' The archer hesitated for a second, then drew the bowstring deadly taut.

Hazel felt the world slow to a glide. The birch-wands gleamed, the frosted earth glittered, and each flicker of movement – the curl of the archer's fingers, the tremble of his eyelid – stretched to an eternity.

Suddenly, as if torn from the wind itself, came the ripping, rolling growl of a predator.

Spine arched, fur spiked, a giant wolf bristled on the ridge of the hill. The Druics backed away.

'Kill it, Sorrel!' one of them shrieked. The archer turned to take aim but, on seeing the white flash of fangs, he fumbled the bow in a panic, then threw it down and scrambled through the icy thickets after his friends.

The wolf's breath puffed and steamed as it watched the assailants stumble into the distance. Then it turned to Arden and padded softly towards her. Arden stared into the beast's flickering opaline eyes.

'Hazel?' she whispered.

The moment Arden said her name, Hazel slipped back

into her human shape. For a moment, Arborean and slipskin stared at each other, wide-eyed.

'Clouds above!' said Arden, her voice trembling. 'Thank you, thank you! I thought he'd shoot.'

'Don't thank me,' said Hazel, voice shaking a little. 'It was the wolf.'

'Same thing,' Arden replied, with a smile.

Hazel could still feel the prickle of fur between her shoulder blades, the sharpness of her teeth behind her lips.

'Right,' she murmured. 'Same thing.'

Arden winced in pain, one hand on her bleeding

forehead. Hazel reached down and pulled her to her feet then, looping her arm over her shoulders, helped her back up the hill.

Arden was silent for a while, eyes on the frost-furred grass. Before they reached the mouth of Boggart Hole, she cleared her throat.

'Perig always believed in you,' she said, 'but I didn't. I'm sorry.'

Hazel glanced across at her and smiled. 'That's all right,' she replied. 'Neither did I.'

As Hazel's feet pressed against the frozen ground, her muscles flowed with a cool energy. The wolf was there, prowling within her, alert and powerful. And, when Perig saw the amber glint in her eyes, he knew that she was ready.

CHAPTER THIRTY-TWO

True Sight

I T WAS A BRIGHT AND BUSY MORNING IN
Kensington Gardens. Londoners hurried down the
frosty avenues, long scarves flapping, as children
cracked icy puddles with their heels. There were newspaper
sellers, gentlemen in fur hats, ladies wheeling past on
bicycles, but not one of them saw an oddly-dressed girl slip
from the hollow of an old oak tree.

Hazel blinked in the sun's white glare. She reached
beneath her cloak and gently patted the breast pocket of her
tunic where Portuna was hiding – a bright orb of fairy light.
Then, dusting the leaf litter from her shoulders, she walked
briskly in the direction of the Natural History Museum.

Only an autumn had passed since she was last amongst
the clayfeet but as she threaded her way along the crowded
pavements Hazel knew she was a stranger now – a visitor
from another world. A group of girls, of about her age, sat on
the steps of a townhouse sharing a bag of hot chestnuts and,

as she passed by, Hazel couldn't help but smile at her secret.

Before long, the crooked gables of the Keeper's Lodge slid into view. She paused a moment, feeling an unpleasant fluttering in her stomach. Pulling her hood closely around her face, she approached the crumbling garden wall and eyed the front of the house. The front door and leaded windows were all firmly shut against the cold, the curtains closely drawn.

'What can you see?' Portuna hissed loudly from her hiding place. A passing gentleman startled at the unexpected voice and glared at Hazel, moustache twitching. She turned her back and scurried further along the garden wall, shushing sharply into her pocket.

The wall bent round to the back of the house where a trail of smoke dribbled from a chimney stack. The kitchen windows glowed warmly and Hazel could see a familiar aproned figure busying about inside.

'Mrs Plover's in,' she whispered.

Portuna peeked over the top of Hazel's pocket and clicked her tongue. 'Yes, but the professor's out.'

Hazel's eyes tracked up to the window of Grinling's study. The curtains were half closed and all was dark and still. She cleared her throat. 'All right. See that rosemary bush under the window? You wait in there.'

Portuna nodded.

'And stick to the plan.'

Portuna nodded again.

'Ready?' said Hazel.

'Yes!' hissed Portuna. 'Hurry up!'

Hazel glanced quickly from left to right, then plucked the fairy out of her pocket and dropped her over the garden wall into a springy shrub. Hazel followed quickly after, swinging her legs over the rough stone. She only fell a short distance, but by the time her feet touched the ground she had taken the shape of a small brown mouse.

Portuna ran up and tweaked her nose.

'Good luck!' she said with a grin. Then, on lightning paws, Hazel darted through the herb garden towards the back of the lodge.

Flattening her ribs, she squeezed herself beneath the door and wriggled into the warmth of Mrs Plover's kitchen. Before her stretched a vast stone floor. She paused for a moment, body bunched and bristling, then darted for cover beneath a nearby dessert-trolley. Whiskers a-tremble, she surveyed the unfamiliar landscape. As a human she had crossed the kitchen in a few paces – every tool, pot and tabletop there for her use – but, as a mouse, the whole world seemed to loom over her, rocking and swaying as if it might topple down at any moment, and smash her to bits. She heard a rummaging in the pantry, and the scuffle of slippers. Mrs Plover was returning to her stove.

Quick as an arrow, Hazel made for the hallway, fur skimming the skirting boards, then up the stairs she flew in great balletic leaps. She didn't stop until she had wriggled under the door of the professor's study, tugging her tail behind her.

A winter light flowed weakly between the curtains, catching wandering motes of dust and illuminating the piles of books on Grinling's desk. As expected the professor was not there, but she caught his scent of oily wool and anchovy paste, and suspected he was not long gone. As easily as breathing, Hazel changed back into her human form and rubbed her nose, still tingling from recent whiskers.

Cautiously, she approached the glass-fronted cabinet and opened the shuddering doors, hastily searching for the deerskin satchel. She found it on the bottom shelf and dragged it, heavy and clinking, onto her lap.

The deerskin was softened with age and dust had settled into its creases and seams. Running her fingers over its uneven shape, Hazel noticed how warm it felt – like a living thing. With a sharp breath, she glanced over her shoulder towards the window. She knew she should hurry but wanted just a moment alone with her mother's things. She undid the wooden toggle and looked inside.

The vials were there, dozens of them, each no bigger than her thumb, all safely corked and tucked into their leather straps. She slid them out, one by one, and held them to the light. Each contained water – some silty or brackish, some clear – and all had been tagged and labelled in a loose, quick handwriting. Many carried the names of rivers, wells and streams. Hazel found the vial labelled MORROW. With a pang, she saw that it was empty and dry. She gazed at it for a moment then slipped it carefully back into place.

She rummaged deeper, looking for the charm. Hurriedly, she inspected the labels. There was one FOR RAINFALL, another FOR THIRST and others with more curious names: FOUND LIGHT, LOVE FROM AFAR, TO FORGET, and a small, cloudy bottle labelled LOST HOPE attached to a tarnished silver chain to be worn round the neck.

Besides the vials there were dog-eared notebooks, green-crusted copper instruments and a dusty chunk of quartz. Then, at the bottom of the bag, Hazel discovered a small moleskin pouch. Her breath caught in her throat. Embroidered on the velvety fabric, in dark green thread, was a Nautilus Strike – the sign of the rebels. She peeked inside. Nestled deep in a clump of moss was a tiny corked bottle. Pinching it lightly between finger and thumb, she slid it out and held it up in front of her.

The bottle was only half full, but the fluid within was brilliantly clear, catching the feeble light of the window and transforming it into fanning rainbows. She held the bottle close to her eye and gasped. Seen through the limpid water, every object in the study stood out in crystalline detail, as if a mist she hadn't known was there had suddenly vanished. She checked the tag that was tied to the cork. In her mother's handwriting were the words: *True Sight*, and on the back: *Dissolves Fae illusion. To be rubbed on the eyelids.*

Here it was – the charm that would get them through the

Wildermist, to the Knoll. The distance between her and Pete seemed to vanish in an instant.

Hands trembling, she repacked the satchel and tightened the strap. Then she dashed to the window and peered down into the kitchen garden where her friend was waiting impatiently in the rosemary bush. Hazel shoved aside the curtain and, as she slid the window open, Portuna sprang back up to her full size.

'Got it!' Hazel whispered. Portuna silently punched the air then stretched out her arms to catch the precious load. Hazel dropped the satchel out of the window then Portuna disappeared into the bush with it – just as they'd planned. Hazel slid the window shut again, so as to leave no sign of a break-in, and secured the brass latch.

Then, just as she made a move for the door, she heard something that made her freeze: the murmur of voices on the landing outside, and the rattle of a key in the lock.

CHAPTER THIRTY-THREE

Mr Emmett Verne

INSTANTLY, HAZEL SLIPPED BACK INTO HER MOUSE'S skin and scampered behind an uneven stack of books piled high on the rug. As the key turned, she heard two gentlemen talking. Straining the large pink shells of her ears, she recognised Professor Grinling's low chuckle.

'Sit down, Emmett, please,' said Grinling as he showed his guest into the study. The guest did not reply. There were footsteps on the carpet and a soft creak of upholstery. 'Mrs Plover will bring the tea.' The professor was putting on his usual cheer, but his voice seemed strained.

Heart humming in her ribcage, Hazel peered cautiously round a book spine. Professor Grinling was behind his desk, busily clearing papers aside, while his visitor sat opposite, deep in a leather armchair. Hazel could see long, black-trousered legs and a thin, spidery hand, but his face was obscured by the wing of his seat.

'Excuse the jumble,' Grinling chortled, pushing his

spectacles up his nose. 'It's true what they say about professors!' The visitor did not laugh. 'Absent-minded and all that,' Grinling added weakly.

The visitor took a nasal breath. 'Let's get down to business, shall we?' His voice was as dry as a fallen leaf. 'What news?'

The professor coughed uncomfortably and clasped his hands in front of him on the desk.

'Well,' he began. At that moment, there was a tap at the door and Mrs Plover shuffled in with a tray of tea and marble cake. The two men waited silently as she fussed with the porcelain, a polite smile stamped on Grinling's face.

'Sugar, Mr Verne?' whispered Mrs Plover, hovering with tongs. The gentleman fluttered his fingers dismissively and the housekeeper bowed then crept out of the room, closing the door behind her.

'You were saying, Bartholomew,' said Mr Verne.

Grinling cleared his throat. 'The thing is, Emmett. They need, well . . .' He paused a moment. 'They need more.'

'The Fae, you mean,' Verne replied brusquely, a shiver of irritation in his voice.

Grinling blushed. 'Yes, yes.' His voice dropped to a whisper. 'The Fae. They're asking for . . . more.'

Mr Emmett Verne leaned forward in his chair, allowing Hazel a better look. He was as bald and pale as an egg with eyes that gleamed like marbles.

'More?' The slits of his nostrils twitched in displeasure. 'Already?'

The professor took off his spectacles and fidgeted anxiously. 'I know, I know. But, Emmett, you should understand that the fairy world is not—'

'And *you* should understand,' Verne interrupted smoothly, 'that we are all growing tired of fairy fickleness and trickery.'

Grinling squirmed and chuckled nervously, but Mr Verne did not blink.

'What I mean,' said the professor with an embarrassed cough, 'is that we need to tread carefully. They are a little skittish at present, you see. There is a slipskin at large.'

Hazel's heart missed a beat.

'You mean the one that escaped from under your nose?' Verne replied drily.

Hazel felt a jolt of recognition. Suddenly she was certain that this man in the leather armchair was the person who had been at the other end of the phone call – the call she had overheard from the herb garden. She remembered what the professor had told him about Pete: *Unimportant*, he'd said. *Of no interest to us.* Fur bristled along her spine.

The professor flushed a deep red. 'Yes. Well, word has reached them that she is in Goblyn Wood and, as I said, they're skittish.'

Verne's lips curled in contempt. 'We don't have time for fairy prophecies and superstitions.' He sniffed. 'If they want *more*, they shall have to show us that we can trust them.'

'I understand, Emmett,' said the professor. 'Dealings with

the fairy world never do run smoothly. But I must warn you, in the strongest *possible* terms, against frustrating the Fae. To do so would be very risky indeed.'

'Is that so?' spat Verne. 'I rather think that the Fae should be mindful of frustrating *us*! Don't you?'

'Of course, of course!' stammered the professor, looking panicked. 'But it would be remiss of me not to tell you the truth. You employ me for my *expertise*, after all.'

Verne regarded the professor darkly. 'Go on,' he hissed.

The professor took a nervous breath. 'Fairies, in my personal experience, do not tend to seek out conflict with humans. But if they are provoked, Emmett, if one encroaches on their world, or offends their sensibilities, or does not honour one's promises, then their fury can be uncontainable. Uncontainable!' The professor's moustache was quivering with worry. 'It has happened before.' He steadied himself and locked his fingers together. 'The last thing we want to do is to put the Fae on a war footing. I'm sure you'll agree.'

There was a long silence. Verne drew back into his chair and slowly drummed his tapering fingers on its leather arm. After what seemed like an age, he spoke. 'They are testing our patience,' he muttered. '*Sorely.* But you may tell them that we shall consider their request.'

'Very wise,' said the professor, looking relieved.

Mr Verne took a pair of gloves from his pocket and stood to leave. He was tall and incredibly thin, like a brushstroke of black ink. 'And don't fret, Bartholomew,' he said with a sneer. 'You shall be rewarded amply for your time. Indeed –' he smiled grimly – 'if all goes well, we shall both be far too rich to fret about anything at all – for the rest of our very long lives.'

At that the professor sat upright.

'Emmett!' he spluttered, offended. 'You know I don't do this for the money. The fairy realm is my lifelong passion.' He puffed himself up. 'My only true reward shall be to have brought the human and fairy worlds one step closer together.'

Verne smiled indulgently. 'Of course,' he said. 'Forgive me.'

Hazel's claws curled into the rug. Who was this man? Was he in league with the Fae? Was *he* behind the death of the forest? Before she could make any sense of what she had heard, she felt a sudden, painful pressure on her tail. She whipped around and found herself whisker-to-whisker with Purkiss, the professor's fairy-hunting cat.

The cat's breath smelled of blood and tiny bones. As he ran his tongue over needle-sharp fangs, every hair on Hazel's body bristled. She tried to run, but her tail was pinned tightly to the rug. A cruel spark danced in the cat's eyes. He lifted his paw but, before she had the chance to scuttle for cover, batted her sideways.

She tumbled, bounced to her feet and rushed for the door. The cat sprang into her path and, with one clean swipe, sent her sailing backwards. Her small body struck the wall and she dropped, breathless, to the floor.

Tail flicking from side to side, Purkiss advanced upon his prey. Hazel leaped onto her four feet, desperate eyes glancing left and right. No chinks in the skirting boards, no doors to slip under. There was nothing left to do but fight. She turned to face Purkiss, up on her hind legs, tiny eyes blazing. The cat hesitated a moment, whiskers twitching in amusement. Then he lowered his head and pounced.

Until that moment, the two gentlemen had paid no attention to the small drama unfolding on the Persian rug. But, as Grinling stood to show his guest out of the room, the air was shredded by terrible screams.

The men turned to see Purkiss locked in a vicious battle with a strange, collarless feline.

The two cats tumbled across the carpet, bodies twisting, tails lashing, hissing and screeching like wildfire.

'Josephine!' howled the professor. Mrs Plover, who had been busy sweeping the kitchen floor, rushed up to the study. 'How did that *creature* get in here?! Get it out!' Mrs Plover swung at the unfamiliar cat with her broom, then chased it down the stairs and out of the back door, hollering and stamping her feet.

The cat hid in the garden beneath a clump of sage and licked her wounded foreleg. Her cheek stung sharply from where Purkiss had planted a claw, and one of her ears felt torn. She waited for the commotion inside the house to die down, then stalked over to the rosemary bush where a small orb of light was waiting.

'Hazel?' Portuna whispered, looking her friend up and down. She was sitting on Erith's satchel, arms folded. *'That wasn't part of the plan!'*

CHAPTER THIRTY-FOUR

The Gift

PERIG TOOK THE MOLESKIN POUCH FROM HAZEL and ran his thumb softly over the embroidered Nautilus Strike.

'Sky above,' he murmured. 'Erith's charm. You found it!'

Hazel and Portuna grinned at each other with pride and delight.

'Lemme see!' cried Sprout, making a snatch for it.

'Not a chance!' growled Perig, lifting it high above his head. 'Arden. Look after this, will you?' Arden took the precious pouch and tucked it carefully away in the pocket of her pack.

The rebels had left Boggart Hole and were now hunkered down in the Babbage family burrow. It was evening. The little ones were tucked in their hammocks and, as Auntie Mag snoozed by the glow of the amber, Pa rustled up a late supper.

'I *knew* you were meant for the Cause,' he told Portuna

as he tossed a batch of prickly leaves into a hissing pot. 'I always knew it!'

The tips of Portuna's ears sparkled happily. 'Where's Corrie?' she asked.

Pa shook his whiskery head. 'Stirring up mischief, no doubt. Been spending too much time with that Webcap lad, if you ask me.'

'Don't worry, Pa.' Portuna gave him a peck on the cheek. 'Everything's going to change soon. You'll see!'

As the smell of browning pastry filled the air, the twins laid the crockery on the cherrywood table.

'Nettle pie!' announced Pa, setting down a piping dish. The others rubbed their hands together with glee, but Hazel's stomach groaned in disappointment.

'Granny Webcap's recipe?' asked Portuna, licking her lips.

'My own!' said Pa. 'With an extra drop of honey for Hazel.' He gave her a wink and served her a crusty slice. Hazel took a cautious bite. It dissolved in her mouth, buttery and warm. No stinging this time, only a delightful tingle on the tongue. After the pie came acorn griddlecakes and thick yellow custard, all washed down with jugfuls of hot damson brew.

'A toast!' said Pa, getting to his feet. 'To my brave daughter, and her brave friends.' Portuna flickered a happy crimson. 'I didn't sleep a wink while you were gone,' he said, shaking his tufted head. 'And I know there will be many sleepless nights to come. There is wickedness at work in this forest, no doubt about it, and terrible danger lies ahead.'

The rebels murmured and nodded.

'But tonight, we are together.' Pa raised his cup high in the air. 'Ley for all! Forever!'

'Forever!' the others chorused.

As the company ate and drank their fill, the mood grew merrier. Pa and Perig puffed on a sweet-smelling pipe, nodding and chortling as they reminisced about old times while, at the other end of the table, Portuna reenacted Hazel's scrap with the professor's cat, hissing and clawing the air.

Arden's eyes sparkled with cheer. 'There's hope now. What you've both done – it brings real hope.'

'Will I get a mention in your next book?' Portuna grinned.

'Ha!' said Arden. 'We'll see.'

When the last dish had been scraped clean, Spud gave a sleepy sigh and pushed himself away from the table, rubbing his taut belly. But there was no time for dozing.

'Look lively!' said Perig, flicking a pastry crumb at him. 'There's work to be done.'

Once the plates had been cleared, Perig hauled Erith's satchel onto the middle of the table. The company hushed down and drew their stools in closer, eyeing the old deerskin bag intently. Hazel unpacked the contents, placing each item carefully on the tabletop.

Amongst Erith's belongings were a small set of scales, a detailed map of the forest and a tarnished water-compass.

'Look here,' said Perig, picking up the compass and turning it between his fingers.

Hazel saw that it was double-sided.

'This side tells you where you are,' said Perig, pointing at a normal compass-face marked *North*, 'and this side –' he flipped it over to reveal an unmarked face with another floating needle – 'this side will guide you to where the Ley runs strongest. Your ma's invention. Clever, eh?' He handed it to her.

Hazel nodded and studied it for a moment, heavy in her hand.

But most precious of all were the dozens of magical vials. Perig slid each one from its leather strap and placed it on a crumpled tea towel to stop it from rolling away. The rebels handled them gingerly, holding their contents to the amber-light, and muttering to themselves as they deciphered the scrawled labels.

'Ooo!' cooed Sprout, pinching a cloudy glass tube between his fingers. 'This one's for thunderstorms!' He began to untwist the cork.

'Don't you dare!' growled Perig, snatching it from his hands. 'Tsk, tsk, I'll give you thunderstorms!' He pushed the cork in firmly with his thumb and passed it to Arden for safe-keeping. Sprout grumbled and turned his attention to the copper instruments, while Portuna delved deeper into the satchel.

As the others quietly examined Erith's belongings, Hazel told Perig about Grinling's mysterious visitor.

'Emmett Verne,' she said. 'I don't know who he is, but Professor Grinling seemed afraid of him.' Perig raised his tangled eyebrows. 'He said something about them both getting rich – very rich.'

The wizard spluttered in disgust. 'Clayfeet,' he muttered. 'Gold, gold, gold – that's all they think about!'

'And they said the Fae know I'm in Goblyn,' Hazel added, 'that they're "skittish".'

Perig huffed with wry amusement. 'I should think they are.' He picked some seeds out of a pinecone and chewed them thoughtfully. 'Emmett Verne,' he muttered. 'Never heard of him. But it troubles me. What are the Fae doing meddling with humans? That's what I want to know.' He frowned and shook his head. 'Don't smell right.'

Hazel was about to ask a question when there was a gasp from the other end of the table.

'Look, Hazel!' said Portuna. 'This one's for you!' She was holding a vial aloft, wiggling it lightly between her fingers.

'What do you mean?' said Hazel.

Portuna reached across the table and handed her the small, corked tube. It looked just like the others and was filled to the brim with a clear, watery fluid. Hazel turned over the tag. There, in her mother's handwriting, were two words that sucked the breath from her lungs: *For Hazel*.

'Where did you find it?' she whispered. Portuna opened up the satchel and showed her the lining.

'Here,' she said, pointing to a torn seam. 'It was sewn in.'

252

The twins scurried to Hazel's side to get a better look.

'Open it!' said Spud.

Hazel held the vial between thumb and finger, a painful fullness in her chest.

'Go on!' urged Sprout. 'Pop it open. Let's see what happens!'

At that, Arden gave him a cuff round the ear. 'Quiet!' she snapped. 'It belongs to Hazel.'

Perig ushered the boys gently back to their stools. 'Indeed,' he said. 'Don't open it now. Wait until it feels right.'

Hazel couldn't take her eyes off her own name, written in her mother's hand. While the other labels had been hurriedly scribbled, this one looked as if it had been printed with care.

'Do you know what it does?' she asked Perig. 'Or how I'm supposed to use it?' She felt tremors building inside. 'Do I drink it? Pour it on something ...?' Suddenly she thought she might cry.

Perig sat down beside her.

'I don't know what it does,' he said kindly, 'but it's a gift from your ma. It's something she wanted you to have. Something you need.' He folded her fingers around the vial. 'Now, keep it safe. You'll know when to open it.'

That night, as she slept in the Babbages' warm burrow, Hazel dreamed the same dream that had come to her on her first night in the Hollows – only this time the details were clearer. She was sinking, water filling her ears, legs pedalling. The sun flashed above her, cool currents tugged at her feet. Then, just as panic set in, quick arms pulled her to the surface and held her tight.

When her eyes blinked open the next morning, she felt strangely stronger, as though somebody had set her down on solid earth. She swung her legs out of the hammock and, as she breathed in the rich smell of the soil, she felt as if every nerve in her body were tangling and joining with the roots and tubers of the trees above. She heard the march of ants through their nests, felt the heartbeats of furred creatures in their burrows and dens – all the life of the forest, stirring within her.

'There she is.' Perig smiled as Hazel hurried to the breakfast table, tugging her tunic over her head. She pulled up a stool and Portuna tossed her a hard-boiled duck egg.

'Here you go, slow-worm,' she said. 'I saved one for you.'

'Thanks.' Hazel smiled, peeling the pale blue shell.

Pa had taken the Babbage clan down to the market early, so the rebels had the burrow to themselves. Erith's map of the woods was smoothed over the table and Perig and Arden were leaning over it. As they quietly studied its lines and contours, the twins wrapped pies in waxy paper, filling the six small backpacks propped against a wall. Preparations were underway for their journey to the Knoll and the air was charged with nervous energy.

'Knoll's here,' said Perig, pointing to a huge hill rising in the north-east of the forest. 'Wildermist all around it.' He circled it with his finger. 'Should take us two days to get near.' He planted a pin on the hill and began to mark a route with a long thread. 'This is the safest way, I reckon. Trees are friendlier down by the Morrow. They'll give warning of any prowling Arboreans.' He traced his finger alongside the thread. 'Then we'll have to cross over Withy Hill. The Ley is weak there, I hear, so it should be deserted. But we'll have to make haste. After that I say we head for Grendel Pond.'

Hazel, Arden and Portuna huddled round the table and listened closely as Perig described the journey ahead. Once through the Wildermist, they would be within the Fae's dominion.

'Nobody knows what lies inside the Knoll,' he said, 'nor what form the Fae have taken after all these years. Time don't run smooth there. The belly of those hills ain't governed by the sun and stars. It's vaster too – higher and deeper. Some say there's a crystal city inside that mountain, others tell of a fortress of shadows. But one thing's for sure: the Ley runs rich. The Fae tell us the Fadings are part of the natural turn of the world, but *we* know they are sucking the forest dry. We must find proof, and bring it back.'

'What sort of proof?' asked Portuna.

'Rock,' said Perig. 'Not any rock, mind. A nice chunk of greenstone's what we need, fresh from the heart of the Knoll. Mark my words, there's more Ley in a chip of Fae greenstone than the lot of us put together.' He looked at each of them in turn. 'Folks need to see for themselves; see that while their families suffer and fade, the Fae are hoarding life, growing stronger by the day. If that doesn't make 'em flare up with rage, I don't know what will.'

'And the captured?' said Hazel.

'We find 'em,' said Perig. 'And we bring 'em home.' The wizard flipped the map over and began to draw a web of intersecting lines with the blackened edge of a cork.

As he worked, Hazel became aware of a hushed muttering near the backpacks. The twins were crouched on the ground, Arden's pack between them. They had dug out the moleskin pouch and Spud was holding the bottle of TRUE SIGHT between his fingers.

'Put it back!' hissed Sprout, reaching to take it.

'No, but look!' said Spud.

Sprout took the bottle and squinted at it. His face fell.

'What's going on?' said Perig, glancing up from the map. 'Oh! You put that back, right now!' He lunged towards them.

'But, Perig, look!' said Spud. 'There's only a few drops!'

Perig pulled up short. 'What do you mean?'

Sprout looked up with anxious eyes. 'We can't all go.'

The wizard took the bottle and held it up to the glowing amber. As he turned the charm between his fingers, the lines on his face deepened to a worried frown. Arden and Portuna hurried to his side, glimmering nervously.

Perig returned to the table and opened Erith's satchel. He delved inside, pulling out notebooks and flicking hurriedly through them. 'If we can find the formula,' he muttered, 'the right proportions, we can make more.' He tugged anxiously on his long moustache. 'She must've written it down somewhere . . .'

'There's no *time* for that, Perig,' said Arden, shaking her head. 'Goblyn will be dust by then.'

The wizard stopped rummaging and planted his knuckles on the table, brow creased. The rebels sat in a numb silence. For a moment, all that could be heard were the muffled shouts of the market floating through the shutters. But Hazel's heart was quickening.

She didn't have to think about what she said next. The words just tumbled out in a heap.

'I'll go . . . me. I'll do it.'

The others stared at her.

'Now, now, hold on a minute . . .' Perig frowned, waggling a finger, but Hazel wasn't listening. A bright energy crackled through her. All at once, she felt a stretching and rustling within: the creatures that lived inside her sniffing the air, pawing the ground.

'I'll go,' she repeated. 'It has to be me. It was my mum's mission. Now it's mine.'

Her friends watched her silently.

'I used to be scared of everything,' she said, 'of myself especially. I had no idea what I could do, or who I was. But you all showed me.'

The wizard's face was cragged with worry, but there was

something else there too. Amongst those deep and broken lines were seams of glimmering hope.

'You told me that when my magic was full, I'd know it,' Hazel said. 'Well, I know it now. It's here. It's running through me. It's in every part of me. It *is* me.' She looked round at her friends. Her eyes were flickering with their strange, changeable light; a fire of golds and greens. 'I'm ready. Please. It *has* to be me.'

CHAPTER THIRTY-FIVE

The Prophecy

THE NIGHT HAD BROUGHT A BRIEF GUST OF snow, patching the forest floor with white. Hazel and Portuna waited, arm in arm, on a fungus-frilled stump while Perig kneeled on the ground, trying to stuff an extra food parcel into Hazel's pack.

'I wish I could come with you,' Portuna whispered.

'Me too.' Hazel smiled.

'I'm good in a fight.'

'I know.'

Portuna was silent for a moment. 'Are you afraid?'

Hazel didn't know how to answer. For as long as she could remember, fear had dragged behind her like an anchor. But now, by some mysterious alchemy, it had transformed from a leaden weight into a silvery quickness, a cold fire in her veins. Portuna smiled and tweaked Hazel's nose.

'You can do it,' she said. 'I know you can. And then we fight – together!'

Hazel squeezed Portuna to her side. 'Together,' she said.

At last, Perig fastened the buckle of Hazel's pack.

'Done!' he said, hauling himself to his feet. 'I'll take you as far as the river, in case of mischief. After that you'd best move alone.' He'd hardly slept and his face was ragged, but he was keeping up a nervous cheer.

Just then, Arden and the twins appeared from between the trees. Spud ran to her with a small wrapped parcel.

'Pear cake,' he said, 'for the journey.'

'We made it ourselves,' added Sprout happily.

'My favourite.' Hazel smiled. 'Thank you.'

The twins flung their arms round her, burying their grubby faces in her shoulders.

When, finally, they let go, Arden stepped forward, hugged her tightly, then stepped back again. 'You're one of us,' she said. 'I know you can do this.' She tapped the wound that was still healing at her hairline. 'I've seen it for myself.'

'I won't let you down this time,' said Hazel. 'I promise.'

Then it was Portuna's turn to say goodbye. Her light was rippling brightly and she was bouncing up and down on her toes. She didn't say a word but wrapped Hazel in a hug so fierce and sudden it squeezed the breath out of her.

The girls clasped one another, two halves of a nut, while the others clustered closely round them. And, as Hazel stood, circled by her friends and sheltered by the spreading branches of oak and ash, the journey ahead seemed suddenly less daunting, the ground beneath her feet more solid.

She kissed Portuna on the tip of her nose then set off with Perig into the waiting woods.

It was still early. A little tangled mist flossed the briar. Somewhere in the undergrowth, larks were nesting, but the morning air was too cold for their delicate throats and the woods hung still and quiet. Perig seemed absorbed in his thoughts. Soon all Hazel could hear was the hiss of frost beneath her feet and the thump of the wizard's staff.

The wide path rose steadily between the silver beeches before levelling off and continuing beneath a pale ribbon of sky. All the while, they kept their ears open, listening for any crack or rustle that could signal the presence of a stalking enemy. But besides the occasional whirr of wings, nothing broke the quivering silence.

At length, the path began to descend and narrow until it sunk down into a shady holloway where shrubby trees curled over them on either side. Here the earth was well-trodden, churned into large frozen clods. Hazel kept her eyes to the ground, taking care not to lose her footing on the icy clumps. Then, as she stepped around a solid puddle, she saw, pressed into the mud, the unmistakable crescent of a horse's hoof.

'Perig,' she whispered. 'Look!'

Perig came to her side and, leaning on his staff, inspected the hoofprint. 'Old,' he sniffed. 'Could've been made days ago.'

Hazel nodded, reassured, though as they continued down

the sunken path, she sharpened her ears and glanced more frequently over her shoulder.

Gradually, the light grew clearer, then they were out of the holloway and walking through scrubbier woodland where nettles and holly grew wild on either side. Before long, they saw the glint of water through the trees. Hazel knew that they were approaching the Morrow and, with it, the moment when Perig would leave her.

She glanced across at the wizard. There was a question that she had been meaning to ask ever since her return from the professor's.

'Perig?' she said. 'Can I ask you something?'

'Always,' he replied.

'Mr Verne,' she began, 'he said something about Fae superstitions, and prophecies.' She noticed Perig startle. 'What prophecies?'

The wizard took a few more steps in silence then cleared his throat. 'Well,' he said uncomfortably, 'it's all hogweed if you ask me.'

'What is?'

Perig frowned and scratched the side of his large nose. 'Do you really want to know?'

'I do,' Hazel insisted.

'All right, then.' He sighed. 'At the time of the Old Wars, there was a foretelling that a slipskin – part human, part fairy – would be the undoing of the Fae. That's why they fear you. That's why they hunt you down.'

Hazel stopped and stared at him. 'Why didn't you tell me?'

'Because it's hogweed. That's why,' he said, a snap in his voice. 'Reading the future's like seeing pictures in the clouds. *You* see horses, *I* see rabbits. Then the wind blows and everything changes.' He thumped his staff on the ground. 'Prophecies, foretellings – no proper wizard touches that stuff!'

Hazel shook her head in dismay. 'You still should have told me.'

Perig's breath wreathed about him, thick and white. Then his gaze softened. 'You're right. I should have told you, but believing the future's all mapped out?' He knocked on the side of his head. 'It addles the brain. Makes for false hope, and false despair. Tomorrow's ours to make, that's what I think. That's real hope.'

Hazel thought for a moment then nodded. 'I understand,' she said uncertainly. ' . . . I think.'

'Now put it out of your mind,' he said, kindly but firmly. 'It won't help none.' Perig placed a reassuring hand on her shoulder and she felt a little calmer.

They walked on together until they reached the ice-crusted edges of the Morrow.

'Best I leave you here,' said Perig. Hazel nodded as he passed her the knapsack. 'Now remember, keep moving or keep hidden. Don't use your powers unless you have to – you need to save your strength.' He tapped the side of his nose. 'And trust your instincts. No funny berries.'

263

'No funny berries.' Hazel smiled. 'I promise.'

Perig looked down at her and chuckled – a warm chuckle that melted the tension they both felt.

'You're just like your ma,' he said. Then he gave her a mighty hug, full of tenderness, before turning and walking away, feet crunching heavily on the snow-speckled earth.

Hazel watched until he was a distant smudge on the mist. Somewhere nearby a thrush was cracking a snail against a stone; in the hollow of a fallen tree, an adder stretched its coils. She was alone in the woods.

A momentary flicker of panic made her reach for the pendant of her necklace. It was there, where it always was, warm and heavy between her fingers. She took a deep breath and made a mental check of her supplies.

She had brought her mother's double-faced compass and map of the forest, Perig's sharpest rock-pick and hammer and as many of Pa's acorn cakes as would fit. In the pocket of the pack were a selection of vials, all snugly wrapped in clumps of moss and, safe in the breast pocket of her tunic, was the bottle containing the few precious drops of TRUE SIGHT – just enough for her to get there and back again, with Pete. She patted it gently through the fabric of her cloak, then she shrugged her pack onto her shoulders and set off down the banks of the Morrow.

As Perig had predicted, the way by the river was sure and safe. Hazel could sense the alder trees watching and muttering, stretching their slim branches to shelter her.

She stayed as close to the river's banks as she could, moving swiftly amongst the mossy rocks and roots. As time slipped by with no whiff of danger, she walked more steadily, eyes on the path ahead. Toads called in marshy pockets; a beaver returned to a snow-dusted lodge, a stick in its toothy muzzle. The life of the winter forest breathed around her, and she moved easily to its rhythm.

After some hours she grew hungry and stopped to eat at the water's edge. A luminous blanket of cloud covered the sky. As she swallowed the last of the twins' pear cake, Hazel felt an alert calm. On the far side of the river, the blue fire of a kingfisher flashed down into the water. She thought of her father out with his binoculars, watching for birds along those same riverbanks. She imagined him meeting her mother there, amongst the bullrushes. Then, as she gazed down into the dark glass of the river, a memory deep within her stirred. Something long-buried was rising slowly to the surface. She tried to grasp it, but it darted away like a minnow.

She unfolded her map and traced the route ahead with her finger. Then she checked her compass and set off once more, keen to make the most of the daylight.

As her route dragged her away from the riverbank, Hazel felt the air become thinner and drier, the woods more bare and grey. With a growing sense of unease, she saw that the undergrowth was badly faded. Woodruff and parsley stood stalky and snapped; claws of hemlock curled into withered fists. The further she walked the more brittle the woods became, until even the tallest trees stood stark and skeletal, branches clotted with abandoned nests.

Hazel paused and sniffed the air, hoping to detect a pocket of living warmth. But there was no reek of foxes or fresh dung, no recently turned earth, only the crumbling scent of dried fur and mouse bones. A shiver ran over her scalp. She hoisted her knapsack up her shoulders and picked up the pace.

By the time she stepped out from the sparse cover of the forest, the pulse of the Ley had dwindled to a murmur. Rising up ahead of her was Withy Hill. Hazel cast her eyes over the stricken landscape and gasped.

It was almost impossible to imagine the hill before the Fading had taken hold. She forced herself to picture thick, dewy grass, rustling copses of bird-filled trees, the drone of bees over heather. Now it was entirely bald save for a few broken stumps, half crumbled to dust. Here and there, the slope was pitted with rabbit holes, but as she gazed at their empty sockets, she knew nothing breathed within. The only sign of life was a scatter of crows orbiting overhead, and even they did not linger.

Suddenly, she felt a dreadful sickening in her stomach. Already, the white earth was sapping her energy, blunting her powers. She fixed her eyes on the ridge of the hill and set off upwards, concentrating on the rhythm of her footfalls, trying to ignore the silence of things long dead.

Her pace was steady, but she hadn't made it to the ridge before a weakness crept into her limbs. With a shudder, she remembered the boy in the tunnel, how suddenly he had faded. She had to make it to the forest beyond the hill before she succumbed.

She struggled on upwards, half walking, half crawling, until she crested the mound. The line of trees stood thickly at the bottom of the slope. Though her vision was blurring, she could see that the undergrowth was thicker there and dusted with snow. But by now her lungs were parched and she felt as if the ground were tipping beneath her. Then, as she started downhill, her foot caught in a rut and she went tumbling and skidding, head over heels, halfway down the slope.

She lay flat on her back, gasping like a fish out of water. The thirsty earth was leaching her remaining energy, the edges of her vision darkening. Gripped with panic, she struggled, half blind, to her knees. The forest was only a short stretch away now, yet it seemed impossibly far. Her limbs were leaden, the earth pulling down on her like a magnet. Then, as the world began to spin, she remembered Portuna's voice in the tunnels – a bright voice that cut through the mists: *Can you run? Here, hold my hand. We'll be there in no time!*

Summoning a last rush of energy, Hazel surged to her feet and ran, tripping and stumbling, for the safety of the trees.

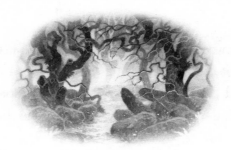

CHAPTER THIRTY-SIX

Wych Elm

AZEL LEANED AGAINST A TRUNK AND retched, the world heaving and rolling. Dizzily, she staggered on, deeper into the woods until, at last, she could feel the Ley strengthening again – life waiting in the buried bulbs and chestnuts beneath her bare feet.

But her legs were still heavy and her lungs felt shrunken and shallow. She stopped to catch her breath. Her magic was weak, she could tell. It needed time to recover.

A stone's throw ahead, she spied the low-drooping boughs of a wych elm. Its branches writhed downwards to form a tangled dome where she could rest out of sight. Pulling the spindly shoots aside, she climbed into its shadows and sat with her back resting against the bark. Her mouth was still parched from the arid air of Withy Hill, so she took the vial marked FOR THIRST from the pocket of her pack and shook a drop onto her tongue. Instantly, a cooling wave washed down her throat, as though she'd drunk from a deep flask. She coughed and spluttered a moment then, thirst quenched, she hugged her pack to her stomach and settled down to doze in the thick shade of the tree.

As she curled up in the shadows, she felt warm energy rising from shimmering underground channels, lulling her into a light and dreamy sleep.

Peaceful images floated by like bubbles on a stream. She saw herself back in the Babbages' burrow. The amber was aglow, and her friends were gathered round the cherrywood table listening to Portuna tell one of her outlandish stories. Perig was polishing a chunk of crystal on his cloak and, by Hazel's side, laughing with the others, was Pete.

It was a lovely dream. So lovely that Hazel resisted waking. But a tiny movement disturbed her.

At first she ignored it. She shifted position, trying to slide back into her fading dream. Then she felt it again – a slithering creak, as if the elm's roots were shifting beneath her. All at once, there was a hard rattle. Her eyes flicked open and she gasped in fright.

The elm's spidery branches were shaking and hissing with unmistakable malice. New shoots sprouted, knitting a quickly thickening web around her, closing her in. Hazel grabbed her pack and struggled to her feet, tearing at the twines that knotted about her, curling round her wrists and ankles, reaching for her throat.

'Let go!' she cried. 'Get off me!'

In a rush of panic, she threw her whole weight forward

towards the dwindling light. The tendrils round her ankles sent her tumbling to the ground, but it was enough for her to wrench herself free and scramble away.

As soon as she was beyond the reach of the strangling twines, she turned and stared back, aghast. The wych elm crackled blackly, muttering its curses, then with a sharp rattle, fell silent.

Hazel wiped a trickle of blood from her cheek and looked warily up at the stark lines of the surrounding trees. This side of the woods was altogether different. Here, the trees were not allies or protectors, but crowded thickly around her, watchful and malevolent.

Hurriedly, she took out her compass and map and studied Perig's route. The Knoll was still more than a day's journey away, and the light was fading, but she couldn't stay in this part of the forest. She waited for the floating needle of the compass to settle, then she pulled up her hood and continued north-eastwards towards Grendel Pond.

The woods were snarled and trackless and after a while it began to snow – fine crystals at first, then large, silent feathers that layered quickly on the forest floor. She pushed on, the thickening silence broken only by the occasional burst of birds, black across the white sky. The snow creaked steadily beneath her feet, leaving a long, lonely trail of footprints. Every muscle in her body cramped and ached and, as the shadows began to gather, she looked more and more urgently for some sign of Grendel Pond.

It was then that she felt a grim sense of foreboding. She stopped dead and focused her senses. She smelled the rot of the leaves beneath the snow, heard the slow creep of ivy up an elder. But there was something else too: an imbalance, a wavering of the air around her. She squinted through the fast-falling puzzle of snowflakes and lurched back in shock.

Up ahead, hunched and black in the darkening wood, was the wych elm – the very one she had escaped from, hours before.

Goosebumps rose on her arms. She pulled the map from her pocket and stared at it in disbelief. Had she turned in a circle? She checked her compass but the needle was steady. With a sudden chill, she understood. *She* hadn't gone astray. It was the trees. They had shifted around her, changing places in the blink of an eye.

She looked helplessly back at the map, but before she could find her bearings, a wind rose from nowhere and snatched it from her hands, sending it dancing upwards through the wet flakes. Hazel leaped to catch it but it spiralled away. In a wild panic, she followed the map through the forest, leaping again and again as it flapped and tore on the unnatural wind. It was tumbling above her, just out of reach, when suddenly a streak of silver split the air. There was a hiss, a thud and a scatter of snow.

She looked up to see the map pinned to the bark of a yew, pierced by a long, silver arrow.

CHAPTER THIRTY-SEVEN

Ruis

THE TREES DREW BACK TO MAKE WAY FOR THE Arborean captain. Hazel stood rigid in the snow, every inch of her bristling. High on his nacreous horse, Ruis glided towards her, face gleaming like a skull, body brimming with violence. His fingers tugged lightly on the reins, bringing his steed to a smooth halt. For a moment, all was silent, the only sound that of the settling snow. Then Ruis spoke.

'These woods are wary of strangers,' he said in a voice that parched the air. Hazel did not reply. Ruis's lips curled. 'Brings out the mischief in them.' He stepped his horse closer and peered down at her with a fascinated disgust. Under his gaze, she felt like some rare and revolting insect – a blot on the crystal-white snow. Ruis watched her, unblinking, eyes pale and opaque. 'I see your friends have abandoned you,' he said with a sniff of amused contempt. Hazel remained stubbornly silent. She knew he was goading her – prodding and flicking like a curious cat. 'But you're not as defenceless as you seem, are you?' Hazel looked up at him, sensing the trap closing round her.

Ruis pressed a heel to his horse's flank and began to circle slowly – head tilted to one side, eyes narrowing.

'I knew I'd seen you before,' he rasped. 'I couldn't place it at first, but then I remembered. You were in that clearing. On the western edge.'

Hazel's heart clenched as, all at once, that first terrible night in Goblyn Wood came rushing back – the staggering blow that sent her sprawling; Pete wrenched away, crying out in terror.

Ruis leaned down towards her. 'You were with that boy. That *clayfoot* boy.' His top lip curled upwards in distaste, baring sharp teeth. 'A dirty clayfoot.'

At the mention of Pete, the forest blurred. Hazel's pupils shrank around Ruis until all she could see, in searing focus, was his hateful sneer.

'But then,' he said, eyes veiling over, 'you're not pure fairy either, are you?'

For a heartbeat everything slowed, petals of snow caught mid-flight. Hazel felt an intense heat spreading from her heart to the tips of her fingers, the soles of her feet, the roots of her hair. Then, as if something deep within her had broken free, a colossal ferocity surged up from the core of her being. The horse whinnied and skittered backwards, green eyes flashing, as the girl in the snow transformed.

Her body grew and bulked: bones stretching, muscles thickening, skin prickling with bristling fur. Claws curled from heavy paws, teeth grew as pointed as daggers.

The bear rose up on her back legs and roared – a shuddering, gut-twisting roar that ripped a hole through the heart of the forest.

Ruis's horse reared and wheeled round, throwing its rider into the snow. Then it turned and bolted through the trees in a spray of powdery white. Instantly, Ruis sprang to his feet, eyes burning with a wild blue fire. For a stretched second Ruis and Hazel stared at each other, pupils locked. Then, quick as a whip, Ruis pulled an arrow from his quiver and drew his bow. But she was ready to strike and, with one weighty swing of her paw, she slashed him down, sending the bow spinning into a snowdrift.

Spitting and growling, Hazel paced back and forth, warm breath wreathing in the freezing air. She had struck hard, but within moments, Ruis was up again, a wicked grin spreading from ear to ear. Crackling with a greenish light, his limbs were far stronger and nimbler than any human's. He rushed towards her; she charged back; but this time Ruis seized her with muscular hands and flung her into the trunk of a tree. Her skull smacked against the frozen bark and she slumped heavily to the ground. Huffing and groaning, Hazel rolled unsteadily back onto her paws, the forest dipping and rising. Hot blood was dripping from her fur, staining the new-fallen snow. Shakily, she turned to face Ruis. But he had gone.

The woods were windless and still. The snow had stopped falling, leaving a twinkling expanse of white. Frantically, she swung around, searching the silent alleys of woodland. But there was not so much as a footprint. She sniffed the air with her steaming muzzle, tuned her soft ears to the muffled forest. Listening deeply, she heard the static crackle of settling snowflakes, the puff of her own breath. Then beneath the deadening white, she detected a muttering. The trees. They were conspiring, plotting.

From out of the shadows came a freezing gust of laughter – a hollow rattle that shook her to the bones. Hazel turned wildly in circles, snapping and snarling. She tried to source the sound, but the trees muddled the echoes, netting her in a web of howls. Blood from her wound streamed into her eyes, her head throbbed and pounded. Then the shadows shuddered and Ruis was upon her.

He clung to her back, arms lashed tightly round her throat. She bellowed and tried to throw him, but he was crushing her, sapping the life from her. She gasped for breath as her body began to weaken and shrink, returning to its human form.

Ruis released his grip and let her fall to the ground. He towered over her, blazing with a cold blue light.

'I know who you are,' he said, gasping from the rush of the fight. 'I've hunted you for eleven years.' With one swift hand he grasped Hazel by the throat, lifted her into the air and pinned her against the trunk of a tree. His face was mask-like in the reflected moonlight, lips twisted upwards in glee.

'You look just like her,' he hissed, eyes freezing to white. 'You're the water witch's child.'

The rings on his fingers pressed hard into her neck and, as her magic sapped away, she felt as if her whole body was emptying, shrivelling to a husk. Then, just as darkness began to crowd her vision, Ruis's grin faded, his hand fell away and he dropped limply into the snow, a feathered arrow quivering in the centre of his back.

Behind the spot where Ruis had stood, between the silver trees, a hooded figure lowered a bow. Hazel blinked in astonishment as the figure rushed towards her through the glittering white. The woman had brambled hair like her own, eyes that glimmered with a fairy light and, the moment she seized Hazel in her strong arms and pressed her to her chest, she knew it was Erith, her mother.

CHAPTER THIRTY-EIGHT

Beneath the Willow Tree

OWLS WATCHED, EYES GLOWING, AS A WOMAN carried her child through the forest.

'Hazel,' Erith whispered, trudging swiftly through the snowdrifts. 'My girl!' Hazel looked up at the long-forgotten face, unable to speak.

It was a strong-boned face with soft lines that spread from the corners of her eyes like sun-rays. Her cheeks were flushed dark red in the cold air, warm breath steaming from her nose and lips. It was the loveliest face Hazel had ever seen.

'Don't worry,' said Erith. 'You're going to be fine. Just a scrape, that's all. I'll patch you right up.'

Not taking her eyes off her, Hazel touched her fingers to her blood-matted hair, then she leaned her head on her mother's broad shoulder and breathed in the musky smell of her cape.

At length, they approached a small shack, tucked

beneath the weeping branches of a willow. Cobbled together from sticks and stones, it looked as if it had grown out of the forest itself. Bearded lichens climbed its sides and clusters of tiny toadstools sprouted from a mossy roof. There, a crooked chimney puffed out a trail of silvery smoke. Erith pulled aside a curtain of reeds, brought Hazel into the warmth and settled her down on a thick straw mattress.

Inside, the shack had the sweet, fungal smell of a witch's den. Bundles of marjoram, rosemary, sage and yarrow were strung from the cobwebbed ceiling alongside dried mushrooms of all shapes and varieties: shrivelled wood-ears, balls of bearded tooth and clusters of candle snuff antlered like woodland coral. And then there were the shelves: shelf upon creaking shelf of water-filled bottles, jars and vials, all glinting in the light of the hearth.

As Erith busied about, mixing a potion, Hazel followed her steadily with her eyes, afraid that if she so much as blinked, she might vanish again and never return.

'Hold still now,' said Erith as she dabbed a clean rag in a bowlful of steaming water. With deft fingers, she parted Hazel's hair and swabbed the liquid onto the cut. It stung sharply, then she heard a faint hissing and felt the wound puckering to a scar.

'There!' Erith smiled, looking pleased with her handiwork. Hazel touched the scar with her fingertips. It felt knobbled and dry.

For a moment, Erith and Hazel gazed at each other in raw amazement, then they held each other tightly.

'You're here,' whispered Erith, kissing her daughter firmly on the forehead. 'You're really here!'

Hazel's heart broke with happiness.

That night, Hazel curled up with her mother by the flickering fire. In the furry folds of Erith's cloak, she slept a deep and heavy sleep, untroubled by even the faintest murmur of a dream. She did not stir until a warbler trilled in the willow fronds outside.

A bluish light was filtering into the shack, and there was a clean rasp of winter in the air. Erith was already awake, quietly grinding seedpods in a mortar. Hazel watched in silence for a moment. Her mother's knotted mane was tied back from her face, and Hazel could see the amber flicker of her eyes beneath heavy lashes. She drew a breath of amazement. Erith was all she had hoped for, all she had dreamed of when, lying in that distant dormitory, she had held the stone of her necklace and wondered how different her life might have been.

Erith caught Hazel's eye and smiled.

'Good morning, my girl!'

Hazel sat up and rubbed her eyes. As the fur cloak fell from her shoulders she shivered in the morning chill.

'I'll make up a fire,' said Erith. 'Get yourself washed and dressed, and wrap up warm. It's cold as a ditch out there.'

While Erith stoked the embers and cobbled breakfast together, Hazel splashed herself at a basin and hurriedly pulled on her trousers and tunic.

As they sat on the coarsely woven mat, eating stewed crab apple and beech-nuts, Hazel tried to unravel her thoughts. She had so many questions she didn't know where to begin. But it was Erith who spoke first.

'I've been trapped here,' she said. 'For years.' The soft lines on her face deepened. 'That's why I couldn't come back for you, Hazel. I'm so sorry.'

Hazel looked up from her bowl. 'Perig said you'd been killed.'

Erith huffed quietly and shook her head.

'Ah, Perig. He must have thought that. But no, I've been a prisoner *here*, in this wandering wood.' Hazel thought of the wych elm, how it had seemed to drift and change places. 'It's a long story, Hazel.' She put down her bowl and took Hazel's hands in her own. They were rough and warm. 'But you must tell me everything. Are you well? How did you come to the forest? Did Perig bring you here?'

Hazel looked into Erith's searching eyes. She wanted to speak, she wanted to tell her mother everything, but she felt a lump in her throat and the words wouldn't come.

'It's all right,' said Erith, rubbing Hazel's hands. 'You've crossed a storm haven't you? I can tell.' She leaned forward and kissed her on the nose. 'No rush. There's time for all that.'

Hazel nodded gratefully. Erith patted her hand, then stood and took their cloaks from pegs on the wall. 'Come with me,' she said. 'There's something I want to show you.'

It was still early morning. A bubble of moon floated in the dawn sky and the forest glowed pink and violet all around.

'It's not far,' said Erith, pulling Hazel's hood around her ears. 'You can climb, can't you?' Hazel nodded then, arm in arm, they trudged through the glimmering woods.

The forest had never seemed so beautiful. Trees drifted past them, luminous and billowing with downy snow. Up ahead, a hare loped gracefully home. In the light of the morning, Hazel could see the clear, strong lines of her mother's profile, her features slightly pointed, just like her own.

'Here,' said Erith, stopping at the base of a giant beech. She swept a mound of snow from the lowest branch and hauled herself up. 'Follow me.' Hazel followed in her mother's footholds, up through the tree's muscular limbs. Once they were high above the forest floor, Erith swung herself onto a broad bough and pulled Hazel up behind her.

Tucked in the crook of the branch, they gazed out across the woods to the white hills beyond. The sun was higher now and Hazel could hear the tinkle of dripping icicles. Erith pointed towards the west.

'Over there,' she said, 'is where I left you.' Hazel peered

into the distance. She could make out Ditchmoor's black cube in the haze – tiny, remote, a distant planet.

'For eight years, I've climbed this tree and stared out at that horizon wondering if you were happy, if people were kind to you, if I'd ever get out of this wood and find you again.' Erith's voice was muffled. 'But now you're here.' She smiled and hugged Hazel close to her. 'I can't believe it's really you.'

'Me neither,' said Hazel. Then she leaned into her mother's arms and clung to her tightly, afraid to ever let go.

That afternoon, Hazel and Erith foraged for acorns, blewits and waxcaps, never straying too far from the shack in case the woods muddled their path home. There were so many questions that Hazel wanted to ask, but somehow they never passed her lips and, as she walked by her mother's side, they drifted away like thistledown.

'I've had to start over, a few times,' said Erith, plucking a soft bloom of fungus from a fallen tree. 'I've become better at reading the mood of the forest. But you can never be certain. It's a wild thing after all.'

Hazel looked up at the bough-tangled sky.

'Don't worry,' said Erith. 'We won't be trapped here forever.' She beckoned for Hazel to come closer. 'I think the trees are softening towards me!' She gave her daughter a brisk peck on the forehead. 'Then we'll get out of here – together.'

By the time they straggled back home, Hazel's feet and fingers were aching with cold but her heart was blazing. As she sat by the fire, ripping sage for the evening meal, she began to tell Erith about her years at Ditchmoor. To her surprise, she found herself laughing and joking about the misery she'd endured there. It all felt so far away now – an ugly, improbable dream.

'Sometimes,' she said, sniffing a bunch of sage, 'sometimes Miss Fitch would lock us in the coal shed, just for *breathing* too loudly!'

'What?!' Erith gasped. 'If I'd known, I'd *never* have left you there – never!'

'Oh, it wasn't all bad.' Hazel shrugged. 'I had friends. Well . . . a friend.'

Hazel felt a stab of guilt. Since she'd arrived at the shack, she'd hardly thought about Pete at all.

A log was blackening in the fire, shivering with tiny flames. Then, as Hazel watched the bark disintegrating, she found with a bitter shock that even her memory of Pete's face was beginning to fade, features blurring, as though he were on the other side of thickening ice.

'Tell me about them,' said Erith. But Hazel didn't want to say any more. She shook her head awkwardly and changed the subject.

After they'd eaten, Erith put a fresh log on the fire and poured two cupfuls of a reddish tea. She passed one to Hazel. It had a subtle, earthy smell.

'What is it?' Hazel asked.

'Rosehip.'

'Rosehip?'

'My father's blend. Your grandfather's, in fact.' Erith took a sip and began to describe the protective properties of flowers, but as Hazel gazed into the steaming russet water, she was unable to listen. A question was forming. Or a doubt.

She stared silently at the scene around her. It was everything she had always hoped for, right down to the smallest detail: the crackling fire, the rosehip tea. It was as if it had all been teased from her deepest longings and woven into a beautiful dream, especially for her. She swallowed hard.

It was just like a dream. Too much like a dream. With a thickening sense of horror, she remembered Perig's words: *Mirage, shadow, vapour. That's the stuff of the Fae.*

Hazel felt a twist in the pit of her stomach. All at once, the comfortable shack beneath the willow and every object within it appeared weightless, unreal, as if, at any moment, it might waver then vanish into thin air.

She stared at the woman sitting by the fire, talking and crushing dried petals between her fingers – all her most secret desires, cut from her heart and made to dance before her eyes. She took a shaky breath and covered her face with her hands, hoping against hope that, when she took them away again, everything would go back to the way it had been just moments before.

'Hazel, are you feeling all right?' Erith's eyebrows were drawn together in concern. She leaned closer and pressed the back of her hand against Hazel's forehead. The touch of her fingers was firm and cool and, for a moment, the world seemed to steady.

'You're burning up.' She frowned. 'Let me mix something for you.'

Hazel watched as Erith selected clinking vials, poured droplets of magical water into a copper bowl and briskly stirred them together. The shack was warm, warmer than before, and Hazel felt a drowsiness spreading through her, fogging her thoughts. The scent of the rosehip was acrid and sweet, the fire hypnotic. All she wanted was to sink back into a blissful forgetting.

Then, glittering in the dusk outside, came the shrill note of a nightbird. Hazel held her breath and listened. The bird broke into full-throated song – sharp, musical whistles, that seemed to clarify the air. As the bird's song twirled around her, she remembered another whistle – a bright, three-note call that, on so many nights, had cracked the darkness and drawn her out of bed, down empty corridors, and up to the rooftops.

Hazel thought of Pete – his surprise gifts, his unlikely stories, his dreams of other possible lives – and, as the bird sang its heart out through the deepening night, his face sharpened again in her mind.

Hazel gazed at Erith. How she longed to believe it was

all real. How she longed to slip back into the comfort of life beneath the willow tree. But as the bird sang and sang, Hazel held onto the memory of Pete – alone, in danger, with no one coming to find him. She took a last look at the woman with the brambled hair, just like her own. She was everything Hazel had dreamed of. But she was not her mother.

Fingers trembling, she reached inside the pocket of her tunic and drew out the bottle of TRUE SIGHT. Then she shook the glowing droplets onto the tips of her fingers and wet her eyelids.

CHAPTER THIRTY-NINE

Falling

THE CHARM STUNG LIKE SALTWATER. FOR A moment, everything was still. Then, like a reflection disturbed by movement below, the willow shack rippled and shuddered. Hazel touched her fingers to the ground to steady herself and, suddenly, with a deafening roar, everything that had seemed so solid, so true, warped and twisted.

She held her breath as the earth gave way, tipping her into a churning whirlpool. Round and round she turned, spinning and falling, legs flailing, hands clutching air. The blood rushed to her fingers and toes until she thought she might tear apart like tissue in water. Then, all of a sudden, her body jolted awake.

She was lying in a soft drift of snow. Above her was the familiar criss-crossing of the branches and, beyond that, the depths of the night. She pushed herself up to sitting and saw that she was back in the glade where she had fought Ruis.

All around there was evidence of the fight. The snow was smashed and churned; giant claws had slashed the bark of an oak; a streak of fresh blood was seeping into the white. With shaking hands, Hazel touched her head and felt for the wound, but it was not there, not even a scar. She got to her feet and checked her body for a sign of injury. There wasn't a scratch, but her arm was heavy and aching. Then she understood.

On the ground beside her, melted through the snow, was a large patch of blackened earth. It was Ruis's shade, scorched on the soil. But there was no feathered arrow in sight. She rubbed her aching arm as she remembered the heavy swing of her paw that had cut him to the ground.

The rest had been an illusion, spun by the Wildermist.

Hazel stood numbly in the cold white woods. The creatures were huddled deep in their nests and burrows; the trees still as stone. Though the forest gathered densely around her, she felt surrounded by acres of emptiness. Images of Erith flickered through her mind, disintegrating quickly, remnants of a fading dream. Then they were gone.

Mechanically, she walked towards the map, still pinned to a yew tree by Ruis's silver dart. With a wrench, she pulled out the arrowhead and tried to unfold the torn and soggy paper. But her hands were trembling and her vision blurred by the tears that were now streaming uncontrollably down her cheeks.

She sat with her back against the trunk and tried to

smooth the paper onto her lap. But the map was a crumpled mess, wet and limp, its ink running in long black rivulets. In a burst of rage, she balled it up and hurled it into the snow. Then she drew her knees to her chest and wept.

The trees watched silently and the moon shone blankly down as Hazel crouched at the foot of the yew and sobbed.

It was the coldest hour of the night. Beads of frost collected on spiders' webs. Snowdrifts crusted over. Hazel knew she should take the form of a rabbit, owl or some other downy creature, and find a sheltered place to sleep, but every part of her was empty and aching and she couldn't muster the strength. Yet, deep within the bitter cold, there was a single speck of warmth.

The pendant of Hazel's necklace lay heavy on her chest, radiating a full and steady heat. She pulled it from her collar and clasped it between her freezing hands. And then she remembered.

Her pack was lying in the glade, half buried in the broken snow. She ran to it and rummaged inside until she found what she was looking for. Kneeling on the ground, she held the vial in her palm and turned over the label: *For Hazel*. She didn't need to think about what to do next: she held the vial upright and gently twisted the cork.

As soon as the cork came loose, the watery contents evaporated into luminous twists of vapour. For a moment they hovered, trembling before her, then they curled and looped around her body until she was entirely enveloped in a shimmering mist. It was as soft and warm as a blanket, wrapping round her shoulders, brushing against her cheeks and hair. Without knowing why, Hazel closed her eyes and then, slowly, she began to understand.

As she breathed the glimmering air into her lungs, her frozen senses started to revive. First there was a scent – the smell of warm skin, particular and indescribable, like no other scent in the world. And, as soon as it crackled through her brain she felt a swirling within, as if the strange but familiar smell had disturbed long-settled layers of her being. Then came the murmur of voices, two voices, rippling within her. She couldn't pick out the words but they were rising and falling, bursting into blooms of sudden laughter.

Then, like a flash of sun on water, a long-lost memory appeared in her mind's eye:

She was a tiny child. A smell of mushrooms, roasting chestnuts and squashed fruit filled the air. She heard chattering, shouting and the creak of heavy carts. All around her were the huge barrels and stalls of Understone market. Her hands were held either side by larger, stronger hands and as she walked through the marketplace, she jumped and swung forwards and backwards, feet brushing the ground.

Other memories followed. She remembered being chased in circles, round and round the standing stone, squealing and shrieking in panicked delight. She remembered the smell of rosemary soap and the feel of slippery hands rubbing her back and shoulders as she sat in a hot, cloudy bath. Then she was down at the river, learning to swim. Nose out of the sparkling water, she paddled forward with her hands, toes still touching the shingle until, suddenly, she was out of her depth. Her feet pedalled water, she slipped, gulping, beneath the surface. A flash of terror, then she was scooped up and held tight, her body pressed closely against that warm, indescribable skin.

As the missing memories swelled and flowed, Hazel felt the hollow space within her filling and closing and, as it did, her whole self took shape around it, everything fitting together, sliding into place.

She held the pendant of her necklace tightly in her hand. The stone was solid, indestructible – a fixed star at the centre of the universe. As its warmth spread through her, she felt every nerve quickening, every muscle, bone and fibre pulsing with a living fire. And, for the first time, she knew the fullness of her power. Every living creature, waiting within her. The whole world, now prowling, snarling, swooping – awake.

CHAPTER FORTY

The Knoll

HAZEL LOOKED UP AT THE STAR-FROSTED SKY. The winter air snipped at her cheeks and fingers but she no longer felt the cold. The forest was asleep, but beneath the crust of snow she could sense the first tingle of change. Midwinter had passed; the year was tilting. Hazel's heart expanded with hope.

She picked up her pack and got to her feet. It wouldn't be long before dawn, and she needed to find somewhere to rest. She eyed a comfortable-looking hole in a chestnut tree: round and deep, just right for a tawny owl. Her skin tingled in anticipation of a changing. Then, from far away, she heard music.

Hazel paused, motionless, and strained her ears. It was the chime of children's voices. At first the song was muffled by the snow, but before long it became clearer and sharper, pealing like silver bells. Curious, Hazel hurried through the woods towards it. Up ahead, many small lights winked between the stems of the trees. A long procession of children was trudging in her direction, swinging lanterns.

She crouched in a clump of bracken, out of sight. The children carried knapsacks and walked in orderly pairs, some with a cheerful bounce in their step. Eyes glowing faintly in the darkness, Hazel watched as they passed. By the shimmer of the lanterns she saw wide smiles and scrubbed faces. These were not Wild Children. There was not a rabbit pelt or bare foot in sight, only the coats and boots of villages and towns.

Her eye was drawn to a girl of her own age swinging her lantern loosely in her hand. She peered closely at her silhouette. There was something familiar about her shape and gait. Then a flash of light cast an upwards glow on her face and Hazel stifled a gasp. It was Elsie Pocket. She was stepping lightly along with the others, hair neatly braided, breath clouding in the cold night air. Hazel blinked in disbelief as she passed by, singing gaily. Was this another illusion? She touched her fingers to her eyelids, but they were still cool from the charm. Everything she saw was real.

As the procession flowed merrily past, Hazel noticed that the children were not alone. Shepherding them along were three figures in white winter capes – three women. Hazel parted the bracken to get a closer look at the woman at the back of the procession. She tried to catch a glimpse of her face, but it was hidden by a heavy hood. Then, just as she passed Hazel's hiding place, she paused. A small boy was tugging at her long skirts.

'I'm cold!' he grizzled. The woman stooped and pulled his woolly hat down over his ears.

'It's not much further, my darling,' she said in a voice that tinkled like a music box.

Hazel frowned. The voice was familiar, though she couldn't quite place it.

'No, no!' the child protested. 'I'm cold, I'm cold!' The woman crouched down to his level, then pulled back her hood to give him a kiss on the forehead. Hazel glimpsed her face in profile and at once, she knew. The elegant nose, the neatly drawn smile, the china-doll eyes. For years, Hazel had waited in a bare stone courtyard as those same eyes had flitted carelessly along lines of hopeful children. Without a doubt, these three women were the *Ladies*.

'We mustn't be late,' said the woman, who Hazel now recognised as the mother. 'They're waiting for us.' But the child wasn't happy. He bobbed up and down on his little legs and began to wail. The woman reached into her cape. 'Here.' She drew out a thick bar of chocolate and tore the corner of the silver wrapper. The child instantly stopped whimpering. She broke off a chunk and popped it in his mouth.

'Thank you, Mrs Verne,' he mumbled. 'Will we meet the fairies soon?'

'Very soon,' she whispered. 'Now come along.' She pulled her hood up around her face, took the boy's hand then hurried after the others.

At the mention of that name, Hazel's breath snagged in her throat.

Verne.

Her mind raced back to Professor Grinling's strange visitor – the man with the spidery hands and sneering voice – Mr Emmett Verne. She stared after the figure in the white cape. Was this woman his wife? She snatched at the fragments whirling through her mind, trying to piece them together. And, slowly, a hideous thought began to take shape.

She remembered the conversation in the professor's study. Verne had seemed angry, the professor cowed. Then one phrase floated back to her: 'They want *more*.' The Fae want more. Hazel looked at the merry lanterns up ahead, and suddenly it was clear. More children.

The procession was moving out of sight. Heart quickening, Hazel slipped into the shape of an owl, beat her wide wings and followed. As she ghosted silently below the branches, golden eyes fixed on the lanterns, she remembered the Ladies' visits to Ditchmoor – the white-gloved hands picking out the 'lucky' ones, whisking them away to a new life. Now she understood. They weren't taken to a family, they were brought here. To Goblyn Wood. To the Fae.

On silent wings, Hazel followed the procession through the midnight forest. Floating behind the winding crocodile of children, she noticed that the trees were becoming taller and thicker, their twisting limbs casting heavy black shadows in the moonlight. From under roots, and from deep in the brambles, wild and wary eyes were shining: rabbits and foxes, badgers and bats, all watching as the children passed merrily by.

Finally the procession came to a halt. The singing died down and the children clustered together, rippling with excitement. Hazel swooped down behind a snow-capped boulder, took her human shape again and crouched out of sight.

They had stopped at the foot of a great snow-covered hill. Steep and treeless, the hill ascended quickly towards a glaring moon. The Ley was powerful here – Hazel could feel it surging through the earth below. But this was not the bright energy of the revels or the Weald. It was tainted somehow, poisonous. Beneath the glittering snow, she sensed a hollow, hungry darkness. She looked up the stark white slope and, with a shudder, she knew that it was the Knoll.

The children waited, gazing up at the hill, whispering and reaching for each other's hands. Elsie was beaming, open-mouthed in wonder. Hazel looked around for a sign of the Ladies, but they were no longer with the children. The three of them had retreated to the line of the trees where they stood, side by side, arms hanging loosely. Their hoods were raised, but Hazel could see the gleam of their faces in the darkness. They were staring ahead, unblinking, motionless as waxworks.

The air began to tighten, stretching like the skin of a

drum. Suddenly, the sky shuddered. A crack of thunder and sheets of blue lightning drowned the moon and stars, sharpening the line of the hill. The children gasped and huddled closer together. Hazel felt the air throbbing and hissing around her, tremors building in the earth below. Up on the hillside, snow was cracking, crumbling, sliding in thick sheets. And with a deep groan, the hill yawned open.

As the mouth of the hill gaped wider, a weird light shone from within, casting nets of green and silver around the gathered children. It seemed to be both fire and water, flickering in waves over their upturned faces. Then, from deep within the hill, a song of pure crystal rang out – lucid, unearthly chimes, calling and beckoning. Slowly, the children shuffled forward, drifting towards the opening. Hazel saw her chance. She pulled up the hood of her cape, slipped silently out of the shadows and, heart thumping, merged into the throng.

The crowd around her jostled and thrilled with excitement as they approached the broken earth. But Hazel kept her feet moving steadily forwards, eyes on the way ahead, and, as the bewitching light danced and shimmered around her, she held on tightly to everything she knew to be real and true. She thought of the belfry with its dusty cushions and stolen lemonade; she thought of her friends gathered round Pa's cherrywood table; of Portuna's hand gripping her own, tugging her to safety. She thought of Perig's rockfall thundering to her rescue; and of those quick arms that had scooped her up and held her tight. And she thought of Pete who she knew, with a sudden and piercing clarity, was close now, somewhere in the hollows of that hill.

As she drew nearer, the crystal song vibrated through her bones and the strange light grew brighter and brighter, dazzling to a searing, prismatic glare. Hazel stood at the threshold of the Knoll. Then she touched the black stone around her neck and stepped into the blinding light.

Acknowledgements

I HAVE HAD A LOT OF HELP IN WRITING THIS BOOK. To begin with, I am lucky and grateful to have had the support of my clever and imaginative agents Caroline Walsh and Christabel McKinley who – in the kindest possible way – took apart my first draft, then gave me the tools to fix it. I am also deeply indebted to my brilliant editor, Lucy Pearse, whose investment in Hazel's journey, and belief in her world gave the story its heart, and to Lowri Ribbons whose thoughtful and inventive line-edit was the final sprinkling of fairy-dust that brought it all to life. Sincere thanks also to Ali Dougal for taking a chance on the trilogy, Emma Young for her eagle-eyed copy-edit, Anna Bowles for her careful and sensitive proofreading, and to the rest of the excellent team at Simon and Schuster for their ongoing support and all their hard work in getting this story out into the world.

I couldn't believe my luck when I heard that the

extraordinary David Wyatt had agreed to illustrate the book. Heartfelt thanks to him and to designer Sean Williams for producing such a gasp-worthy cover, and astonishing illustrations.

Along the way I have also had a great deal of help from friends and fellow writers whose notes produced a whole goblin's market of ideas from which I merrily stole. Amongst these helpers were Sylvia Bishop, Archie Cornish, Julie Landau, Kate Tunstall, Ashley Williams, Natasha Davis, Judy Dendy, Nikki van der Gaag, Stephanie Nightingale, Elizabeth Crowley, Clare Carswell, Sam Stanton-Stewart, Geneviève Helleringer, and my kind and generous parents who read far more drafts than is reasonable – and will now have to read this one.

Special thanks must also go to Alice Harman for her insight and encouragement at our weekly chats, Sal Drennan and Rachael Powers for their sensitive readings and spot-on edits, and the excellent Megan Kerr of The Writers' Greenhouse whose inspiring course 'Imaginary Worlds' set Hazel's story in motion.

Though my fairies do not map onto traditional fairy lore in every respect, Hazel's world draws on the work of some wonderful scholars of Faerie. In particular, I owe much to Professor Diane Purkiss's brilliant and beguiling book *Troublesome Things*. I hope she doesn't mind my lending her name to a fairy-hunting cat as a strange sort of homage.

Finally I thank my much-loved husband and son,

whose presence is better than anything fairy glamour could conjure.

It is notoriously dangerous to thank fairies, so I shan't risk it. I shall just have to hope that none is offended by what they find here, and that I won't get pinched black and blue . . . or worse.

ANNA KEMP writes both picture books and middle-grade fiction. Her books have been nominated for a number of prizes including the BookTrust Early Years Award, the Roald Dahl Funny Prize, the Waterstones Children's Book Prize and Oscar's Book Prize. Her work has been adapted for a variety of media including TV, puppetry and theatre. Her picture books include *Dogs Don't do Ballet* and *The Worst Princess*, both illustrated by Sara Ogilvie.

DAVID WYATT's first professional work appeared in British comic *2000AD*, illustrating a strip for Neil Gaiman. Since then he has focused on Children's books, working with authors including Philip Pullman, Diana Wynne Jones, Terry Pratchett, Geraldine McCaughrean and Philip Reeve. In 2017, he won the Blue Peter Book of the Year for his work on *Podkin One-Ear* by Kieran Larwood. He recently moved from Dartmoor to North Wales; two equally dramatic and ancient landscapes that provide plenty of inspiration for his work.